THE GLAMOURIST

T0021785

ALSO BY LUANNE G. SMITH

The Vine Witch Series

The Vine Witch

THE GLAMOURIST

LUANNE
G. SMITH

Published by 47North, Seattle

www.apub.com

Amazon, the Amazon logo, and 47North are trademarks of Amazon.com, Inc., or its affiliates.

ISBN-13: 9781542019613
ISBN-10: 1542019613

Cover design by Micaela Alcaino

Printed in the United States of America

THE GLAMOURIST

PROLOGUE

She emerged from the layer of mist too late to avoid colliding with the rose-colored window three stories up. Her right wing smacked against the glass, leaving behind a feathered streak of dirt as she tumbled to the ledge below. Reeling at her precarious position, the little bird dug her claws into the stone ledge. The reflection of a startled sparrow blinked back at her from the bottom of the glass's surface. In the midst of her confusion, the pain in her shoulder announced itself smartly. Shaking all over, she settled her ruffled feathers back into place.

The bird had no recollection of flying, no idea how she'd come to crash into the side of a building. Or how it was she'd come to have feathers, for that matter. A string of red silk trailed from her left leg, teasing her with the half-shadow of memory. It meant something, it must, but no matter how hard she tried to grasp the significance, the meaning drifted from her avian mind, elusive as mist. She made the mistake of trying to force the thought by pecking at the string, but vertigo set in the moment the river came into focus in the foreground. In a panic she flapped her wings.

Forced aloft by an updraft, she wobbled higher until she touched down on a narrow terrace surrounded by a stone balustrade. It wasn't the direction she'd wanted to go, but at least there was room to hop about without fear of falling over the ledge. And the view! She could see the whole of the city from so high up. But which city? She hopped a little farther along, peeking out between the Gothic cutouts in the stone railing, until the lean outline of a metal tower arose in the distance. It pointed skyward, looming over the low profile of modern buildings and stone bridges. A wagging finger taking aim at a new age. It ought to have been an inspiring view, yet her heart pounded at the sight. The skyline was too familiar, too weighted with the threat of danger. She shouldn't be there. She didn't know why, and yet instinct told her to fly, to get away.

The sparrow spread her wings, ready to catch the wind and fly to safety, when a plume of white smoke flooded the terrace, stinging her nostrils with its burnt citrus scent. Her eyes watered and her throat clenched. She beat her wings, desperate to escape, but the string of red silk squeezed tight around her leg, holding her down. Surely, she would choke to death, a poor bird that'd lost her way, smothered by the polluted exhale of a city breathing in an industrial age.

The smoke grew thicker, tainted by the heavy perfume of frankincense. Dizzy from the scent, she flopped over on her side, certain she would die from lack of oxygen. Her eyes fluttered on the verge of closing for good as a dark-eyed woman stepped out of the smoke to stand over her.

"You're not dying, Yvette," the jinni said, straightening her red-and-gold garments. "Get up."

The jinni nudged her tail feather with the toe of a worn sandal, blew a puff of hot breath over her tiny head, and uttered a foreign word full of hard consonants. A warm zephyr swept the sparrow up within a column of smoke that churned like a chimney fire, as a whirlwind of energy buoyed her off her feet. The feathers singed away, the beak receded, twig-light bones calcified and grew human-heavy, until Yvette stood once more as a spritely young woman, still in the red-and-black harlequin costume she'd worn when they'd hastily escaped from the cellar and *les flics*. She rubbed her sore arm as her mind expanded with all the memories that had been too big to hold in her tiny sparrow brain. And then she saw it again, the narrow tower in the distance pointing skyward.

Yvette gripped the balustrade with both hands. "No, no, no, not here!" she said, taking in the expanse of the city as the lights came on along the river. "Sidra, you have to take me somewhere else."

The jinni, alarmed by the reaction, leaned over the railing, and she, too, gave a look of terror as she spotted the tower, the river, and the bustling street below, with its automobiles, *bicyclettes*, and wagons all vying for a path through the evening congestion. Beside her a stone gargoyle gazed placidly at the view. "We're in the city of a thousand lights? I did not will this." She turned on Yvette. "What have you done? I will turn you to ash for this, I swear it!"

"*Me?* I didn't do anything. *You* turned *me* into a bird, remember. You could have killed me, you crazy desert witch."

Sidra glared, radiating a heat wave of hatred. "I should have bound you and left you to the authorities. Let the drop of the blade take that useless head of yours. It's obviously doing you no good where it is."

The jinni pushed her sleeves up as if she meant to strike with magic. Yvette reached for her sharpened hairpin, the one she kept tucked in her sloppy pompadour for self-defense, but it wasn't there. She backed away, pointing a warning finger. "Don't you even think of turning me into anything else."

"Missing something? Your mortal trinkets are of no use against me anyway. We're not in prison anymore, girl." The jinni waved her hand, a thin seam of mist trailing in the air.

Yvette cringed, waiting for the smiting move to sweep her off the balcony and into some pit of vipers. But it never came. She opened her eyes to find Sidra shaking her hands out and staring at them as if they had betrayed her. "Well, that's interesting," Yvette said, gripping the balustrade.

But she didn't dare relax. Not yet. Jinn were tricky. Dangerous. And this one was a known murderer.

She'd been bolder around the jinni when they'd both been locked up inside Maison de Chêne, the prison for witches. There they'd been on equal footing, each stripped of magic while they awaited their fate. But here, alone on a ledge against the jinni, she was as helpless as she'd ever been. A stub witch with no more than a handful of parlor tricks.

Sidra lifted her robe to check that she wasn't manacled. But there was no chain, no restraint on her magic. "What have you done?"

"Don't go blaming me. Maybe you're too old to do proper magic anymore."

Sidra's forehead creased with worry as she stared at the tower. "I vowed never to return to this stinking city. Prophets protect me, I should not be in this place."

"Then maybe you shouldn't have magicked us here."

The jinni's lip lifted in a snarl, revealing an ivory eyetooth engraved with gold. "*I* am not the one who brought us here."

"Well, we didn't just land here randomly, did we?"

Sidra adjusted her silken shawl, rattling the gold bracelets on her wrists as she thought about it. "No, we didn't," she said and leaned against the railing so that her profile matched the gargoyle's. She stared out over the city, eyes glittering like black diamonds, as she scoured the rooftops below.

Yvette, still watchful for any sudden move, wondered what the jinni was on about. Sidra might yet toss her over the railing, but the jinni's genuine puzzlement suggested she was safe for the moment.

Sidra clicked her tongue as she thought out loud. "You smuggled something in your heart," she said, finding a thread of logic worth following. "Something you desired above all else. At the moment I did the transformation. It must have gotten caught in the magic. That must be what carried us here." Sidra spun on her. "You stole a wish!"

"Did not."

"Did."

"Oh là là, is it a crime to want something now?"

The jinni shook her finger in Yvette's face, then marched to the end of the terrace, her silk robes billowing out behind her. There she reached over the balustrade, where an abandoned bird's nest sat tucked below a decorative stone scroll. She plucked it loose and cradled it in her hand, still managing to cast a stern look at Yvette. "We'll see now the value of your heart's desire."

"What's a bird's nest got to do with it?"

Sidra folded her robes around her and sat on the terrace with her legs crossed. She pointed a finger. "Sit and close that mouth of yours."

Yvette feared a trap but had no choice. Even from five feet away, anger radiated off the desert sorceress, making Yvette feel as small and defenseless as she'd been as a girl on the streets below years earlier. She sat in front of the jinni and folded her legs.

Sidra held the nest in her hand and blew gently across the dried sticks and grass that had been woven together with instinct and care. Fluffs of feathery down stirred inside the shallow depression as the nest caught fire. The flame spread but didn't consume the small nest or feathers inside. The nest glowed orange as the fire danced in a circle in the jinni's hand. Sidra's eyes followed the flickering light like one might read a newspaper.

"How'd you do that? I thought your magic went out."

"Not out, only dimmed. Now hush. One's fate must not be trivialized by idle talk. Not even yours."

One's fate?

Sidra's head tilted to the side, and her eyes narrowed as she squinted at some vision. What did it mean? Yvette chewed nervously on her thumbnail, waiting to see if the jinni intended to throw her over the side of the building after all.

"It's as I suspected," Sidra said, placing the nest on the ground, unharmed from the flame. "It was your desire that brought us to this city of infidels."

Yvette shook her head. "I didn't. I swear!"

"The fire does not lie." Sidra stood and nudged her chin. "Get up."

"Why, what are you going to do?" Yvette looked quickly around for a door. Surely there must be an escape.

"Stand, girl. I need to give you something." The jinni reached in the silken folds of her robe and brought out a small perfume bottle made of green glass with an intricate overlay of gold in a leaf pattern. A crystal bird served as a stopper. Exquisite. The sort of thing found in the bourgeoise shops along the rue de Valeur. Sidra placed the bottle in Yvette's left hand.

"What'd I do to deserve this?"

Sidra scoffed. "Nothing. And it's not yours to keep. But you stole a wish, so now you must do this thing for me."

Always the tit for tat with these jinn. "I told you I didn't—"

"Do not deny it. Your heart was pointed here when we escaped, and now you've dragged me to these dirty streets as well."

"I don't know why you keep going on about it. You're a jinni, for heaven's sake. Poof off if you don't like it here."

Sidra advanced, her hands balled into fists. "You know nothing about the rules of magic."

"No, but I know what this is worth," she said, holding up the bottle in a way that suggested she might drop it at any moment if Sidra didn't back off.

"Do not test me, *sharmoota*! That bottle is worth ten thousand of your heart's filthy desires."

Yvette tossed the bottle in the air so that it flipped once, then deftly caught it in her right palm. "Then why give it to me?"

The jinni reached out a panicked hand. "I've no time to explain, but because of your reckless wish I am now confined inside the city boundaries. I cannot leave. And neither can you."

"I can leave right now, if I want."

"No, girl, you can't. The thing you desired with every ounce of your heart is here, and until you find it and satisfy your wish, you cannot leave." Sidra shivered, a thing Yvette had never seen her do before. "In the meantime, that bottle cannot be found in my possession," she went on. "Not while my powers are dimmed."

"So, you want me to stash it for you?" Normally she'd be happy to continue tormenting the moody desert witch, but there was something different in Sidra's eyes this time. Something desperate. Fearful even. It strummed a sympathetic chord inside Yvette, layers and layers beneath the tough facade she'd built up from years of living on the streets. She knew the feeling of offering something of value to someone, only to have it broken from lack of care.

Yvette closed her fingers over the bottle and slipped it inside her costume. "I guess I owe you for helping me escape. I'll keep it safe, if that's what you want."

Sidra gave a firm nod, her relief obvious. The jinni seemed to consider the matter settled, as if a debt had been paid. Standing aside a horned gargoyle, she scoured the skyline and pointed to a hill on the far side of the city where a domed roof rose above the summit. "You're not too late. The one you're looking for is still there."

Yvette's mouth watered with fear. She didn't know what dream the jinni had seen in the flames, but watching her correctly pick out the neighborhood atop the butte where she was born told her the vision had been rooted in truth. Or as near a version of the truth as she'd ever known. She understood partly why she'd been swept back to the city. Perhaps she *had* wished to return from some deep place inside. Before Sidra turned her into a sparrow, she'd seen proper magic done by a proper witch, and for the first time in her life she'd wanted that for herself. Magic was in her blood, always had been, tingling on her skin at the tips of her fingers, in the roots of her hair, and along her spine. And yet she'd never been anything but a failure at spells. There'd never been anyone to show her how to do them properly or teach her how to channel the restless energy that seemed to flow through her. No one who cared, anyway.

But now that she'd seen a vine witch wield her magic and knew what was possible, Yvette wanted power for herself more keenly than she ever had before. That was the thought she'd folded up and tucked away in her heart just before she'd been caught in the jinni's sorcery.

Yvette leaned over the railing, scanning the city as the streetlights twinkled against a purple sky. The image gave her the courage to confess. "I want to learn magic for myself, is all. I want to know what kind of witch I was supposed to be before everything went to shit and I ended up in that prison."

Across from her, a fat gargoyle stuck its tongue out and rested its head in its hands.

"That, girl, is why I decided not to kill you." The jinni side-eyed Yvette as if waiting for her to flare up and then smiled when it didn't happen. "There is no greater journey than following one's fate," she said, her voice softened, perhaps on reflection of her own circumstance. "Even if it's to be found in this stinking place."

"It's been three years," Yvette said, finally gazing at the white-domed cathedral on the butte in the distance.

"A blink in time."

"There's usually some hell-broth on the boil at a little café at the top of the hill, if you're hungry. That is, if you want to come with me."

The jinni shook her head and pointed her chin in the opposite direction toward the south bank of the river. "My path is that way. In the maze of narrow streets where I can disappear."

"So that's it? We crash-land in the city together and then go our separate ways? How will I return your bottle to you?"

Sidra adjusted her shawl so it covered the top of her head. "For whatever reason, fate has bound us together. We will find each other again. This I do not doubt. Until then, take care with that bottle or I will curse you and your children, and your children's children, to an eternal blistering hell of torment, as though a thousand fire ants feast on your brain."

"Honestly, it's a wonder you haven't got more friends."

Sidra showed her teeth—half grimace, half smile. The gold scrolling engraved in the ivory gleamed in its secret incantation.

"Not one scratch," answered the jinni. And with that she climbed onto the ledge of the balustrade and shimmered into a screen of smoke that vanished over the head of a pouting gargoyle, leaving Yvette alone to contemplate her own way down.

CHAPTER ONE

Elena and Jean-Paul arrived in the city on the afternoon train, leaving themselves just enough time to forward their luggage before hailing one of the now ubiquitous motorized cabs. They were headed to the campus of ancient buildings on the south side of the north bridge, summoned there by the Ministry of Lineages and Licenses. The address written in bold type at the top of the telegram clearly stated Elena was to report to 333 rue de Courbé. After double-checking the number above the door, she tucked the summons back in her purse and tried to hide her nervousness with a tight, confident smile.

"Are you sure this is the place?" Jean-Paul glanced up and down the street as if they'd somehow made a mistake. He tried the door, finding it locked.

She supposed to the mortal eye the plain blue door tucked in the alcove at the mouth of the narrow lane did have a rather unremarkable appeal. There was no name on the doorplate, no welcoming urn of flowers beside the threshold, and, well, not even any evidence the door was anything more than a servant entrance, rarely used. And yet it radiated with the proper hum of official witch business, that droning buzz of documents being psychically scrutinized and signed just on the other side. She could almost hear the muttering of inkspell incantations.

"I'm certain," she said and turned the handle without feeling the least bit of resistance.

Jean-Paul removed his gray homburg and followed Elena inside the official entrance to the Ministry of Lineages and Licenses. He was often forced to trust her instincts when it came to the world of magic, something he'd gradually come to accept in the short time they'd been together. His willingness to open his heart and mind to a world mostly invisible to his senses was one of the many things she admired about him. Inside, the lobby smelled of layers of bureaucracy, built up over years of casual disregard for logic and ease of function, but with the not unpleasant aroma of freshly prepared café au lait wafting in from a nearby office. Papers shuffled and reshuffled themselves between in-boxes. Enchanted typewriters filled out forms, then spit them into piles to be sorted and mailed. And against the far wall sat a row of doves on a perch waiting to deliver messages within the city limits. Every time one shook out its feathers, a downy fluff rose up to further bedeck the portrait of the prime minister hanging above them. Elena tried hard not to inhale the listless office air too deeply, lest the smell invade her lungs and render her as permanently apathetic as the clerk greeting them glassy-eyed over the tops of his half-moon glasses.

"Mademoiselle Boureanu here to see Minister Durant," Jean-Paul said in his most lawyerly tone.

The gentleman lowered his gaze and rummaged through a stack of forms on his desk. "Ah, yes. The double-licensing case. This way," he said after plucking up a stack of yellowed onionskin papers. The documents appeared to be handwritten in a florid old-world style of calligraphy, unlike the typewritten ones piling up on the desk behind the clerk.

Elena and Jean-Paul followed the spectacled man through a swinging mahogany gate to a private office at the rear of the hall. The clerk knocked three times before opening the door and escorting them inside. He placed the documents on the oversize desk beside the new application already there, then retreated, leaving the couple to wait in the pair of hard wooden chairs provided.

Not a minute later a lean gentleman in a mauve frock coat and matching bow tie entered and shook Jean-Paul's hand. To Elena he bowed his head curtly. "Mademoiselle, I appreciate you coming to the city on such short notice." Minister Durant sat behind his enormous desk, tapping his fingers in an odd sort of rhythm, as though conducting a silent drumbeat spell. The faint scent of ink bloomed in the air. She watched him take a quick inhale before opening his desk drawer and retrieving a fountain pen and magnifying glass.

"Mademoiselle Boureanu is happy to comply with the court order," Jean-Paul stated, brushing a smudge of coal soot from the train off his hat.

"Quite so." Durant inspected the onionskin documents on his desk while rubbing his fingers in the odd way Grand-Mère often had, as if testing the air for the static energy of spells. Though perhaps with Minister Durant it was merely a work-related tic, the aftereffect of having to deal with so much paper and ink on a daily basis. He slid the newer-looking application from the corner of his desk and seemed to compare it to the older papers the clerk had brought him. "It says here, mademoiselle, that you have made application to register as a *venefica*, per the agreement derived from a criminal court hearing one month ago."

Elena nodded when Durant looked up. He bit at the corner of his lip, raised his brow at her, then returned his gaze to the documents on his desk once more, scowling as if confused by the order.

"And yet you are already registered as a vine witch in the Chanceaux Valley. Is that correct?" He held up the corner of the newer document to indicate where he'd read the information. The official seal featuring Liberté wearing her crown of seven stars had been stamped on the bottom.

"She is," Jean-Paul volunteered. "We produce wine at the Château Renard vineyard. She's the resident vine witch. And my fiancée," he added.

"Yes," Durant remarked in a rather disapproving tone. He rubbed his fingers together and leaned back in his chair. "Well, that news aside, what I can tell you is that normally in this office, when we deal with witches from the outer provinces, it is for those who have not yet complied with registration under the 1745 Covenants or who are wishing to change their status from one art to another. For instance, a gentleman was in earlier this week who felt he was better suited for working with electricity rather than fire. An easy fix for the modern age. We simply amended his registration to reflect the change and monitor for any abuse of magic." He tapped his fingers again on the desk, a one-two-three rhythm repeated three times. "However, from what I understand of your request, you are wishing to retain your status as a vine witch while *also* registering as a *venefica*, is that right?"

"Yes. You see, I was adopted as a child and trained as a vine witch by my mentors. My parents . . ." She hesitated, feeling her heart constrict at denying Grand-Mère and Grand-Père as being anything but her mother and father. "I was always told Raul and Esmé Boureanu were country hedge witches, selling curatives and healing potions out of their wagon. It was only recently I learned the truth about my parents' bloodline."

Durant shuffled back and forth through the onionskin papers. "The problem, however, is that . . . ah . . . here it is." He slid a document from the pile and turned it around so Elena and Jean-Paul could both read it. "Your parents were convicted and hanged for the poisoning of three mortals. Because of those deaths, the court, in its inimitable way, has deemed you must register as a *venefica* and continue as such under probation until the magistrate is satisfied you pose no threat."

"That's why we're here." Jean-Paul scooted closer to the edge of his chair, as if sensing trouble.

"Yes, but surely even a mortal like yourself can understand how the one art is in direct conflict with the other. Someone wishing to continue working in the food and beverage industry cannot also have an affiliation with poison. It would be disastrous."

Elena felt a sting at the back of her mind seeing her parents' names listed in the register with the word "executed" printed in the margin. "I don't understand. What is it you're trying to say?"

"I do apologize for neglecting to be as straightforward in my telegram as I could have been, but the reason I summoned you here was to inform you your license to continue working with wine must be revoked, so long as you bear the designation of a potions witch who specializes in poison."

"But I'm not!" Even as Elena denied it, she had to swallow the flutter of guilt that rose up, knowing she had recently intended to poison someone in an act of revenge. And that the poison she'd concocted for that revenge had unintentionally contributed to the deaths of two people.

"And yet the court has said otherwise, mademoiselle." Durant twisted a signet ring on his finger, a crude pentagram engraved with a motto too small to read from where Elena sat, though she didn't need to guess what it said. "I understand that being a vine witch is your vocation and that you are quite adept at it; however, this is a matter of public safety. Those who purchase your wine must have every assurance that the product is safe to consume. To be blunt, they cannot drink your wine in confidence if you simultaneously carry the designation of *venefica*, which the court insists upon."

Jean-Paul massaged the outline of his jaw as he absorbed the news. "He's right. We'd be ruined if our buyers connected the two." He avoided Elena's eye for a moment, then took her hand. "But there must be some recourse, some appeal to be made under the Covenant Laws. She's no poisoner. It was her parents who were convicted, not her."

"Forgive me, monsieur, but you are a *mortal* attorney, am I correct?"

Jean-Paul nodded slowly, defensively. He hadn't missed the pejorative tone in the witch's use of the word. "Witch law is so much more complicated than the regulations mortals are expected to abide by. Though it perhaps makes little sense to you, our laws are often enforced based on instinct and intuition. Ancient rules that have evolved over a millennium of practical application."

"I'm familiar with witch law. I've read the 1745 Covenants. The abbey in our village fortunately retained a copy."

"*Non*, monsieur, I'm afraid that would be the provincial country code for witches." The man retrieved a fat leather-bound book the size of a small travel valise from the credenza behind him. "*The Treatise on the Code for Witches*, which governs the entire country and its supernatural inhabitants, is much more complicated and reaching in scope. For example, there's a one-hundred-page section on the rules overseeing poisonings within the capital limits. After the panic of 1647, the local constabulary insisted there be defined parameters of intention. Motive and intent being only partial considerations of a crime. In some instances, mere possession of the right combination of ingredients is a crime for someone with the lineage of Mademoiselle Boureanu. For that reason, I'm afraid I'll have to restrict her from working or residing at the vineyard until such time the court deems her safe to return."

"I can't return home? But that's ridiculous. That's not even reasonable. You'll ruin our livelihood if I can't return. Besides, we're to be married."

Fear sank full-bodied into Elena's bloodstream until the truth of her past and the uncertainty of her future collided midstream. The vineyard, Château Renard, she and Jean-Paul—they might all be ruined because of the lies she was told as a child. Her parents' guilt gripped her by the wrist as sure as any manacle devised by the Covenants Regulation Bureau.

"It has to be a mistake." Summoning as much rebellion as she dared before the minister, she straightened her back. "Surely there has to be a way for me to continue my work at the vineyard while this gets sorted," she said, looking to Jean-Paul for reassurance. He had none to give.

Durant blinked back, his mouth pursed in smug assurance, as if he'd been anticipating her reaction. He drummed his fingers in their odd rhythm against the desk. "There is *one* stipulation that might allow me to relax my powers of enforcement in this case."

"Tell me, please."

The minister reached in his desk and removed a silver hairpin, its edge filed to a stiletto-sharp point. The same hairpin a certain young woman in prison had once threatened Elena with before they'd escaped together and found common ground as witches who never knew their mothers. Elena shivered at the implication of it in the minister's hand.

"Mademoiselle, I see from your expression you recognize this rather crude weapon as one belonging to Yvette Lenoir. It might interest you to know that it was recovered from the cellar where I believe you were last taken into custody."

Before she could reply, Jean-Paul put a cautioning hand on her arm and asked, "What is it you're after exactly, Minister?"

"Mortals. Always so eager to get to the point. Very well." Durant leaned forward, steepling his fingers. "In short, mademoiselle, I've been given the authority to overturn the revocation of your position as a vine witch in exchange for information."

"What information?"

"You must reveal whatever knowledge you have of the whereabouts of Mademoiselle Lenoir. She is known to have been in your presence moments before your recapture. It stretches credulity to believe you had no part in her further escape."

Elena gaped at him. "But I have no idea where she is. I already told Inspector Nettles I haven't a clue what happened to her after she disappeared."

"You cannot hold her responsible for the law's incompetence," Jean-Paul insisted. "This is coercion. The law is willing to take away her livelihood simply because it wasn't resourceful enough to apprehend the young woman when it had the chance."

"A young *witch*, monsieur. And may I remind you she is a murderer who has proven herself both dangerous and elusive after so many weeks on the run. If your fiancée knows anything about her present location, I suggest she tell this office at once or I'm afraid the law will have no choice but to permanently enforce the forfeiture of her status as a vine witch."

The pins in Elena's hair scratched, her shoes pinched, and her corset seemed to squeeze even tighter around her ribs. She stood, unable to sit with the uncomfortable news. "How can I tell you something I don't know?"

"The burden is yours to bear out, mademoiselle. I suggest you use your particular talents to find Mademoiselle Lenoir, if you wish to return to your vineyard in your former capacity. In the meantime, here is my business card. Send a dove, or a telegram if you find mortal communication more to your taste," he said with an eye toward Jean-Paul. "When you're ready to talk, your status will be reinstated."

"The law is an ass," she said.

"Regrettably for you, that is often how the law functions," Durant said, then took his rubber stamp, plunged it against the ink pad, and stamped her vine witch registration as Revoked.

CHAPTER TWO

The couple emerged onto the street outside the minister's office as dazed as if they'd been shell-shocked by mortar fire. Jean-Paul paced the sidewalk, slapping the brim of his hat against his trouser leg before securing it atop his head again with a squeeze of his hand. Elena dug her heel against the pavement and folded her arms around her middle to keep her hands from casting spellfire at the two-story apartment building across the street with the wrought-iron flower boxes. And still she fumed, the faint aura of burnt cinders radiating off her as strong as any char girl selling roasted hazelnuts in the street.

Blast that man, blast the court, and blast everyone who ever lied to her about her past.

"I nearly lost the vineyard once before. I cannot be on the verge of losing everything again," she said.

"You're not going to lose the vineyard. Or me. I promise you." Jean-Paul squared his shoulders and buttoned his coat as if affixing the last strap of armor. "What an insufferable man, that Durant. Their ultimatum cannot be allowed to stand. It's legal blackmail. And did you hear the way he used the word '*mortal*'? As if it were a disease he was trying to avoid."

"There must be some lawyer trick you can do."

A man in a bowler hat and three-piece black suit strode toward them, checking his pocket watch. He had the scent of authority about him, but it was the mortal kind, full of self-importance. They held their conversation until he passed by, acknowledging him with a nod of their heads, and then watched as he continued past the blue door completely unaware of the idiotic supernatural bureaucracy it contained.

"Do? I don't even understand the context of the question anymore." Jean-Paul stared at the surrounding street in bewilderment. "I lived and studied in this city my entire life growing up. To think all the while there was a secret society of witches living beside me and, just like that man, I hadn't a clue. You have your own rules, your own laws"—he waved his hand at the inconspicuous office they'd exited—"your own damn buildings, for God's sake. He might be a bureaucratic bastard, but Durant is right, Elena. I studied mortal law. I have no idea of where or even how to establish your basic right to protest their preposterous terms, given the scope of laws he referred to in there."

She listened to his uncomfortable confession, adding it to the pains already building from the discomfort of her city clothing. "We're not a secret society," she said, tugging at her too-tight sleeve. "Witches have always lived in the open, especially in the city."

Jean-Paul checked that the man had walked sufficiently far enough away. "You should keep your voice down."

"Mortals simply function better if they're allowed the freedom to not notice us," she said, raising a brow at him. "Ignoring our existence makes it easier for you to accept your own limitations." He gave her that stern-eyed look that suggested she'd verged on insulting his intelligence, so she added in a whisper, "I meant as a species. Not you specifically, my love."

"Well, that's a relief." Apparently mollified, Jean-Paul slipped his arm around hers and led them down the street. "I am sorry, Elena. I wish there was something I could have said or done back there. I was simply outmaneuvered by my own ignorance." He veered them toward the main avenue, where the noise of city life galloped at them on a wave of sound. Horse carts and omnibuses, taxis and *bicyclettes* all vied for the road, creating a cacophony of honking horns and shouts of warning. The exhaust from the automobiles hanging in the air was new since her last visit to the city, though not the overpowering stench from the *pissoirs* situated on every other corner for the men to relieve themselves. The combination of foul scents carried the whiff of a bad omen.

The unnatural bustle of the city at full throttle worked like friction to heat Elena's already agitated aura. She was more accustomed to the hum of bees in the vineyard than the drone of cars and buses on the street, and the noise weighed on her mood. She thought it best to do a quick calming spell, lest she attract every charlatan selling a healing charm within a three-block radius. She reached in her purse to pull out a sprig of sage she'd tucked inside for precisely this sort of occasion. It had crumbled slightly, leaving bits of leaf in the bottom of the bag to mingle with the loose rose hips. Honestly, how did witches in the city cope without large pockets to store their herbs separately? She motioned for Jean-Paul to stop beside a lamppost, explaining her need.

"Here? Now?" He looked around. "On the public street?"

"It will only take a moment. No one will be the wiser."

"Yes, of course." He nodded even as his eyes watched for any onlookers. But they were in the heart of the city. No one had time or inclination to notice anyone but themselves, which is how witches had survived in the open for so long among the busy streets and booming population in the first place. She doubted Jean-Paul had even thought twice about the woman drinking from the tin cup at the *quatre femmes* water fountain they'd passed. An obvious water witch paying homage as she splashed water on the ground to encourage the cycle.

Elena dabbed the sage over the blue veins running under the skin at her wrists, invoking a moment of calm. This couldn't be happening again. Why did the All Knowing insist on making her fight for every last scrap of serenity? Then she caught Jean-Paul's eye and was reminded of the worth of remaining engaged in the struggle.

"There are some who think we ought to be more assertive with mortals," she said, feeling her agitation and disappointment yield to clearer thinking. The minister's words still prickled like a nettle in her shoe, but she felt better able to bear the bad news after her blood carried the sage's healing properties through her veins.

"More assertive than conducting magic in the middle of the street?" he asked.

She took his arm so they might stroll as the newly engaged couple in love that they were. The warmth of his body next to hers created its own calming spell. "I meant politically. Our status might be that of the minority because of our population, but we're a rather potent faction when we wish to unite. I suspect Durant feels quite emphatic in that direction. You noticed his ring, no doubt."

"In fact, I did not." He guided them toward the interior pathway running through a grassy park with raised garden beds as a horse and automobile jockeyed violently for the eastbound lane of traffic in the road beside them.

"A clear Magus Society supporter, judging by the pentagram he wears on his pinkie finger. Doesn't approve of mixed marriages, would be my guess."

"Mixed marriages?"

Elena plucked a narrow leaf off a chestnut tree and passed it under her nose, inhaling. "Yes, you and I. Mortal and witch. You must be aware there are some who think it unnatural."

"I hadn't considered . . . there are witches who don't approve?"

Had he thought only mortals judged those who were different? Of course, there'd always been mortals who disapproved of magic—Jean-Paul had been one himself when they first met—but there were a growing number of witches, too, who believed the mingling of mortal and witch blood somehow diminished the connection with the All

Knowing. She hadn't revisited the city for nearly ten years, but even a decade earlier there had been small protests, propaganda, pamphlets, and salon chatter calling for stronger rights for magical folk, given the general weakness of mortals, both morally and magically. It was mostly nonsense, but not all. At times she thought the Magus supporters had a point. The law's insistence that she register as a *venefica* despite her obvious talent with wine was certainly proof that mortal fears could be taken too far.

"Sometimes the mark of prejudice settles in the eyes of those with limited vision, much like cataracts," she replied. "The Magus Society believes witches should be running the show, not mortals."

After pausing for Elena to clip several blushing pink rose petals from a bloom whose scent nearly arrested her in her tracks, Jean-Paul asked, "Do you know where she is?"

She, too, had been thinking about the minister's request concerning Yvette's whereabouts. "No, I don't."

"Not even with your . . . you know . . . special vision?"

It was perhaps possible. If she had that hairpin of Yvette's, she might be able to find her. But then what? Turn her in and let her feel the kiss of *la demi-lune* against her neck? She may want to have this *venefica* business out of her life and go back to the vineyard, but could she really turn in the young woman who stood by her after she was falsely accused? Who helped her confront the demon-loving murderer in the cellar? She had the girl to thank for saving her life.

"She's no innocent," he said as if reading her thoughts. "Yvette and Sidra were both convicted of murder. You weren't, because you didn't kill anyone."

"Not directly."

"Not at all. Not in the eyes of the law and certainly not in mine."

"So, I should give her up? Her life and freedom in exchange for my livelihood as a vine witch? Like coins given over for a tin of cigarettes?"

"It's merely an option." She tensed, and he held up a hand. "A last one, I hope. If I can find another solution, I will. But, Elena, you cannot protect her at the cost of our life together at Château Renard."

"And yet I can't bear the thought of betraying her like that. And don't you think it's odd that they only want Yvette? Why didn't they ask me about Sidra? Perhaps she's long gone and they know it. Much more likely Yvette would return here to the city or somewhere nearby."

She squeezed his arm as they emerged from the park on the street opposite, where a newly opened hotel stood, a lily among the stones with its art nouveau lines of sinuosity and rebellion. Truly, the man responsible for every building in the city being cast from the model of white stone and a gray roof was the epitome of mortal monotony. She much preferred the witch aesthetic of curved iron balconies, stained glass, and suggestive symbolism, which this new building showed off proudly.

She detached herself from Jean-Paul's arm to explore a remarkable engraving she'd spotted to the side of the front door. Her eye traced the almost musical quality of the lines and numerals carved into the marble facade. Math, music, time—all ticking along to the same cosmic rhythm, in this case in the form of a sundial strategically placed by the building's designer. She checked the needle's shadow against the position of the daylight stars and found it reliably accurate.

"Your mother will be expecting us soon," she said.

They were, in fact, due to meet her future mother-in-law for the first time in less than an hour. The second reason for their visit to the city. Elena wouldn't admit it to Jean-Paul, but doubt had dug a cozy burrow in the back of her mind at the prospect of meeting his mother, the reason for her ridiculously uncomfortable outfit. She'd actually hoped to impress the woman on mortal terms by donning a fashionable burgundy travel suit with far too many buttons and far too few pockets. There was a matching hat as well that insisted on staying put atop her overly teased pompadour only with the aid of several sharp pins. The entire outfit threatened to unravel at any moment. She couldn't help but assume the exquisitely dressed women she passed on the street, with their hair, hats, and hobble skirts in perfect polished order, were the result of some stitch-witch spell she had yet to learn. Oh, to be back at Château Renard in her comfortable wool skirt and apron and muddy clogs so she could muck about in the vines.

"You still haven't given me your decision." Elena turned from admiring the sundial to watch the expression on Jean-Paul's face. "Time's nearly up."

"That sundial is in shadow. You can't possibly read that."

"I can read a sundial in the dark better than your thoughts right now."

"Ah . . . right."

Yes, he'd come around to accepting the existence of magic, to accepting the presence of witches, but by the sudden greening of his gills it appeared he had not yet accepted the idea of telling his mother he was about to marry one. She would be angrier at him for his indecision, but so rare was the opportunity to find Jean-Paul on the defensive, Elena let the matter slide into its usual channel of conversation.

"As I've said, it's often easier for mortals to believe the world they see is the world they live in."

"It isn't like that, Elena. I simply think we ought to give her some time to get to know you first, don't you agree? As the woman you are."

"The woman I am is a witch. A vine witch, despite what that imbecile minister tried to imply. Though I suppose for the moment I really am nothing in a legal sense. Not a poisons witch, and not a vine witch. I'm simply an ordinary woman on the street."

"Oh no, my darling, I don't think you could ever be ordinary," he said, holding her tight in plain view. He kissed her under the sundial, then hailed a motorized taxi to take them to the fashionable arrondissement where his mortal mother awaited.

CHAPTER THREE

Yvette reached the door at the end of the catwalk. From the reconnaissance work she'd done two nights earlier, she knew a stairway waited on the other side that would take her to the street. The door, however, was bolted tight, as if winged thieves might attempt to rob the Palace Cinema from on high. Well, she *was* technically committing burglary by hiding inside the converted theater's inner workings, but she'd had little choice. If that damned jinni hadn't magicked her into a bird and abandoned her at the top of one of the nation's oldest cathedrals a month earlier—where a gargoyle had sat watching her every move, its concrete lip curling in a judgmental sneer, until she finally found the courage to descend the cathedral's winding staircase into the mob of the capital city—she might instead be enjoying her new life of freedom on a warm beach on the Mediterranean rather than hiding out in darkened buildings she had to ensure had multiple egresses before snuggling in for the night. But, no, since her escape from the cellar, she'd had to hustle every day to survive within the city, destined to remain within its boundaries until her accidental wish was fulfilled, according to Sidra. Not such an easy thing when you're wanted for murder and every witch-hunter in twenty arrondissements is looking for you.

The smell of damp wood and mildew permeated the upper chamber of the cinema where the outdated spotlights and pulley ropes dangled from the narrow walkway over the stage. There'd been a distinct shimmy to the suspended bridge as she tiptoed across it. The men working backstage had heard the noise and now were on the prowl, investigating. So much for stupid mortals being afraid of ghost stories and haunted theaters. She'd hoped to stay hidden inside the cinema for at least three more nights and perhaps watch a midnight showing of *Le Voyage dans la Lune* one more time. Alas, she had only enough time to snatch the red velvet curtain she'd been using for a bedcover before running for the exit. *Au revoir*, man in the moon!

Yvette focused her attention on the locked door at the end of the catwalk. For a witch, she'd always been piss-poor at reciting spells, but she wasn't completely without guile. Ignorant, maybe, but even she'd picked up a trick or two from the gutter mages who worked the cabaret district looking to shake a little luck loose from rich men's wallets. She would never have survived the streets of the city as a girl if she hadn't.

The metal lock was cold to the touch. She rubbed her hands together to create some heat, then pressed her palm over the mechanism. She squeezed her eyes shut in concentration and spoke the burglar's charm. "You keep your secrets, and I'll keep mine. Open for me, and we'll get along fine." The bolt quietly slid in its track, and she opened the door, a smug smile perched on her lips. "Much obliged," she said and skipped down the corkscrew metal steps to the street below.

With a little clever arranging, she wrapped the curtain around her shoulders so it resembled one of the fashionable cocoon coats so popular with the city elite on their way to the Palais Opéra. Never mind it was a warm autumn evening; the dictates of fashion gave a woman ample permission to wear whatever outrageous confection she liked if the sky foretold of a chance of rain, which it did. The overlords of fashion encouraged it, even. And, at any rate, it covered the dreary workaday skirt and blouse she'd stolen from the laundress, though not the shabby acrobat shoes she still wore, even though the soles were as thin as newspaper.

It had been three years since she'd had to survive on these streets, yet the only thing that appeared to have changed, as she refamiliarized herself with the city's charms and aversions, was the number of people. They were everywhere—gaggles of women in feathered hats stepping out of taxicabs, men in frock coats and spats jumping nimbly out of the way of motorized automobiles as the streetlights flickered on one by one. On the sidewalks and in the public squares, vendors selling *glaces et sorbets*, hawkers offering pairs of lovebirds in brass cages, and flower girls carting bouquets of zinnias and dahlias clamored for the day's last customers amid the hiss of trains running along electrified rails on the overhead bridges.

A pickpocket's dream.

Her fingers itched with the old habit. After a few short years working the carnival circuit, she'd forgotten what it was like to sit in the shadows and watch the city's wealthy step out under the streetlights, eyeing the pocket watches and diamond earrings, the purses and dropped coins. Waiting for the bump, the distraction, the apology, quietly slipping a month's worth of food and rent in the shape of a gold ring into a hidden pocket, while the mark shook off the unfortunate encounter with a member of the working class as one more dastardly disappointment of the day. One smart grab could set her up for a week in the city. She might even earn a few nights' rent at a flophouse. And bread! An entire loaf all to herself. Her stomach rumbled from the thought.

A fair number of the *bon chic* class were headed to the ballet, judging by their impressive satins and silks. Predictable as ever, a dinner of escargot and cognac at Maurice's would follow. Her mouth salivated as she spotted the outline of a fat wallet beneath an older man's breast pocket. Returning to the streets on an empty stomach was turning the lure of the easy snatch-and-run into a serious temptress.

But she was done with that life, wasn't she? Hadn't she accidentally stolen a wish because she yearned to be a proper witch? As light-fingered as she'd always been, there had to be a less conspicuous way of earning a living in the city than exploring men's pockets when they weren't looking. Especially for a witch on the run from the law. Elena might have been innocent, and good for her for trying to find a way to prove it, but that wasn't going to happen here. Not for this girl. She couldn't risk losing the little scrap of freedom she'd stolen with her escape, albeit a tenuous one that threatened to unravel at every opportunity.

Merde. Why did she have to lose the safety of the Palace Cinema? It had been a rare warm space with good protection. Plus she'd liked pretending to be a phantom haunting the old place. Now, if she didn't wish to go back to life as a thief by relieving the portly gentleman waddling toward her of his wallet, she'd have to find another means of staying dry and fed.

There *was*, of course, another theater she could head to for the night if she wanted to eat, though it wasn't the sort of ritzy establishment women in grand hats and genuine mink stoles patronized. No, it was the place their husbands scuttled off to in horse-drawn black *fiacres* after the dinner conversation with the family was over. And where a girl wrapped in stolen velvet wouldn't garner a second look. All part of the grand illusion of life imitating art imitating life.

"Spare a coin for the homeless?" she asked the portly gentleman on impulse, hoping for one last, honest reprieve.

The man's nose flared in disgust as he noted the scar on her jawline, then ignored her as he walked up the steps and disappeared behind the great mahogany doors of the Palais Opéra. Their decorative windows glared like sigils, warning those who didn't belong to stay away.

Yvette cursed her grumbling stomach, but she had no choice but to journey down one of the many darkened streets that radiated out from the center of the city. It was something she'd done a hundred times before. Proper magic had always evaded her, but since she was old enough to remember, she felt she had a secret ability to make herself invisible, to fade into shadow and not be seen. Not truly invisible, but a street sweeper could pass right in front of her with his broom and dustbin and not pick her out among the cobblestones if she willed it. It was a talent that had served her well in her years working the streets as well as on her last day inside the city three years earlier. After she'd washed the blood from her hands.

An hour later, footsore and weak with hunger, she stood under a shedding elm tree, staring at *les escaliers* leading to the top of the butte. A string of streetlamps ran up the center of the stairway, their globes aglow with orbs of soft white light that seemed to float in the air. A sudden breeze whooshed down from the top, sending a rustle of warning through the leaves in the trees. A sliver of doubt burrowed under her skin. The jinni had been right. More than right, really, about her stolen wish. She *had* wanted to come back to the city. But it wasn't just about finding her mother's magic. There was something else riding on the currents in the ether. One wish sewn to the other. A wisp of hope that she, too, could somehow clear her name and start her life over.

Oh, she was guilty of killing the man, no question. But there was murder and then there was *murder*.

Yvette stood contemplating whether she should turn around and give up when a black cat slunk by with his tail in the air. She couldn't remember if it was a good omen or a bad one for a witch to have a cat cross her path. One more thing she ought to know but didn't. She twitched her finger at the cat to see if he would tell her which sign to obey. The animal paused, green eyes narrowing as he apparently recognized her for what she was. He dropped his head and trotted off without a second glance.

Even the cats knew her for a failed witch. But the snub only made her want to know even more what was wrong with her and why she'd been abandoned to fend for herself in a world of mortals. The pain she normally stuffed deep in her psyche ballooned to the surface, fueling her legs forward toward an answer one way or another.

She scaled the stairs in one extended effort, emerging at the top of the butte where the great white dome of the new basilica asserted its squatter's rights. "*Mon Dieu*," she whispered, catching her breath. "They'll never finish that beast." Skirting west around the wooden scaffolding that flanked the church's base, she was reminded again how easily they could have provided food for every soup kitchen on the butte for a decade for what one shiny dome must have cost to build. But even Yvette knew the real reason monuments were built was to outshine and outlast the bodies of the men who built them.

She walked one street over, remembering to avoid the busy square at the heart of the hilltop village where the smell of the vendor's fried potatoes would drive her mad with hunger. As she did, a couple strolled in her direction, the heels of the woman's ankle boots clicking against the sidewalk. Yvette lifted the velvet drapery over her head and shrank back under the overhanging branches of a chestnut tree to let them pass before she walked on. The man donned a top hat and frock coat. The woman wore a black straw hat with a large red flower pinned to the brim. When the woman spoke, her hands played with her black feather boa, punctuating her drunken words with a flounce of her wrist. It was like watching a ghost from her past life walk by.

She waited for the couple to duck into a street where the café chatter was beginning to bloom. Once their laughter trailed off, she continued down the lane on the left where it quietly angled toward the backside of the butte. The streetlamps were farther apart here, and the people moved differently than the bustling, proud city below. No grand parades, no contrived pivots on high heels to show off the fashionable cut of a dress. The men were drab in their corduroy jackets and scuffed boots and the women almost shrunken under their petite hats and thin shawls. No automobiles, no *bicyclettes*, no clattering omnibuses. Only the steady one-two rhythm of slow horses being led over worn cobblestones.

She was close now. As the lane dropped, she could make out the amber glow of the gaslit globe above the door that illuminated the cabaret's hand-painted sign. LE RÊVE. Skulking along a line of trees, she made a move to step out of the dark when a shiver like cat's claws needling her spine stopped her in her tracks. Beneath the halo of light appeared a man in profile. He wore a three-piece suit in gray flannel and a derby hat with a distinct dent in the top. He leaned back against the wall and took a bored puff of smoke from a cigar as he bent one leg up to prop the sole of his shoe against the building. Definitely with the Covenants Regulation Bureau. So, *les flics* were still watching for her. Which meant there'd likely be a pair of agents inside as well, sitting at the back tables where the stage lights didn't reach the men's faces.

She retreated a step to consider her options. It was still too early for the bread-and-butter cabaret crowd—the absinthe drinkers, cocaine sniffers, and spell-fetish types who returned as often as three or four nights a week. The building wouldn't be bustling with their manic energy for hours yet. Even if she could slip past the stiff at the door, she'd have to cross in front of the stage to get to the apartments upstairs. Yvette would be spotted in a flash among the well-behaved early arrivals quietly sipping their warm-up glasses of champagne. She could wait it out until the crowd was drunk and rowdy enough to create a distraction, but by then Tante would have her hands full watching the movement of money and girls, making sure everything was flowing in the right direction.

Merde. After a month of watching the old place and waiting for *les flics* to give up, tonight she thought she might actually be desperate enough to *act* no matter the danger. She was so hungry, so tired of trying to find a safe place to sleep. And even more, the stolen wish was churning like a dervish inside her, desperate to be fulfilled. She'd fought it for weeks, afraid of the risk, afraid of the answers she might find, but something had changed. She'd felt the quiver in her blood when she woke up that morning, separate from the usual faintness she felt from eating only vegetable peels and gristle out of rubbish bins.

Yvette had no family, but she had Tante, her only tenuous tie to her long-absent mother. That was why the police were still watching the cabaret a month after her escape. They'd assumed, correctly it turned out, that she'd swim home like a spawning salmon returning upriver. Though "home" was a loose term, the drive to breach the cabaret's walls and cross the threshold was turning into a compulsion she couldn't ignore. But how to get inside without *les mouches* swarming all over her?

Yvette backtracked until she came to the narrow lane around the corner from Le Rêve. "One house, two house painted blue, three house, four house, say *adieu*," she whispered as she walked past the two-story boardinghouses, remembering her old chant for getting in and out of the cabaret unnoticed as a young girl.

And there it was. The Perezes' place, built on a wonky slant to accommodate the steep incline it sat on. There, tucked between the walls of house number three and house number four sat a narrow corridor leading to a hidden courtyard. It was where the women hung their laundry to dry during the day. In the old days, drunks needing a place to piss at night sometimes staggered in, too, hence the locked gate. Yvette watched the upstairs windows for movement. When no one stirred, she put her palm over the lock and whispered her burglar's spell. After aiming a little spit at the hinge, the gate opened, squeaking no louder than the rise and fall of a carousel horse in the Jardin des Fleurs.

With one hand pressed against the bricks to guide her, she passed through the darkened corridor to where the rear apartments of Le Rêve overlooked the courtyard. A prickle on her neck made her turn and look up. A faint light, like a match held to a cigarette, glowed in one of the windows, but it quickly went out again. What if it was one of *les mouches* buzzing around the back? She held still, ears and eyes tuned to any movement. When no one came out to investigate or raise the alarm, she turned her attention to the window of her old room, one story up. The once convenient ladder was gone, but there was a wooden wheelbarrow leaning against the building she might stand on. She could drag it across the yard, but the scraping of metal would make a hell of a noise, and the only stealth spell she knew wasn't worth the effort. Never buy a spell off the back of a wagon, she thought, even if it does come wrapped in a fancy decorated tin covered in testimonials.

Preoccupied by her dilemma, Yvette almost didn't notice the prowler who had joined her in the shadows. The black cat that had ignored her earlier tiptoed through the corridor, flicked his tail, then walked to the opposite end of the courtyard. There, stacked in the corner, sat a tower of vegetable crates still ripe with the smell of cabbage and turnips.

Ah, merci.

She threw off the velvet curtain and, as quietly as she could, stacked two crates under the window. The long skirt and blouse would be a hindrance. Not made for climbing, those. But on the streets, you couldn't afford to throw anything away. She kicked off her clumsy shoes and shimmied out of the stolen skirt and blouse until she stood in the harlequin leotard she'd been wearing when she arrived in the city. It hadn't fared well from the grime of the gutters, but it was made for performing just the sort of acrobatics a climb like this required. And, as she'd learned from working the carnival, so was her body. She put her stockinged foot atop the bottom crate and tested her weight on it. It held, so she scrambled onto the ledge of the first floor. The cat curled up in her discarded velvet, preening his paws, unimpressed.

Yvette brushed the brick dust off her hands. "You may not know this, Monsieur Whiskers," she whispered in her thief's voice, "but I've been called as nimble as a cat myself."

What she didn't say was that she first heard those comments come from behind the glass of the apartment window she now peered through, by men she never knew beyond the phrase, "Whatever you like, monsieur."

The room was dark, so she lifted the sash a mere inch. She'd have bet her last centime it wouldn't be locked. She'd broken the mechanism years ago during one of her midnight escapes, and Tante Isadora was too tightfisted to spend precious coins on such a minor concern as a girl's security. Yvette pushed the window all the way open and slipped over the sill. A feather-light tingle brushed over her skin as she stood inside her old room. The scent of male musk and rose-oil perfume mingled in the air above the unmade bed. Three years gone by and still the smell lingered, transporting her back to those last moments she'd stood in the room, blood spilling everywhere.

Her eyes adjusted to the inky darkness. The furniture was the same: bed, vanity, wardrobe, and washstand. But they'd been moved, rearranged to suit another's spatial comfort. Or maybe to cover the stain. She hadn't come to snoop, but a glint of starlight reflecting off a metal blade on the vanity caught her eye. She reached for it as the door swung open.

"Stop right there!"

A young woman wearing a pink corset and petticoat over black tights and ankle-high lace-up boots stood in the doorway, a fire poker hoisted in one hand, a blue flame cupped in the other. She kicked the door all the way open with her foot. Her gaze shifted to the table where Yvette had picked up the decorative knife, an athame, the sort of fancy blade witches used in their magic rituals.

"Put that down."

"I only—"

A bolt of energy hit Yvette in her midsection, knocking her flat against the bed.

"We have a thief," yelled the young woman, as Yvette reflexively felt for damage to her ribs. The sound of women's heels running on the wooden planks in the hallway followed. "Move again and I'll skewer you to the floor with this poker," whispered the pink-frocked woman.

There hadn't even been an incantation, not a single utterance to birth the spell, and yet Yvette had been thrown clean off her feet. "How'd you do that?"

"Never mind, you. Just be glad I didn't shove you out the window. Though you may wish I had. Here she comes."

"What's all this?" asked the stern voice of a woman accustomed to zero nonsense.

Yvette recovered enough from the blow—and the shock of hearing that voice again—to sit up.

"Hello, Tante. How's tricks?"

CHAPTER FOUR

Marion Martel greeted her son in the foyer of her city apartment with a kiss on each cheek, then pivoted like an animatronic woman to formally welcome Elena. The hem of the woman's gray silk evening gown swept over the tile floor as the intricate beading caught the light from the chandelier above. Electric light, Elena noted.

"My dear, we meet at last." Marion leaned in for an air kiss on each cheek as the women shook hands. "You are as beautiful as my son reported. Do come in, please. I've arranged for the most wonderful dinner of *soupe à l'oignon, confit de canard,* and *niçoise* salad. And if you're very good and let me get to know all about you, we'll share a chocolate soufflé with a coffee afterward." A smile bloomed on her lips in obvious delight at her proposal. "Come, I know you're famished from the train ride."

Elena barely had time to say yes before they were escorted into an extravagant dining room with three floor-to-ceiling windows. An eight-foot potted palm had been precisely positioned on either side of the center window, their leaves arcing in seemingly effortless sync with the curve at the top of the windows. Above the linen-draped table hung a chandelier adorned with teardrop-shaped crystals that glimmered in the sunlight coming through the glass. The effect was absolutely magical.

They ate, commenting now and again on the quality of the bread, the seasoning of the duck, and the freshness of the eggs and tomatoes in the salad. If Elena didn't know better, she might believe Marion Martel employed a culinary witch in her kitchen. Every crumb was as sumptuous as the next, each as buttery and flaky as any *sorcière* could produce. She vowed to peek in the kitchen before she left to see if she could detect the aura floating above the chef.

And then there was the wine. Well aged. A special bottle, one of Grand-Père's last vintages. Her tongue perceived the telltale grapes from the old vine. The weather had been perfect that year, full of sun and rain in the right proportion, encouraging just enough sweetness in the grape's flesh. The wine filled her mouth with a mix of currants and cherries, plum and smoke. That particular red had always been one to savor, but even more so now because Marion Martel had served it with purpose. A gesture of acceptance? She hoped so.

"Now that we have satisfied the palate, let us satisfy our mutual curiosity," Marion exclaimed as she led Elena and Jean-Paul into her salon to drink coffee on a lush velvet sofa. The divan was the color of deepest red wine, like a young cabernet, Elena thought. Above it hung a curious painting full of complex color combinations depicting a family at the beach. The paints ought not to work with each other, yet they came brilliantly together in a kaleidoscope of hues that grew more distinct the farther one stood from the picture.

"Tell me about your family, my dear. Do all your people come from the Chanceaux Valley? Philippe, my late husband, and I enjoyed many a summer holiday there as newlyweds, and later as a family, didn't we, Jean-Paul? It's most certainly why my son ended up settling there."

In keeping with their prior arrangement, Elena only admitted half-truths. "It's where I grew up. My people have worked in the vineyards there for centuries."

"That long? That's quite a legacy. But, of course, the wine is what the valley is famous for. That and the witches. Always an adventure when one of the local women reaches out for your palm to offer to read your fortune." Marion's shoulders shimmied, as if the prospect of mingling with the occult gave her a little shiver.

Jean-Paul nearly spit out his coffee.

"All right, dear? As I was saying, I've always enjoyed the summer market days in the valley. The atmosphere puts a little pep in my step. In fact, I aim to do a little supernatural investigating here in the city as well. Oh, don't look so shocked, Jean-Paul; a little psychic mischief is good for the soul now and then."

"*Maman*, what are you on about?"

Elena wondered, too, leaning slightly to her left to see if there was any hint of an aura tucked under the collar of the woman's gray silk dress. But, no, Marion's halo was as dull as hen feathers.

"I'm visiting a medium later in the week. She does séances to communicate with those who've passed over to the other side. Several of my circle have been already and highly recommend her."

"A séance?" Jean-Paul shook his head as if he hadn't heard right. "To speak with the dead? Why would you do that?"

"To speak to your father, naturally." Marion took a sip of her coffee, raised a brow, and smiled at her son. Then she spoke to Elena. "I noticed you studying that painting a moment ago. It is beautiful, isn't it? And yet it's quite ordinary in comparison to the one I had hanging there prior."

"The colors are so . . ."

"Bold! Yes, I agree. It's all part of the modern sensibility. But, before Philippe and I were married, I had a portrait done by a splendid new artist. But I cannot for the life of me remember the man's name. Something foreign sounding. Tell her, Jean-Paul."

"It was a portrait of my mother. His take was . . . different. I can't remember who the artist was either, though he's apparently grown quite famous."

"That's right. His works are highly valuable now," his mother inserted.

"Which is why the painting was stolen."

"Stolen?" Elena asked.

Jean-Paul explained how weeks before his father died there'd been a break-in. Jewelry, cash, some paper bonds, and the painting—all taken in a brazen daytime robbery. The police couldn't figure it out. There was no sign of the door being forced, no way anyone could carry so much out the window, and none of the neighbors or passersby apparently saw a thing.

"There were a rash of burglaries that summer along the rue de Jardin," Marion said, pointing out the window to indicate the park view. The woman shook her head at the state of the world. "But it wasn't as bad as Madame Chevalier's loss. A million in gold stolen."

"Who keeps that much in gold?" Elena asked.

"Precisely. I think there was some foreign deal she was involved in that required cash. Enough money to fund a small country as I recall. Nearly destroyed her financially. It happened years and years ago, but no one was ever caught. She's quite recovered from the theft now."

"Oh, and while we're on the subject." Marion opened the drawer of a bureau desk and removed a small velvet box. "I found something the other day among your father's things. I thought for sure they'd been stolen as well, being solid gold. They're from his time in the service in the colonies."

Jean-Paul opened the box. Inside were a pair of gold cuff links, each sporting a crescent moon and star emblem, immediately sparking a chain of memories in the mother and son about the father's brief post in the desert. While they reminisced, Elena stared at the window Marion had gestured to earlier. She let her shadow vision seep in ever so slightly, lowering her eyes as if she were listening in deep concentration.

There, near the latch, the faintest trace of a spell, like a cobweb that showed only in certain light. Someone had used magic to get in and out. A masking spell of some sort, based on the cloak-like webbing that spread to the glass. That's why the police couldn't figure the case out.

"So, you see, dear"—Marion had begun speaking about the séance again—"I need to talk to my late husband so I can ask him who the artist was. I might like to hire him again."

Elena felt Jean-Paul's hand squeeze hers. She shook loose from her shadow vision and nodded and smiled at her future mother-in-law as if it were perfectly normal to want to pay a swindler a large sum of money to speak to an empty crystal ball in the hope the dearly departed might respond. A few reputable necromancers did exist—at least Grand-Mère had mentioned one she'd seen raise the dead in her youth—but she knew of none who took money from mortals on a whim. She wouldn't be surprised if this medium turned out to be one of the infamous Charlatan clan. Their brand of fraud seemed to be everywhere lately.

"Perhaps I could accompany you," Elena said, curious to see if it was a witch involved with these hapless mortal women. "We do see a lot of that sort of influence in the valley."

Jean-Paul sat up. "Really?"

"Oh, that would be splendid! I'd love to show you off to my social circle." Marion clapped her hands together in delight. "And now that you've surprised me with this wonderful gesture, I have something wonderful I'd like to show you both in the morning. It will require an excursion through the city. Please say you'll come."

Elena sensed Jean-Paul inwardly groan, but they agreed to accompany Marion in the morning, not wishing to deny her the pleasure of presenting her surprise.

CHAPTER FIVE

Tante Isadora, the woman who'd taken Yvette in when her mother had abandoned her, stood in the doorframe silhouetted by the smoky glow of the hallway's gaslights. Her auburn hair, streaked now with filaments of gray, was parted in the middle and swept atop her head in a pile of marcel curls. Her cheeks were heavily rouged in an effort to revive the youth long gone from them. A stiff corset held her middle-aged form inside a purple silk evening gown. The double flounce above the hem was a common stitch-witch trick to make the dress appear more expensive than it was.

Tante Isadora stared at Yvette and exhaled. "Leave us, Louise."

"But she—"

"I said leave."

The pink-ruffled witch opened her mouth to protest being tossed from her own room, then thought better of it. Tante had no magic, but one look of displeasure from her could shrivel even the bravest heart to a prune.

The young woman left. Tante closed the door, leaning her back against it with her arms crossed, as if to reinforce the one truth every girl who worked Le Rêve came to know: *she* controlled who came and went through her establishment.

"I didn't believe them when they said you might actually show your face here again."

Yvette stayed seated on the bed, though she inched closer to the open window under the guise of finding a nonlumpy edge of the mattress to get comfortable on. *They*, she knew, were the Bureau agents downstairs.

"Any chance you have a ciggie on you? I'm dying for a smoke."

"*Mon Dieu.*" Tante advanced and pulled a small blue tin out of the beaded reticule dangling from her wrist. "Don't you ever tire of testing my patience?"

"Missed you too," Yvette said and took two cigarettes from the case. One she slipped between her lips, and the other she tucked behind her ear. She waited for a match, but Tante nudged her chin toward the vanity, where an Aladdin's lamp lighter sat. "Well, doesn't that beat all," Yvette said and felt for the small bottle tucked between her breasts, still safe and secure.

"Don't you dare steal it. It was a gift from a generous *abonné*. He's quite taken with our Louise."

"She's a witch."

"Yes. Only this one actually knows how to do spells. Brings in the money you never could."

Yvette lit her cigarette and squinted through the smoke as it stung her eye. Tante leaned in and lit one as well before sitting down on the upholstered bench with the gold fringe in front of the vanity. Yvette had always wanted a seat with fringe.

"Thought there were laws about tricking mortals into handing over money."

Tante balked. "Did you come here to give me a lecture on the law? Spare me the hypocrisy. Besides, if you'd been any better at the game, you wouldn't still owe me money." She raised her eyebrow and blew out a trail of smoke, as if she almost believed it was possible to see the cash materialize.

"And why *is* that?" Yvette asked. Now that she had survived the initial threat of coming face-to-face with Tante Isadora again, she grew bolder. "Why don't I know more spells? Why don't I have a Book of Shadows of my own, or potion jars?" She stooped to pick up the dropped athame. "Or one of these?" She leaned closer to Tante, her grip a little too tight on the handle. "I'm a witch same as anyone. Why didn't my mother leave me any of these things?" She swallowed before her emotions could well up and make a mess all over the room. "Where did she go that she couldn't take me with her? Why didn't I get to learn all that stuff?"

Tante inhaled deeply, as if arming her emotions. "Ah, so that's why you're here." She reached for an ashtray, her eye steady on the knife. "You've finally come looking for your *maman*."

She didn't like the glint in Tante's eye, the familiar calculations going on behind them—pros and cons, profits and loss, truth or dare.

"What happened to her? Why did she leave me to be raised by a—"

"A cabaret whore?"

"Oh là là, I was going to say mortal."

Tante tapped her cigarette three times, flicking the ash into a tray shaped like a palmistry hand—the heart, life, and fate lines crisscrossing the white porcelain in black paint. It was *she* who insisted she be called Tante. All the girls who came to work the cabaret were required to think of her as Aunt Isadora, though only Yvette had grown up within the guts of Le Rêve, as near as anything resembling a blood-related niece. Left in the care of a fellow dancer and supposed friend of her mother's when a mere babe, she'd been given a bed, two meals a day when there was money enough, and, as she got older, a new dress once a year, though always bought second- or thirdhand from the church's charity shop. In exchange for her room and board, she wiped down the drinking glasses, mended costumes, and mopped up the stomach contents of drunks too off their feet from the absinthe to make it outside.

Of course, there had been "lessons." At least at first, when Tante still offered rare but regular sugared treats and bedtime kisses. Yvette recalled a spindly fellow in a worn frock coat and scuffed shoes who had shown up three times a week when she was a girl of seven or eight. At first, he taught her the alphabet, followed by reading and writing, and then subtly the lessons shifted to recognizing runes, suits of tarot cards, and working out how to put words in the right order to perform a simple spell. But even then, she could barely control the frenzied energy that would surge into her hands. It would start with the promise of magic and the feeling she could shape the thing forming on her fingertips, only to have it fizzle into nothing, her hands left with the sensation of holding a dripping pile of wet newspaper. After a few short months the man gave up, sneered at her ugly scar, and declared her a stub—a useless witch without talent in the eyes of the All Knowing. Following that proclamation, Tante's sweets and kisses fermented into sour regret at having taken her in.

No return on investment, it would seem.

"Your mother and I were friends," Tante said. "I've told you that before. Better you were placed here with me than left in the orphanage with the filthy urchins running up and down the streets like rats. And in the end, what difference did it make if a mortal raised you? You've no more powers than a common country charlatan."

"Maybe if my mother had been around to teach me what she knew, I'd be different."

Tante shrewdly narrowed her eyes. "Something's changed. You never cared about these things before. You always managed with your limitations. And yet you risked coming here when you know the police are looking for you. And for what? To find some lost magic that will never be yours?"

It's true she hadn't cared before. She hadn't thought there was any point in working at something she obviously wasn't any good at. There was more money and exhilaration to be had in enabling the whims of men's desires. And then she saw a real witch work serious magic and felt the sizzle rise in her blood to know more. To *be* more.

"You're not a witch," Yvette said, thinking of her conversations with Elena, the only proper witch she'd ever known. "You wouldn't understand how important a mentor is to learning the craft."

Tante answered with a cynical laugh. "No, I'm a businesswoman, and I have a cabaret to run." She stubbed her cigarette out on the ashtray's heart line and stood. "So, if you're not here to pay me what you owe, I think it best you hop back out that window, my dirty little harlequin."

"Wait."

Tante picked up the train of her gown, ready to leave, then paused, imparting one last ounce of patience.

Yvette sucked in a breath. "Tell me if she's still alive. If I can find her somewhere in the city." She would not cry and beg in front of this woman, but she had to know. She reached out and gently touched the pale, freckled skin of Tante's forearm. "Please, where can I find my mother?"

Tante's eyes, glistening ever so slightly, flicked from her arm to Yvette. "There was a time, in the beginning, when I thought I could be a mother to you. But even as a child you were different from most girls. You see it in dogs sometimes, too, the way one pup gets culled from the rest of the litter. A runt." Tante sighed. "With your mother's genes, I thought there might be a chance . . . but it simply wasn't meant to be."

"You mean to be a dancer like her?"

"Your mother wasn't merely a dancer," she said, twirling away from Yvette so that her skirt swept the floor with a flourish. "She was a star. She commanded the room. The stage was her domain, the audience her subjects. Oh, how the men adored her. She had the face of a gilded angel. All done by magic, of course, but she wielded it with such grace it never took on the tawdry hue of the common witchcraft you see on display from so many these days. Like those slatterns in the street selling

46

their potion bottles while lifting their skirts." A moment passed, and the dream of shadows past drifted from her eyes. She looked again at Yvette, her gaze shifting to the unfortunate scar. Something in Tante finally softened. Relented. As if she'd grown weary of keeping up her resistance. She reached toward Yvette's face, tentative at first, as if petting a stray dog for the first time, uncertain if it would bite, then lightly touched the ridge of scar running along the cheek and jaw. "Such a shame," she said before taking her hand away again. "I don't know where your mother is. Or if she's still alive. To my knowledge, no one has seen or heard from her since the day she left you in my care. She simply vanished."

Left? Not abandoned? Yvette's heartbeat sped up, that racing speed that said something in her life was on the verge of either disaster or miracle.

The former dancer walked across the room, seemingly floating above the rough wooden planks with her light, rhythmic steps. "However . . . ," she said, stopping before the wardrobe closet.

Yvette lifted her chin. Her life always seemed to be hanging on the hope of a "however" or a "but" or a "maybe."

Tante opened the closet door and took down a pair of hatboxes that had been stored on the top shelf. "So dusty," she said, setting them aside and waving a hand over them to clear the air. She returned to the closet, reaching up even higher this time. She gave a quick glance over her shoulder, shrugged as if to say everyone had their secrets, then slid open a panel in the ceiling of the wardrobe. Her arm stretched to feel for something in the deep recess of the hiding place, then came away with a packet the size of a deck of cards tied up in faded blue ribbon.

Yvette gaped. All the years she spent in that room and she'd never once discovered the hidden compartment. The contraband she could have hidden!

Tante blew on the packet to clear away a tiny cobweb clinging to the ribbon. She tested its weight as if there might yet be a stack of money inside, double-checking the balance against her sharp instinct for things of value, before handing the envelope over.

Yvette turned the package around, inspecting it from all sides. "What is it?"

The flick of a dismissive hand. "I opened the wrapping once. Just to see. I don't know why she wanted me to save it. A bunch of nonsense, if you ask me." Tante replaced the hatboxes on the shelf, then delicately brushed the dust from her hands. "But your mother insisted I keep it safely hidden away for you. Even gave me a gold coin to ensure I do so. Mind, it was never enough to cover the cost of feeding you all those years."

"Why didn't you ever give it to me before?"

"She implored me to wait until you turned sixteen. Of course, by then you'd already run off as a murderess."

Down the hall the musicians began to play a new melody featuring the piano and accordion. Rowdy. Jaunty. A song to get the blood moving and raise a thirst so customers would order more drinks. Shrewd Isadora, always worried about where the next coin would drop. Yvette knew the thing in her hands, if it had been a family heirloom like a silver locket or gold ring, would have been pawned long ago, despite any wish of her mother's. And yet the shabby envelope wrapped in blue ribbon with a sprig of dried rosemary had value to her beyond the measure of mortal reasoning.

She could feel the energy humming against her palm.

A gift. From her mother.

She untied the ribbon and peeled back the brittle paper, all the while sensing Tante's watchful eyes. She turned her body a little to the right and slid what looked like a booklet free of the paper. The unadorned black leather had dried over time, bearing a faded crack in its skin, but the pages—handmade paper with a deckled edge—still had the suppleness of fine cloth. She fanned them open and saw that the pages were filled with small handwritten symbols. Triangles, circles, swirls, and dots inked in black, all arranged in different positions. Some, though, had been double traced with gold. Yvette touched the symbols with the tip of her finger, feeling the raised ridge of the paint.

"What is it?"

"I thought you might know, being a 'witch.'" Tante rolled her eyes and closed the wardrobe closet. "Like I said, nonsense."

Was it a spell book? A book of curses? A pawnbroker's coded ledger? There wasn't a speck of explanation, a title, or even a pair of initials to claim it. The booklet simply hummed like a bee against her skin.

Yvette was having difficulty holding back the twist of emotions vying for dominance. She was one part confused, one part brimming with hope. Riding on the tail of the latter, she dared to ask, "Can I stay till morning? I'll sleep on the floor. Or backstage after closing. It wouldn't bother me."

"With *les flics* hovering like fireflies at the door? I don't think that would be wise for either of us, *mon petite chou*. My bribes only buy me a blind eye for so long." Tante's gaze flicked to the window. "Best you go the way you came, if you don't want to wake in a cell tomorrow engaged to Monsieur Guillotine."

For any other girl it would have been as harsh a blow as a palm against her cheek, but not for one holding pages full of buzzing promise in her hands. The cold, wet street would be no match against Yvette's buoyant heart tonight, and so she left.

⚬⚬⚬

An hour later Yvette curled up on the floor beneath a painted dome aglow with starlight. Dozens of candles flickered from an altar below. Seeking refuge for the night, she'd slipped inside the great beast of the butte, as it was the warmest place she could think to hide. Staring up at the cathedral's grand interior, it certainly lived up to its name. The exposed ribs arched three stories high, giving her a feeling of having been swallowed whole by a great white whale. As long as the overgrown beast held her safe, she didn't much mind being fish food for the night.

People from the neighborhood came and went, one or two at a time, to show their adoration at the altar. But no one seemed to pay her any attention, once she'd tucked herself away in the shadows at the back behind a confessional. A woman wrapped up in a black shawl lit a candle and knelt nearby, speaking an invocation. Yvette drew her velvet curtain up under her chin and stared at her booklet, passively listening to the rhythm of the woman's foreign words being said over and over again.

Even in the low light she could make out the gold-and-black symbols, as if they created their own luminescence on the paper. She tilted the pages, watching how the triangles and squiggly lines seemed to bend with the light. Like tiny golden fish. Her mother's magic. It had to be. But it was no kind of magic she'd ever seen before. The symbols meant nothing to her. They could be magic symbols from another country for all she could tell, or the very same words the shawled woman was muttering. If so, she knew even less about her mother than she'd thought. Sidra might know what the symbols meant. But Sidra . . . no. That was a dead end. She'd rather tear all her hair out than listen to that self-righteous jinni explain magic to her.

She trailed her finger over the paper, liking the soft tingle of communication between the strange marks and her bare skin. The booklet was only seven pages long, with each page containing seven lines. And, she noticed, there were seven symbols in each line. A definite pattern. What did it mean? She looked for more telltale signs of patterns, but nothing stood out. Things repeated, but not in any order she could recognize. She was going to need help. And she knew enough about magic to know it could go one of two ways: good or very, very bad.

Yvette went over the names in her head of the witches she knew from her former days in the city. She'd spoken a few times to the rag lady Consuela, who always set her cart up on the street in front of Jardin

Antoine to watch the spirits of the dead come and go between the catacombs and the park cemetery. Then there was Desiree, who used a levitation spell to become a juggler in the circus that did shows on the other side of the butte. And Rings, of course, who wasn't really a witch but a thief who taught her how to charm locks and slip fat wallets free of their protective pockets. How he learned the burglar's charm as a mortal, she had no idea, but it had never failed her. And while any one of them would probably help her for the right price, it was unlikely they had the know-how to contend with a conundrum like this. No, she was going to need the help of a properly trained witch.

She was still thumbing through the booklet and considering her options when the same black cat from earlier found her in the cathedral, only this time she noticed the animal was wearing a silvery collar around his neck. "Monsieur Whiskers?" she whispered. "What are you doing here?" She lifted her head to see if he'd come inside with anyone, perhaps the woman in the shawl, but no one accompanied him. Though a tad suspicious of his sudden fondness for her, she was grateful for the animal's company. "You looking for a warm place to hide too?" The cat blinked up at her with stoic green eyes that neither confirmed nor denied the animal understood what she'd said. At least he seemed to accept she was a witch worth his attention. "Well, lucky for you I have a little something for both of us."

Yvette slipped the booklet back inside the paper cover and stuffed it under her blouse for safekeeping. Then she reached beneath the velvet curtain turned blanket and brought out a small wedge of cheese wrapped in a wine-stained napkin. "It's from Tante," she whispered to the cat. "She's not always as hard as she likes to pretend." None of us are, she thought, and pinched a finger full of the cheese and held it out. The cat accepted the offering, smacking his tongue against the roof of his mouth, then swallowed with what looked like disappointment. Yvette unwrapped a portion for herself and took a bite.

"Leftovers that would have been thrown out," she said with her mouth full, "but not so bad compared to an empty stomach. Would be better if we had some of that altar wine to wash it down with, but such is life for those on the run, eh, monsieur?" The cat meowed, and she held her finger to her lips. "Shhh, you'll get us tossed out of here with your complaining." She patted her hand against her thigh. "Come lie down."

The cat yawned and needled her velvet cover with his sharp claws. She slid over enough so that he could curl up in the space behind her knees. He really was a scraggly, wretched thing, but his small presence, no matter how transient, made her feel less alone. She gave him a scratch behind his ear, and he purred with his head resting against her leg.

Yvette put her head down knowing she didn't have a centime to her name. She was also wanted for a murder she most definitely committed and forced to take shelter inside the belly of a bloated beast that could spit her onto the street at any moment. But between the humming of the booklet against her heart, the promise of the jinni's fire prophecy, and the comfort of the tiny windup motor purring inside the cat beside her, she fell asleep to the vibrating thrum of hope for perhaps the first time in her life.

CHAPTER SIX

The wet asphalt glinted in the morning sunlight. Marion made a remark about the swirling colors on the wet pavement being like a work of one of the impressionist masters. Elena politely agreed, though she rather thought the effect was more like a mushroom-based jinx that caused light and color to dance in the eyes.

The overnight rain had deterred them from getting an earlier start, but Marion had promised a surprise worth venturing to the other side of the city. Now that they rocked from side to side atop the northbound omnibus, the trio greeted the outing with the spirit of joie de vivre it deserved. The sun was shining, the sky was clear, and summer's impending death hung in the air.

Of course, they were cut off at nearly every turn by one of the myriad two-seater automobiles that seemed to have reproduced like rabbits on the streets since Elena's last visit.

"To think your father nearly bought one of those disasters of human progress." Marion waved her handkerchief in the general direction of the traffic below.

"*Maman*, it was a race car. He meant to sponsor a driver in Le Concours Ville à Campagne."

"Oh, pish, it was always something to try and stir the blood with that man."

Elena recognized the look on her fiancé's face, knowing he felt strongly that the vigor of a man's blood should not be taken lightly. Left to pool, it had the tendency to congeal into a sort of sticky mud that left the heart choking from a lack of ambition. From a witch's perspective she wholeheartedly concurred with his assessment. The nurturing of one's well-being was of utmost importance, pleasing the All Knowing. Which is why she had to question the peculiar murmur that had fluttered beneath her solar plexus since she'd awoken that morning. It was small at first, like the beat of a butterfly wing against her heart, but the farther north they traveled the more distinct the rhythm became until she feared her fellow passengers might hear the knock of a raptor's wing against her rib cage, her intuition banging on the door of her third-eye perception.

"Everything all right, dear?"

She'd noticed. Marion was no witch, but she had a keen eye for a mortal. Not many details slipped past her powers of observation when it came to matters of etiquette and fashion. Earlier that morning she had asked Elena if her suit was from the House of Enrique. It was, but from the father, not the son. She had one new ensemble to wear on this trip—store-bought from a mortal—and she meant to wear that on their outing to Maurice's later in the week. Almost everything else was at least ten years old, dating back to the time before she'd succumbed to the curse that had taken seven years of her life. Her clothes were dreadfully out of style, judging by the sea of beautiful women walking past on the streets below with their feathered tricorn hats, shapely skirts, and velvet cocoon wraps.

Elena pressed a hand on her chest to calm her rattling intuition. "Oh, I was merely wondering if we'd be taking the bus all the way to the end of the line at Place Blanco?"

"Ah, so you've guessed my destination but not my surprise," Marion said with a shake of her finger. "Not another clue until we get there."

Yes, of course they were headed toward the butte. The energy there was overrun with old magic, not all of it under the eye of the All Knowing. Elena had felt the hum before when she and Grand-Mère had traveled the back lanes looking for a bit of this and that for spells requiring rare ingredients, like the pale-yellow marula oil bought in small glass vials and the lardish chunks of ambergris sold in wrapped muslin. Could that vortex of questionable energy be the thing calling to her? Warning her?

A barge honked like an ailing duck and a train rattled from a nearby elevated track as they lumbered north across the river. Elena stirred from her wandering thoughts. Her future mother-in-law was watching again. Marion narrowed her eyes before looking away to admire the impressive Musée Couloir, home to the works of the old masters, on the left, a wink in her smile. Straightening her posture, Elena, too, concentrated on admiring the architecture for the remainder of the journey. From her lofty perch she took in the view of the Royal Gardens, the austere facade of the Palais Opéra, and a charming domed theater on a busy street corner offering midnight showings of a moving picture: *Le Voyage dans la Lune*.

At last the omnibus halted at a busy junction where five streets converged across from a dilapidated-looking nightclub with a bright-red windmill in the midst of the cabaret district. The odd tilt to the structure, the film of grime on the windows, the scent of urine and wine rising from the sidewalk—Elena wondered briefly if the place could be a witch's tavern. But despite the radiant aura materializing above the roof (the probable result of an abundance of supernatural exuberance), there were no detectable spells or jinxes affixed to its perimeter to thwart the curious mortal venturing too near. She could only conclude the establishment was open to anyone. Curious. The boundaries between witches and mortals in the city had blurred more than she'd observed before, at least at this particular urban crossroad.

Jean-Paul appeared somewhat embarrassed for his mother to be standing on a street in her fine fur collar in front of such an establishment, but the woman was on a frolic. An adventure. She beamed, lit up by the power of her secret, urging them onward past the workingwomen with their rouged cheeks and low-cut bodices.

"Is it much farther? Should I hire a *fiacre* for the rest of the journey, *Maman*?"

"Pish, we'll walk from here," she said, urging them to follow. "Exercise is invigorating, don't you find?"

Ten minutes later, after climbing up the ever-narrowing lanes of the butte, it wasn't just Elena's heart that was beating faster from the exertion. Her pulse thumped to keep up with her revving intuition. Nearly driven to compulsion, instinct told her something urgent waited for her.

Marion's smile grew more genuine, revealing her small, straight teeth, as they reached a cobblestone courtyard. A pair of benches sat under a canopy of chestnut trees. The shade was sparse given half the leaves had already fallen from the trees, but it was a welcome relief to stand beneath the bare limbs and catch one's breath. Marion continued to smile like the cat that swallowed the canary as Jean-Paul and Elena took in their surroundings. There were no shops across the street—no tailor, no patisserie, not even a café where they might sit for a coffee, though Elena knew such places were nearby. There was, however, a sharp scent in the air, as if someone were boiling the bark of a pine tree and infusing it with tar or petrol. They'd passed a laundress's shop a block away, but, no, the smell was coming from the run-down building on the other side of the courtyard, the one that listed to the side like a ship in rough water.

"So, *Maman*, what is this surprise of yours?" Jean-Paul asked. He removed his hat to let his head cool. "Please tell me it involves a wineglass."

"Perhaps later," said his mother. "For now, there's someone I want you to meet." Remarkably, she headed for the entrance at the base of the tilting building.

"*Maman,* are you sure it's safe? The place doesn't even look like it should be standing anymore."

His mother crooked her finger, and they followed, if only to protect her from being buried beneath the wobbling walls of the obvious flophouse.

The sharp pine scent hit the back of Elena's throat again as she adjusted her eyes to the dark interior. Once inside, she recognized the source of the industrial tang. Turpentine! And paint. Yes, the muddy smell of oily pigments emanated off the floorboards, the walls, and even the ceiling. The place was steeped in the earthy scent. Pretending she was correcting her balance, she placed her hand against the cracked wall to allow herself a moment to sense what else might run through the wood and plaster. Through her shadow vision, she saw the golden filaments of an odd spell encircling the place, as if that were the only means holding the structure upright. The crumbling building had been bewitched. But by whom? And for what purpose? She walked farther down the hallway and peeked through the crack of an open door. The room was spartan, full of canvases and paints and a tiny stove with a single pan. The windows were large and let in the daylight, lifting the overhanging gloom.

Marion sashayed down the rickety hall strewn with rubbish, overturned cans, and the occasional yet obvious rat dropping, lifting the hem of her skirt in the worst spots as if it were a path she'd taken many times before. On the third door down on the left, she knocked three times. A moment later a short man with full round eyes and a painter's palette balanced in his hand answered. "Ah, *buenos días,* Madame Martel." He grinned at Marion before embracing her warmly and kissing her cheek. When they parted, he stuck his free hand out and welcomed them inside.

The man introduced himself as Pedro, a painter of portraits, though after taking a peek at the canvases lining the walls, he was unlike any artist Elena had encountered before. Many of his subjects were women, prostitutes with kohl-rimmed eyes and smudges of rouge to highlight their cheekbones. Their faces defiant. Proud. Rendered in a palette of reds, blues, and yellows that spoke of pluck and nerve on the part of the models. Pedro showed not only talent but ingenuity. A willingness to try new things. Art was one of the disciplines her kind was drawn to as a vocation too. She'd read some witch artists ground up sacred herbs and bits of bone or rock into their pigments to enhance their paints and infuse a scene with an element of enchantment. She could see the allure, though she'd never shown even a mortal's gift for the arts.

"What do you think of my surprise?" asked Marion, gesturing with open arms at the loft full of canvases.

"I'm still not sure what it is." Jean-Paul turned around, eyeing the jumble of tins full of brushes, the pots of pigments, the loose rags splotched with a rainbow of colors, and the bottles of sinus-burning solvents lined up along the floor. His gaze stopped on the unmade bed against the wall and he swallowed, as if bracing himself for the worst. "Is there something more you need to tell me?"

"Yes," his mother answered, unaware of his innuendo. "I've commissioned a portrait. Isn't it wonderful? Pedro is going to paint Elena. It's my wedding present to you both. He's quite inventive, this one. You'll see. He's already had a showing with that dealer, what's his name, Vieillard. Very up and coming. I admit he doesn't speak the language that well yet, but no matter. There's no cultural barrier when it comes to art. I'm sure you'll get along swimmingly."

"Oh." Elena wasn't expecting that. And yet as surprised as she was, the announcement wasn't the sort to arouse her instinct, not to the level of panic she'd felt since they hopped on the omnibus and headed for the butte.

"This is the one?" Pedro asked, arms folded as he squinted at Elena. He had her stand in the light of the window as he took in the angles of her face and shoulders.

Marion waved Jean-Paul over, his mouth still agape, to see some of the artist's other finished works. "Come, tell me what you think of this one for the entryway."

Pedro rotated Elena's head to view her from cheek to cheek, then nodded, his lower lip protruding in approval before obliging his patroness by turning out more of his canvases. Some he propped on the furniture, two rested on easels, a few sat along the floorboards leaning against the wall. To Elena's surprise, Jean-Paul did, in fact, take an interest once his eye seemingly caught some spark of undiscovered genius in the paint strokes before him. He turned once to smile at Elena but otherwise embarked on a scavenger hunt through the stacks.

Based on the sphere of small lights hovering around his aura, Pedro was favored by the All Knowing, but he was definitely a mortal. And possibly a bit lascivious in his nature, judging by the leering looks he shot her way while the others dug through his work. Elena resigned herself to enduring the rest of the morning's visit as best as she could, but then she was going to have to politely decline her soon-to-be mother-in-law's "surprise."

After circling behind the others to be closer to the exit, Elena wondered if it would be better to use a wishing string or merely a suggestive tea on Marion to get her off this idea of having a portrait done. Lost in contemplation, she almost didn't register the first whisper-soft brush of fur against her ankles. But when it happened again, she looked down to find an ebony cat had sidled up against her. Having got her attention, he purred loudly and insistently, winding back and forth against her legs.

Unlike Marion's announcement, the sight of the cat immediately set her intuition on alert. Just when her heartbeat sped up in recognition of the animal's significance, the feline waved his tail and ran out of the room. Obeying her instinct, Elena followed. While the artist answered Jean-Paul's question about the mood he'd intended to depict by painting an old man with azure skin, she slipped back down the hall and out the door to the courtyard. The cat looked over his shoulder once, as if making sure she'd followed, before trotting up the cobblestone lane.

Chasing after the cat as he crept up one alley and then the next seemed to unspool the thread of tension that had been building inside Elena since she awoke that morning. She had no idea what the cat was playing at, only that she must follow. As she chased behind, Elena tried to discern if he was a spirit creature, some cursed human, or perhaps a psychic guide. It was also possible he was merely a hungry cat looking for food, but she banished that thought as soon as he pranced past a café full of afternoon diners enjoying bowls of soup and bread at their outside tables.

The cat veered left after the café, his nimble feet more urgent in stride. Elena turned the corner. The cat stopped and sat in the middle of the lane as a man and woman argued ten feet beyond. Was that a nudge of the cat's chin, as if to say get on with it? The man shoved the woman hard against the wall and slapped her face. He pulled his arm back to hit her again, and Elena darted back to the café tables.

"I'll take a sprinkle," she said and held her hand below a pepper mill as a waiter hovered it over a customer's plate.

The waiter gave the mill a twist, and she ran back to the crooked lane with the pepper cupped in her palm. The man stood over the woman, who cowered on the ground with her hands held over her blonde head, demanding a key.

"Right, that's enough of that," Elena said to herself. She held her palm up and whispered, "Pepper black, sniff and sneeze, deliver your sting as a swarm of bees."

The crushed pepper lifted from her hand as the illusion spell took shape. A moment later a hive of swarming bees descended upon the thief, stinging him from head to backside. The cat mewed in apparent approval. And as the woman sat up to see what had driven off her attacker, lowering her arms to reveal her face, the astonishing accuracy of Elena's intuition struck home.

CHAPTER SEVEN

"*Cochon!*" Yvette shook her fist at the man as he ran away. Her head stung and her arm would likely be left with a bruise, but she was otherwise in one piece. Turning, she meant to wave a quick thanks to the woman who'd scared off her attacker, then run to the top of the lane before anyone had a chance to recognize her. Instead she clutched her velvet wrap around her, feeling shabby and poor standing in the long shadow of the witch before her.

"What the hell are you doing here?" Yvette wavered on her feet, still dizzy from the smack to her temple, as a trickle of blood wove its way through the roots of her hair.

"I could ask the same of you," Elena said. "Are you all right? Did he hurt you badly?"

"I've had worse."

Yvette wiped a smear of blood away when the trickle got too close to her eye. She looked past Elena, suspicious of the coincidence of finding her old cellmate on the street, then spotted the cat waving his tail and licking a paw. So, that's where he'd gone this morning after leaving her to wake up alone in the belly of the beast. Instead of dragging a dead mouse home, he'd gone and fetched a proper witch. Some cat.

"Better if we do this up here," Yvette said, nudging her chin away from the people at the café tables still chattering and laughing about the odd woman who demanded a handful of pepper. The cat tromped behind her, proud as can be.

Halfway up the lane, Yvette ducked into the mouth of a private courtyard. She leaned against the wall as Elena caught up.

"How'd you do that?" she asked, thinking of the bees and the way they'd attacked the man out of nowhere.

Elena smiled as though impressed with her own spell. "It was only an illusion, but the pepper gave it some real bite." She took some green leaves from her purse and rubbed them between her fingers. "Do you want to tell me why that man attacked you?"

"I have no idea why. Crazy lunatic. I was checking the trash bins for something to eat. Don't look at me like that; I've been out here for a whole month already. Today even the throwaways were rotten, so I skipped down here to swipe some leftovers off a plate before the waiter could clear the table. My mugger must have followed. He grabbed me from behind and threw me against the wall. Don't know what he was on about. Kept telling me to give him some key. When I said I didn't have one, he hit me."

"May I?"

"Sure, go on," she said, remembering how Elena had saved her sore feet once before with a bit of leaf and a spell.

She let Elena dab the oily substance from the crushed leaves on her hairline. It stung at first, but once Elena recited her incantation, nearly all the pain subsided. All except for that nagging prickle of envy at not being able to do the same magic for herself.

When she finished dabbing at the cut, Elena checked up and down the lane. "So are you going to tell me what you're doing back in the city? Sidra was supposed to take you somewhere safe."

The trickle of blood dried, and Yvette's head stopped throbbing. "Something went wrong." A row of stone steps led up to a locked gate guarding the narrow close. Yvette climbed halfway up and sat down. She explained about the stolen wish and her desire to find her mother and her magic and how she hadn't found the courage to confront Tante Isadora until yesterday. "Something changed. I got this fluttering inside. Felt like one of those big moths you see at night banging its wings against a streetlight. Like I *had* to go to the cabaret, even though I knew it would be dangerous. And I think it was because the wish was waiting for you."

The vine witch narrowed her eyes. "How do you mean?"

Yvette removed the book from under her velvet cloak and held it out. "What is it?"

"A book from my mother. Her book of spells, I think. Or maybe a diary. Or a list of debts? I have no idea."

"I thought you said you never knew your mother."

"Didn't. But she left this for me. For when I turned sixteen. Tante had kept the book for me that whole time, only I'd left the city before she could hand it over. Because of, you know." A couple strode by on the lane below, and Yvette ducked her head so she wouldn't be seen. "Because I'd stabbed that man. And let me tell you, he was just as crazy as the guy who did this. It was self-defense, same as this time, but no one ever listens to that part. I'm starting to think my magic talent is being a human magnet for lunatics."

It wasn't the first time Yvette had the thought or the first time she'd said the words out loud, but after this latest attack out of the blue, she was beginning to actually believe something was wrong with her.

"What makes you think your wish was waiting for me?"

She watched as Elena held a hand to her midsection as she spoke. The same place she'd felt the strange compulsion too. "Because you're a proper witch. Book smart. You know how magic works. So maybe my wish couldn't come true until you showed up to sort out what these pages say. And maybe even"—Yvette bit her lip—"maybe even teach me how to sort them out too."

"Sounds like you know more about how magic works than you let on."

"I know what I know. But it makes sense, don't it? Like Sidra said, maybe our fates are tied up together somehow." The cat purred and rubbed his body against Yvette's leg. "Even he thinks I'm onto something."

"May I take a look?"

Yvette handed over the soft leather book, her eyes wide with expectation. Though Elena had put on a fancy dress for the city, the smell of the vineyard still oozed from her skin—musty, earthy, a tinge of oak and red wine. Something else was there, too, like the scent of one of those flowering plants that lure you in with their fragrant petals, daring you to lean in closer to experience their beauty, even knowing a single seed held within could stop your heartbeat in an instant. Yvette didn't trust most people, but she'd thought this one was all right. It was Elena, after all, who'd saved her from going back to prison even knowing she wasn't exactly innocent.

"Can you feel it, the buzzing?"

"The words hum for you?" Elena had been turning the pages slowly, running her finger over the raised gold paint that adorned some of the letters. She shook her head. "I don't feel anything out of the ordinary, but if it's yours, and only yours, the magic might only speak to you."

The comment stopped her breath in her chest. Yvette had never once believed there could be anything in the world meant only for her. "What do you think it means?"

Elena thumbed through the pages again, back and forth as if affirming something. "I'm not quite sure, but I'm not convinced it's a spell book. I've never seen markings like these, at least not in any grimoire I'm familiar with. The odd part is the pattern."

"Repeated sevens. I saw that too."

"Precisely. Which makes me wonder if it isn't something else. Like you said, a diary or book of debts of some sort?"

The booklet couldn't be a boring old diary, not with such a strong infusion of magic beckoning to her.

"But the tingling energy when I hold it . . . Elena, you have to help me with this. You have to help figure out what the symbols mean. This book is the only thing I've got that my mother ever touched. It has to mean something."

"I'd help if I could, only I'm visiting the city briefly with Jean-Paul. We're staying with his mother—"

"Weren't you the one who told me how important a witch's intuition is in magic? Well, mine is telling me this means something. But it's also bigger than I can deal with on my own. You've got to help me figure out what it is."

At the bottom of the lane a man's voice called out for Elena—her man, the one she remembered from the cellar. Desperation sped Yvette's breathing.

"Look, I can't leave the city until my wish comes true. Sidra told me so. But I don't know how much longer I can keep hiding from *les flics*. I have to know why my mother left this for me. This book is the key to finding out who she was, who I'm supposed to be—I know it is. And I know you're the only one who can help me. Your being here has to be fate."

The man called out again for Elena, heightened worry creeping into his voice. The cat mewed and swished his tail, his green eyes intent on Elena. The vine witch smirked at the animal before smoothing her fingers over the cracked leather cover and exhaling.

"Very well. But we don't have much time. You have to promise me, if we do this, you'll do as I say."

Yvette stuck out her hand, willing to risk contact with the poisonous innards of the beautiful bloom to get what she wanted. "Deal."

CHAPTER EIGHT

One week. It wasn't much time to teach a hotheaded naïf how to wield her magic, discover the code to her mother's diary, and fulfill the demands of a stolen wish, but that's what fate had given them. Because that's how long Marion Martel believed it would take for Elena to sit for the artist's portrait.

Elena finished brushing her hair out before bed, then opened a jar of face cream she'd infused earlier with a few of the crushed rose petals she'd plucked from the city garden. The botanical scent was heavenly as she smoothed it over her face, whispering a self-indulgent charm to fend off the sooty effect of the city's dirty air. The curse she'd suffered from had weakened her magic for a time, but as much as she hated to admit it, the constant sloughing of skin as a toad had left her with a renewed blush in her cheeks.

She stared at her reflection, tilting her chin to see what an artist might see. Yes, she'd meant to refuse the portrait, seeing little point in a witch having a painting done of herself if the artist was a mortal. Their vision fell short of capturing the complete form. There was never any attempt to portray the spirit, only the rough-skilled depiction of skin, bones, and hair beneath silken clothes. Perhaps with the accessory of a flower pressed to the nose. A photograph created a more accurate depiction. The verdict was still out on whether that particular form of portraiture was invented by a witch, though Elena suspected it was. Under the right circumstances, the camera was actually quite capable of revealing one's true visage on film, sometimes even capturing the halo of one's aura as a white, ghostlike shadow in the photograph. How would a mortal artist do that?

With a sigh she realized her original rationale for refusing the portrait verged on echoing the ugly refrain of the Magus Society fomenters by disparaging the shortcomings of mortals. Nevertheless, she now saw how she might benefit from Marion's wedding present. The need to report daily to the butte under the guise of having her portrait completed ought to give her ample time to check in on Yvette. And so she'd accepted the gift and the opportunity to escape the city center for the rural annex atop the butte each morning during their visit.

Besides, the odd little book intrigued her. She'd never seen anything like it before, though there was something eerily familiar about the words and pages. She didn't think Yvette had noticed, but she'd tried using her shadow vision to see beyond the symbols, to possibly get a glimpse of the girl's absent mother. Strangely, the vision was blocked, as if the book had been wrapped in the equivalent of butcher's paper. So then how to unravel the mystery and help the young woman trace her only connection to her mother and her magic?

And she did intend to help her. For the briefest of moments, yes, she'd fixated on the young woman as the leverage needed to get out of her appalling situation with the Ministry of Lineages and Licenses. All Elena would have had to do is stun the girl, then turn her over to Durant so the Covenants Regulation Bureau authorities, namely Inspector Nettles, could come and collect her, and she'd have her standing as a vine witch reinstated. Her worries would be over.

Except giving the girl up was never a real possibility. The idea rejected before it could take root. She and Yvette had little in common, and yet they'd been bound at the wrists by fate and the secretive deeds of long-gone mothers that still reverberated through their lives. She recognized the sudden pang of sympathy she felt for Yvette, the same one that had made her vow a month earlier during their prison escape that she would mentor the young woman should they reunite.

But how would she know what discipline to steer the girl toward to help her find her natural talent? She certainly couldn't go to the records office and look up the Lenoir family bloodline. That would be a dead giveaway. They'd have to begin with the fundamentals and see where it led.

Elena was trying to recollect her grade-school spells as she put her cream away when a soft tapping came at the door.

"You're far away." Jean-Paul stepped into her room. He listened at the door for a moment, then shut it behind him. "And I have the distinct impression you're keeping a secret," he said as he lifted the hair off her neck and kissed the tender place behind her ear.

"Am I?" She let the shivers work their magic along her skin.

"Yes, ever since you disappeared down the lane this morning," he said, guiding her to her feet. "And I don't buy it for one second that you were chasing after a cat. Unless, of course, it was some lost relative of yours?"

"Wouldn't be out of the question."

"The possibility of truth in that statement still gives me a chill."

She settled into his arms and kissed him. She didn't wish to deceive Jean-Paul, yet how much could she divulge of her plans without him interfering? His devotion to Yvette was nil. He would try to persuade her to turn the girl in so she could get back to her work in the vineyard and be done with the whole ugly business. And she wanted that, too, only she rather thought they ought to go about it another way.

Before passion carried her too far, she pulled back, yet she kept her arms around his neck so she could feel the heat under his skin and the threading pulse keeping him alive. "Do you know about the Bibliothèque Suprême near the university?"

"*Suprême?*"

"It's a witch's library."

"There's a witch's library near the university? The same one I attended?"

She nodded while trying to suppress a smile. "I'd like to show it to you tomorrow."

"I'd very much like to see it. Among other things," he added, slipping her robe off her shoulder to expose her skin.

The touch of his lips against her neck sent a flutter of ecstasy through Elena's core. "I rather think your mother wouldn't approve of you visiting my room at night."

"Maybe you could work a sleeping spell on her so we can be alone."

She considered it before giving him a mock slap against his chest. "You know I can't do that. Besides, I feel as if I'm on some sort of probation as it is. With her *and* the court. This whole mess is Inspector Nettles's doing, I'd wager."

"Possibly, but I doubt he'd have the authority or means to coordinate this sort of political extortion against you. My guess is it's someone higher up, though I can't imagine what their game is, expecting you to turn in that strange girl in exchange for something that's already yours." Jean-Paul kissed her shoulder before closing her robe again. "And, only a hunch, but I'm guessing they keep a copy of *The Treatise on the Code for Witches* at this library where you're hoping I might find a loophole in the law," he said, touching his forehead to hers.

"Yes, darling, that would be wonderful. But it's a restricted area. I'll have to escort you, at least on the first visit."

"Meaning they don't allow mortals to wander the stacks unsupervised?"

A door clicked open down the hall. His mother was on the prowl.

"Exactly," she whispered. "But you're perfectly welcome to browse the shelves, once a witch sponsors your entrance."

"I think half the time you've got me under a spell," he said and agreed to look at the treatise.

"I believe they call it love." She kissed him again, reconsidering the sleeping spell before thinking better of it. "But for now, you'd better go, mortal," she said, her hand lingering in his before he said good night and slipped out the door.

The next morning a motorized taxi dropped the couple off in the section of the city long termed the Latin Quarter due to the prevalence of the dead language at the core of scholarly pursuits (*and* the creation of dusty old spells that withered on the tongue like brittle paper) when the original university was founded seven hundred years earlier. Academia was not then sympathetic to the idea of preternatural beings peacefully coexisting in the world. Quite the contrary. The school was established, in part, to disavow the existence of magic and to put it on par with evil—a contradiction in itself, but it was the Dark Ages, after all. It took several hundred years, and not a little bloodshed on both sides, for the scholarly elite to finally come to terms with the prevalence and legitimacy of *others* among them. One outcome from the truce, in addition to the 1745 Covenants, were the co-efforts of witch and mortal in the construction of an eighteenth-century church turned crypt in the heart of the city's center of learning. With its neoclassical dome and pillars, the structure loomed over the heads of the other buildings, a tribute to the changing of hearts and opening of minds. Few mortal citizens who walked in its shadow knew the truth of its origins. The builders, having the forethought to recognize the potential for misuse and exploitation, restricted the true history of the crypt to those mortals with a need to know, leaving the information as a footnote at the base of the tomb of the famous philosopher and poet Vérité.

Today, Jean-Paul needed to know.

"I thought we were headed to the witch's library," he said as Elena led them toward the neoclassical colonnade fronting the domed building.

"Just through here," she said, smoothing the front of her burgundy travel jacket as she waited for him to open the door for her. By now he'd learned to trust, and so he followed her without further protest.

Inside, Elena strode past the murals, the grand columns, and the center circle under the dome where she remembered a decorative pendulum once hung from the ceiling to demonstrate to the masses how the earth turned. Such elementary stuff, but education of both witch and mortal was the main thrust of the building, after all. The heels of her lace-up boots clicked against the marble floors as she continued on to where a fair number of tourists had gathered around the sculpture of a great hulking man who appeared to be lost in deep thought, chin in hand. He'd not been there the last time she'd visited the city, but she thought him a worthy ambassador as she took the stairs down to the crypt.

"Are you sure you're going the right way?" Jean-Paul cast a last curious look at the statue before descending into a tunnel with numerous alcoves and side hallways veering off. "I've been through here many times and I've noted no books, only bodies encased in oversized marble tombs."

"As the library is only open to witches and their guests," she whispered over her shoulder, "it would hardly be practical to make the entrance obvious to the general public, would it?"

Jean-Paul nodded to a mustached man who looked up from reading about a long-dead general. "Pardon my ignorance," he said to her, then nodded again to the man as if to apologize for their intrusion.

"You're forgiven." Elena stopped beside the mustached man and said, "*Bonjour, après vous,*" and by the time Jean-Paul looked again in the man's direction, he was gone.

"Where . . . what just happened?" He walked to where the man had been standing and then raised his hand up as if feeling the air. "Ah, spiderwebs, which means there's a spell."

"You're catching on." She took her fiancé's arm and they walked forward past the marble edifice, taking a left into what probably appeared to Jean-Paul as a stone wall. But in truth they were standing before an arched metalwork door composed of gears and pulleys, which the mustached man held open for them.

"*Merci.*" Elena smiled at the gentleman, and the door closed behind them. The gears turned, their teeth engaging with cogwheels and spokes, until a secure locking noise sounded behind them, not unlike the click of a cell door, as she uncomfortably recalled.

Jean-Paul whistled softly, suggesting his first impression fell somewhere between fear and awe. She couldn't help but take a little pride in his reaction.

"Psyché Iatreion?" he asked, staring up at the inscription carved into the header at the entrance.

"It means apothecary of the soul."

He nodded as if he understood as she led him inside. Mahogany shelves, many with leaded glass doors, lined both sides of the room. Above, a hand-carved banister ran along a second story that was supported, at least aesthetically, by gold-topped pillars, all of which led the eye to the ceiling. There, a constant illumination spell was kept in place to replicate the cycle of sunny day to starry sky.

She'd always found the stacks remarkable, but from a mortal's point of view they must have appeared utterly mesmerizing. Naturally there were books, thousands on everything from spellcasting and transmogrification to love potions and wart removal. Some of the original grimoires kept behind glass were a thousand years old. Held together by catgut and vellum, their pages were still fragrant with the scents of spells calling for dried hellebore, ground burdock, and oil of toadflax. A few of the medieval spell books still radiated soft halos of light from the strong magic bound inside the heartwood of their spines. There were scrolls, too, from other nations, whose foreign letters glowed with pigments too rich to possibly come from local earth.

While contemplating the scrolls, it occurred to Elena she might also benefit from their visit to the library. If she were quick. Yvette would be waiting for her at the same time and place where they'd met the day before. The prearrangement was the only way to coordinate their next meeting since the girl was too ignorant to know how to receive a dove. First things first, she'd need to teach her the spell on how to talk to birds.

Elena and Jean-Paul approached the reference desk, where they were greeted by a petite redheaded woman in a green-and-white-striped blouse, matching green hobble skirt, and button-up ankle boots that peeked out beneath her somewhat immodest hem to reveal turquoise silk stockings. The woman smiled coolly at Elena, then appeared puzzled when her gaze sailed over Jean-Paul's head, expecting to find an aura.

"We'll need a dispensation," Elena said. "For a mortal. Can you help us with that?"

"I . . . give me a moment." The woman searched through a filing cabinet embellished with the astrological signs for Jupiter, Saturn, and Uranus. She flipped through a few files until she pulled out a parchment, holding it up triumphantly. "It's been an age since I've done one of these," she said before instructing Jean-Paul to put his hand flat against the parchment.

"Why?" he asked.

"Think of it like a fingerprint," she said. "We're required to keep a record of each mortal hand that's allowed to touch the books so we know where to look when, or if, something goes, um, awry." She smiled as if to reassure him, though there was too much deception in her expression.

Jean-Paul reluctantly did as he was told. When he lifted his hand again, a perfect imprint of his palm remained on the parchment. Several of his palm's lifelines had been denoted: head, heart, health, fate, and love. The librarian cocked an eyebrow and aimed an improved smile full of charm at him. Elena felt a twinge of jealousy, but then what woman wouldn't swoon at the combination of intelligence, faithfulness, and sexual prowess revealed by the indentations and angles of the man's palm lines.

"Right, you're all set. You're allowed to look at anything on the first floor. I'm afraid everything upstairs or under glass is off-limits, but come to me if you need assistance and I'll see what I can do."

Jean-Paul brushed his hands together as if to rid them of whatever supernatural substance had been used to copy his palm. "Which way to the overly complicated treatises on witch law?"

"Right over there," she said and pointed to the bookshelf lined with dozens of identical-looking leather-bound books. Then she twitched her nose, as if she'd detected something beginning to rot, and turned to Elena. "Books on potions and poisons are kept in the back room under the old gaslights."

"I'm not . . ."

But the librarian had already moved on to helping a young man inquiring about enchanted atlases featuring sea monsters.

While Jean-Paul settled into his familiar territory of books and legal notes, his glasses perched firmly on the bridge of his nose, Elena went not to the potions and poisons section but to the archival birth announcements. There she flipped through the book of clans, searching for the Lenoir name. She had to guess at Yvette's year of birth, but the document wasn't so enormous that she couldn't explore the difference of a year or two either way if she were wrong. She found Yvette on her second guess, though the last name had an asterisk beside it for no discernible reason. Below was a picture of a young blonde woman with pale eyes and skin and a distinct scar on her left cheek. It was customary to keep the personal information updated with notable events, and so the photo was from her arrest at Le Maison de Chêne, with her prisoner number stamped on the bottom.

Beside the photo of Yvette was Elena's own somewhat angry mug shot as well, with the words "known accomplice" and "exonerated" written below in cursive script. Not her best likeness, yet a fair representation of her mood that day. After scanning further through the documents, however, she discovered that nothing else had been kept up to date. In fact, there was little else in the file besides a birthdate. She'd hoped she might find a notation on Yvette's designated magical discipline based on her bloodline, but there wasn't even a mention of family relations. The space where her parents' names ought to have been filled in had been smudged out with a blocking spell, not unlike Yvette's book. The traces of the spell's bond to the paper still shimmered around the edges.

Perplexed by the missing information—not merely omitted through dereliction but deliberately hidden—Elena closed the book, but not before she removed the photo of herself from the corner tabs holding it in place and dropping the image in her purse. If no other information was deemed important enough to include in the young woman's file, then neither was the addition of her likeness. Besides, she had a better use for the photograph.

Elena ensured that Jean-Paul was comfortably ensconced in his corner of the library before leaving to make her way to the butte for her appointed sitting with the artist. Thank the All Knowing Marion had a previously arranged engagement with her Union Pour le Suffrage des Femmes group and did not accompany her.

An hour later, the artist Pedro greeted Elena in the hallway of the shabby collection of rented rooms, his charcoal already in hand. The black cat was there, too, slinking around her ankles, rubbing his silver collar against her leg, eager to escort her to Yvette's location. "Patience," she said to the cat and then proceeded to enter the artist's work space.

But before Pedro could place one finger on Elena's chin and tilt her face to the light to check the angle of her cheekbones, she presented him with her photograph. He was confused, naturally, so she had him stand before his easel while she explained by way of an incantation.

"Catch the light and paint the lie, render the face before your eye."

She blew a pinch of ground-up morning glory seed in his face to seal the spell, and by the time she reached the door the artist had settled down and begun sketching her outline on the canvas, speaking to the photo as if Elena were really sitting in a ray of light from the single window. The enchantment was, perhaps, verging on interfering with a mortal, a clear violation of the covenants, yet there was no real harm done. Nothing to alter his mind or thoughts, merely a little trick of the eye to focus his attention on something other than her. With luck, the portrait would turn out no different than if she'd sat in the stiflingly dreary room for four hours a day for the next week. Tedium at its upmost, to say the least.

"Lead on," she said to the cat as she stepped into the hallway again, though instead of trotting outside to find Yvette as expected, the animal wound his skinny body through a crack in the nearest doorway. Elena pushed the door open and followed. The cat sat in the middle of the floor, twitching his tail at her excitedly as if to say, "Look around!"

She soon understood his intention. There was a cot, a washtub, a tiny stove, and the same light-filled window as the room next door. Only this apartment appeared to have recently lost its tenant—another artist, judging by the dabs of fresh paint on the floor, the broken brushes in the washtub, and the dirty turpentine rags strewn across the floor.

"Clever cat," she said, and together they left to speak to the landlord about a short-term lease.

CHAPTER NINE

"You're late."

Yvette sat against a wrought-iron fence, tucked in among the Virginia creeper that had already begun turning a brilliant shade of seasonal red. She knew she was practically invisible there, except to the cat who pranced straight for her, picking her out of the verge with those perceptive green eyes of his.

"For good reason," Elena answered back.

The vine witch was wearing a smart burgundy skirt and tailored jacket. Not new, not even a modern drop-waist cut, but smartly embroidered around the collar. Witch-made, no doubt. She suspected the ensemble was Elena's sole travel suit. But it was one more than Yvette owned, so who was she to judge.

"Your friend here has found us something we can use. Come take a look."

Yvette peered up and down the lane, eyes searching for anyone—namely *les flics* or their informants—who might be watching without looking like they were watching. The telltale sign was a person leaning one shoulder against a building, their head down to stare at a newspaper, with seemingly nothing better to do in the middle of the day than hold up a wall. But everyone she spotted was either busy tossing wastewater into the gutter or dragging an empty cart up the steep slope toward the Moulin â Farine, the old flour mill turned cabaret. Knowing her blonde hair worked like an electric light for drawing attention, she covered her head with the velvet curtain and followed Elena down the lane. A few streets later, they came to the notorious Maison Chavirée, so named because the building slanted toward the courtyard like a ship that had run aground. So, the tilt wasn't just the effect of the drink, Yvette mused, recalling the last time she'd been inside the flophouse and felt the floor go out from under her feet.

"What are we doing here?" she asked.

"You need a place to stay, somewhere safe, where no one's going to ask questions."

Yvette balked. "This place is a dump."

"It's cheap and it's dry. *And* it's convenient, at least for me."

Still wary, she stepped over the threshold, careful not to set her foot in a suspicious wet spot on the hallway floor that reeked of the sewer. Elena opened the door to the vacant apartment. "What do you think?"

In all honesty, it wasn't the worst place Yvette had slept. At least the cot was off the ground. The stove came with a pan for boiling water. And there was a small chunk of leftover soap sitting on the windowsill for washing up. A set of curtains might give the place some charm.

"So now what? Is this my new jail?"

"It's our new work space. Here," Elena said. "Give me your hand."

"What for?" Like a stray dog that had been kicked one too many times, Yvette constantly questioned people's motives, on the alert for harm especially from those appearing to do her a favor. They were the ones you had to watch the most.

"You said you wanted to learn about magic. That's why we're here. But first, I'm curious to know how well attuned you are with the All Knowing. There's something I noticed about the building on my first day here. Take my hand and tell me if you can see it too."

Yvette tossed off her velvet covering and grudgingly stuck her hand out. She held on while Elena placed her other hand to the room's exterior wall and did that familiar trance thing.

"Anything?"

A second later a shiver ran from the curve of Yvette's back to the base of her neck until her head felt like it was full of aluminum tinsel, abuzz with electricity. "What the hell is it?"

"A spell of some sort encircling the entire building. It's woven into the walls, the floors, the roof. Can you see it? The golden strands like a web? Almost like the spell's the only thing holding the place up in one piece."

Yvette couldn't see anything but slanting walls and dirty windows. Still, she felt . . . something . . . tingling within her veins, her brain, her heart. And the book. It vibrated against her middle with the hum of a tuning fork. She let go of Elena's hand as if the touch burned her skin. The electricity, or magic, or whatever it was, stopped.

"What's wrong?"

Yvette spun around, checking all around her. "I didn't see anything, but I felt it. All tingly like. What was that?" She ran her hand over the walls herself but didn't sense it again. "I've never felt magic like that before."

"In that case, I'd call it an encouraging sign."

"Truly?" Yvette reached under her blouse and removed the book she'd strapped around her waist. "It was buzzing against my skin. Like before, only stronger."

Elena held her hand out to examine the book again. "It responded to the room's energy? That's interesting."

"What kind of spell would do that?" Reverberations from the magic skittered over Yvette's skin. It wasn't an unpleasant feeling, or even all that eerie, but it did leave her rubbing the gooseflesh on her arms and wondering what kind of trouble she'd gotten herself into by making that damn wish.

The cat jumped up on the cast-iron stove and licked his paw, though he stopped mid-lick when Elena opened the pages of the book. His eyes gleamed emerald bright in the dank space as she tried an incantation.

"Words of mischief or worldly wise? Reveal your purpose. Cast off your disguise."

A page ruffled as if lifted by a breeze, and then . . . nothing. Yvette looked over Elena's shoulder and saw that none of the marks on the paper had changed. The symbols were still as mysterious as they'd been before. And just as nonsensical.

"It was worth a try," Yvette said.

"Yes, it was." Elena sat on the edge of the cot with the book. "Judging by the resistance, the pages have likely been charmed, but it doesn't explain the way the book reacted to the magic encircling the building, which is highly peculiar."

"Maybe my mother had been here before?"

Elena peered up at her, her face serious. "What do you know about your parents?"

"Don't know anything about my father. Don't even know if he was a witch or not."

"But your mother was a witch?"

Yvette nodded and pirouetted closer to Monsieur Whiskers. "Must have been. But she was a dancer, too, so maybe that had something to do with her magic," she said, stroking the cat's head. "That's how she and Tante Isadora met."

"What was her name?"

"Cleo."

"Lenoir?"

The cat meowed and jumped down to sniff at a gold paint splotch on the floor.

"That's Tante's name. When I was a kid, she said I belonged to her now, so I had to use her name." Yvette shifted uncomfortably from one foot to the other. "Are you going to teach me how to do proper magic?"

Elena emerged from her thoughts and brightened. "Not in a week, but if we can figure out where your natural magical abilities lie, we can make a good start."

"How'd you know you were meant to be a vine witch?"

"My . . . Ariella Gardin, the woman who took me in, taught me her craft. She'd sensed I had an affinity for vine work when I was a child."

Yvette knew liars. Elena wasn't lying exactly, but she wasn't telling the whole truth. "What kind of craft did you say your mother did?" As soon as she asked, she knew she'd hit a soft spot. The color fell from Elena's face as though she was ashamed, the same look certain family men at Le Rêve got years ago when they'd learned Yvette was only fifteen. They were the ones who handed her some cash, grabbed their coats, and left quick as they could, though not before getting what they'd paid for.

"She was a potions witch," Elena said, not looking up from the book. "She was especially good with poison I'm told."

"You mean she was one of them green-bottle witches you see riding around in the painted carts? There's one that rides up and down the butte three times a week. Sells some nasty stuff, if you're in the market."

"No, I'm not," Elena snapped. "So why don't we focus on figuring out what this book is for, since that's why I'm here."

"Oh là là, I'm just telling you what I know about poison witches."

She liked Elena, she didn't want to upset her, yet sometimes the urge to pester people until they felt as bad as she did was too strong to back down from, especially once she knew where they were vulnerable. This time she did stop. The compulsion to learn more about the book proved stronger than her instinct to inflict harm, so she sat on the cot beside Elena and behaved. The cat leaped onto her lap as if affirming she'd done the right thing, purring as he rubbed his collar against her chest.

"So how do we even start?"

"A few of these symbols are universal, but I don't know how, or even if, they're part of a code. Most of the rest are foreign to me. If your mother was some kind of word witch, a writer, or even a linguist, it would have made sense for her to keep a journal like this. However, as far as you remember she was a dancer, which makes me think she was some kind of kinetic witch. And that would involve movement of the body."

"I am pretty good at climbing walls and throwing knives."

Elena stood. "Let's conduct a little test."

"What kind of test?"

"One for magical aptitude." Elena narrowed her eyes at Monsieur Whiskers. "Yes, I think you'll do for this," she said and ordered the cat to sit on the cot. He reluctantly jumped from Yvette's arms, though he sat with his shoulders tensed as if ready to run.

Yvette reached out to pet the cat and reassure him when Elena stopped her.

"There, hold your hand just where it is," she said. "Let it hover over the cat's back. Now I want you to concentrate and see if you can make him lift his fur. If you're a kinetic witch, the command ought to come through naturally. Just breathe in and out—feel the energy rise beneath your fingertips."

Yvette held her hand steady as she closed her eyes to concentrate. Inhale. Exhale. Inhale. Exhale. She pictured the cat's fur standing on end. A slight tickle reached her fingers. Was it working? Her heart opened to the possibility as she squinted to take a peek.

The magic she thought she'd felt was only the cat's whiskers brushing against her skin as his fur remained as smooth as ever.

"It's okay," Elena said. "We'll try something else."

And for the next hour they did just that, trying everything from lighting a candle with a snap of her fingers to boiling water in the washbasin with a simple fire incantation, all without luck.

Frustrated, Yvette returned to her mother's book to look at the pages again, wondering if she was ever meant to be a witch at all. "Do you think she made it up? Could this all be a bunch of nonsense?" What she didn't ask was if her mother might have been afflicted. Mad. Locked away in an asylum.

"It's not nonsense, Yvette. There's something there."

Relieved by Elena's answer, Yvette handed her the book when she held her hand out. "Sometimes I can feel the energy. Almost like the book is alive and trying to tell me something."

"It's infused with magic," Elena said, studying the binding. "I just don't know what kind yet. Perhaps something meant only for you. Which makes me think we're going to require some professional help."

"I thought that's what you were."

"Oh, no. I'm quite good with fundamental magic and anything to do with plants, but my intuition tells me we might need someone who specializes in the outer parameters of the supernatural to sort this out. As luck would have it, I may know the perfect witch for the job."

"Sounds good to me." Yvette grabbed her stolen velvet as if ready to head out the door.

Elena closed the book and handed it back. "I was going to suggest I go alone, but I think you're right. The magic bound to that book seems especially attuned to you, so you should probably come with me."

"Right. Let's go see this witch friend of yours."

Elena stood up and tugged her jacket taut over her skirt. "Two things. One, I'm afraid my time is up. I have plans for the evening and if I don't leave now, I'll be missed. And two, we have to be smart about this, Yvette. You're still a fugitive. Before we go anywhere, we're going to have to do something about your appearance." She pointed to Yvette's hair and clothes, then tapped her finger against her jaw to indicate the telltale scar on the lower cheek as well. "We cannot take any more chances of you being spotted in the city."

Yvette glanced down at her outfit. There was nothing wrong with the way she looked for the butte. No one offered a second glance at someone dressed in an old curtain with harlequin tights under their skirt in this neighborhood. But of course, a professional witch was probably going to be located in the heart of the city, which meant she'd stand out like the misfit she was. And standing out meant getting caught. Going back to prison now, when she was on the verge of discovering the secret from the mother she never knew, was not going to happen.

"All right," she said, agreeing to the terms. She picked up the pot on the stove and blew out a speck of dirt, determined to settle into her shabby new surroundings until she could emerge in public as someone other than Yvette Lenoir, the murderess with the golden hair and unsightly scar.

Monsieur Whiskers curled up on the cot as Elena rubbed her fingers together to light a fire in the stove before waving *au revoir*.

CHAPTER TEN

Now that she thought about it, the scar was unusual. A pale mark that ran along the girl's left cheek and jaw. Not thin, as though made with a knife, but like someone had swiped the skin with a stick of chalk. Elena had never asked about it out of politeness, but she'd always harbored a curiosity. Naturally, the imagination made up the worst stories, though with Yvette any one of them could be true. Perhaps when this book mystery was settled, she'd work up the nerve to ask about the circumstances.

"My dear, I don't believe you've heard a word I've said." Marion smiled coyly as she wrapped her fox stole over her shoulder and clipped it in place by the clasp implanted in the animal's teeth. "Oh, you are in love, aren't you? Daydreaming about the big day? We'll be sure to ask Madame Fontaine if she has any insights about your matrimonial future. She's quite good, you'll see. Oh, here we are."

Elena smiled wanly and stepped out of the carriage onto the quiet residential street. A halo of soft lamplight landed on the cobblestones in front of a white marble facade with a black door. Petals from a faded geranium fluttered down from a wrought-iron flower box bolted beneath the window overhead. While curious to see what passed for a spirit medium in the mortal world, Elena's mind *had* been elsewhere, otherwise occupied with thoughts of foreign magic that might explain the strange notations in Yvette's book. But all that would have to wait until this ridiculous outing was over.

A pair of ladies in draping velvet and overly plumaged hats disembarked from a second cab, their semi-inebriated husbands right behind. While the couples arranged themselves on the sidewalk, Marion whispered in Elena's ear that the woman with the enormous black feather in her hat was Madame Chevalier, the one she'd told her about who'd lost all the gold. She then made a locking motion over her lips as if to suggest no one ever spoke of the scandal in public.

Marion made introductions between the women, kissing each on the cheek and clucking her hellos. Each greeted Elena with the same cheek-to-cheek kiss, though their lips never reached her skin, and afterward their husbands shook her hand politely.

"But where is your son? Your fiancé, Jean-Paul?" the women asked of them.

Marion gave a small lift of her shoulders, making the fox head on her stole appear to grimace. "A born skeptic, that one. Science and facts are his one true religion."

"He's at home reading," Elena added, knowing he preferred to search for a legal solution to her clerical blackmail rather than partake in an evening of obvious charlatanism. "But I have no doubt he would have found the evening just as entertaining as I expect it to be, had he come along."

The women all nodded their agreement, assuring Elena she would be most impressed with Madame Fontaine as their husbands marched up the steps to the black door and banged the knocker three times. A dour woman in mourning lace up to her chin answered the door. After a modest bow of welcome, the assistant, for that's how she introduced herself, showed the group into the main salon, explaining that they should take a seat. Madame Fontaine would arrive soon.

The salon was standard size with tall ceilings, a fireplace, and a six-panel paned window overlooking the street they'd come in from. Green damask wallpaper graced the walls in a fleur-de-lis pattern, though the paper had noticeably begun to split and peel along the seams. A pair of gaslit sconces, their globes tarnished with sooty streaks, glowed against the emerald green, fumigating the room with their oily scent. And near the window, framed by a set of cordoned drapes, Elena gazed upon a round table with eight chairs squeezed together. In the middle sat a fat candle in a brass holder. The largest chair, the one with the raised back, sat in front of the window. An eerie backlight from the street conveniently fogged the glass. But there was one encouraging sign, Elena noted: no crystal ball atop the table. Definitely not the sort of supernatural paraphernalia an amateur ought to play with in a room full of mortals.

"Oh, Elena, isn't it exactly how you pictured?" Marion peeked out the window at the abandoned lane before letting her eyes roam over the room. "Can you feel the energy? I'm positively tingling all over with anticipation."

"Yes, it certainly has met my expectations so far," Elena said.

Marion peered out the window once more, only this time her face tightened noticeably. Elena moved closer to take a look as well. Below, a black coach had pulled into the lane, stopping in front of the door. A man in a top hat and cloak stepped out.

"It's the comté," Marion said. "A client of my late husband's. I didn't know he was on the guest list."

"Comté?" The nobility had become as rare as passenger pigeons.

"Hmm, the Comté-du-Lac du Nord." Marion snapped open her fan. "Single and reportedly quite wealthy. Come, let's find our seats."

Disobeying the assistant's suggestion they sit across from each other to even out the energy, Marion had Elena sit on her left and held open the seat on her right, even when Madame Chevalier attempted to squeeze in. A moment later the door to the salon opened and the comté entered, removing his hat and gloves. The assistant took his belongings with a bow and friendly smile, gesturing for him to enter and sit where he liked. Marion paid him absolutely no attention whatsoever until he'd said hello to everyone in the room but she and Elena.

"Charmed," he said to Elena when Marion introduced them at last. "And Madame Martel, I must say, the supernatural air suits you. You're positively beaming with spiritual energy this evening."

"Am I?" Blushing like a schoolgirl, Marion invited the comté to sit, which he did.

It was then Elena noticed the aural specter peeking out of the comté's collar. For some reason he'd tried to dim his glow, though none of the guests, besides her, were witches. Perhaps he lived as a mortal. Despite the covenants and their rules concerning relations between mortals and witches—namely, that it was a crime to persecute anyone for their inherited powers—there were still occasional violations that sometimes resulted in violent encounters. Some witches simply found it easier to live in anonymous peace, especially if they were heavily invested in the world of mortals. And yet here he was at a séance.

Madame Chevalier removed a pamphlet from her purse, a conjurer's magazine for magicians, and slid it in front of the comté for him to peruse. "Our first issue," she said proudly.

His lip curled almost imperceptibly beneath his mustache as he opened the booklet. There could be nothing in there to impress a witch, and yet he licked his finger and turned each page as if he were fascinated. Finally, he congratulated the madame and tucked the pamphlet away in his jacket pocket, expressing his intention to subscribe at once, the least he could do.

The comté caught Elena staring at his collar and nodded curtly in recognition as his eyes sailed over her head to trace her aura. The awkward moment was remedied quickly when the lights dimmed and Madame Fontaine entered the room. The men stood and the women turned their heads, expectant, as if a stage show were about to begin. It was a wonder they didn't applaud. The medium—every inch of her imbued with an air of the theatric—held her arms out so that her draping sleeves spread open like moth wings at her sides. Her head was covered in a matching band of black-and-gold silk. She was perhaps fifty, perhaps thirty—it was difficult to tell with the low lights—but there was no mistaking the determined look in her obsidian eyes rimmed in kohl. This one was eager to make her way up the psychic ladder, hungry to make a name for herself in the city. If the professional skeptics didn't eat her alive first, of course.

A wave of silent static traveled throughout the room, and then their host spoke. "Good evening, fellow spirit seekers!" Madame Fontaine lowered her arms and welcomed the circle of gaping admirers. She worked her way around the table to greet each person with a palm to their forehead, as though taking their psychic temperature. Those who'd attended before thanked her for her uncanny gift, to which she raised her open hand up to a vague source of energy overhead that she claimed gave her the power.

"My, my, my, you are searching for some specific answers, aren't you?" Madame Fontaine said when she stood in front of Marion. "A dearly departed husband, is it?" Her eyes glittered in the lamplight as she awaited confirmation.

Marion nearly swooned from the touch of the medium's hand placed against her brow. "Philippe, yes! Oh, I have so many things I wish to ask him."

"And he has many things to tell you." The medium's gaze traveled over the cut of Marion's dress, no doubt evaluating the expense of her hat and the likely weight of her pocketbook. "Yes, we may have to have a long conversation with your departed husband. Even now I feel his presence making itself known nearby."

Marion exhaled in breathless awe.

"And who do we have here?" Madame Fontaine asked as she approached Elena and placed her hand on her forehead. "Such a young woman. Do you have someone you wish to contact this evening?"

To Elena's surprise, her emotions overrode her intellect and she spoke before she could stop herself. "My mother, perhaps."

Elena was under no illusion this woman could do any of the things she claimed, so why did she confess this barely acknowledged desire? Ever since she'd learned the truth about her mother and her crime, she'd borne a strange yearning to know the details. Arriving in the city and discovering how her mother's shadow still held sway over her future had only embedded the curiosity deeper.

"There are unresolved issues with your mother, are there not? Hmm, we'll need to call her gently, encourage her to speak with us. Shall we get started?"

The medium took her hand away, locked eyes with Elena as if accepting some unspoken challenge, then asked the men to take their seats.

"She really is special," the comté said to Elena, leaning deliberately close to Marion. "You'll see."

Madame Fontaine sat in the high-backed chair and extended her hands across the table, palms up, to those seated beside her. The entire table completed the circle of handholding, then the medium asked the spirits for a sign that they were ready to communicate. The sconces on the wall dimmed further, as if by their own accord, though it was entirely likely that the dour assistant had access to some sort of remote knob by which to control the flow of gas. The chorus of "ahs" from Elena's fellow attendees confirmed the effectiveness of the trick on the mortal imagination. Swallowing a smile, she couldn't help wondering what kind of response *she'd* get if she offered to light the men's cigars with a flame from the tips of her fingers.

As soon as she had the thought, the flame on the candle in the center of the table came to life, though in this case it was from an *allumette* produced from the assistant's pocket. The light formed a yellow halo in the center of the circle so that the eye was drawn away from anything else but the flame.

"Madame, I feel an exceptional energy tonight," one of the intoxicated husbands said, giggling. "I do hope my poor aunt Ophelia will make an appearance."

"It is up to the spirits to decide who will join us. Let us begin." Madame Fontaine closed her eyes and took several deep breaths, encouraging others to do the same. Elena felt a quick squeeze from Marion, as if the excitement was too much to bear. "Breathe and let the spirits know you're here to welcome them in."

The group inhaled in unison, sonorous and exuberant. The candle-wick fluttered. The drapes shifted. The scent of orange blossoms filled the air.

"Spirits, if you're here, give us a sign."

On Elena's left, Madame Chevalier began to sway from side to side. The others soon joined in until it felt as if the entire room might break into a hymn at any moment. And then they heard a knock. Followed by another. One came from under the table, the other from inside the wall. A door hinge squeaked, the curtains rustled, and a floorboard moaned as if someone had walked into the room.

"I feel your presence, spirit, and we welcome you," Madame Fontaine announced. "Spirit, can you identify yourself?"

Elena had never witnessed a true necromancer at work, but she didn't think one would be reckless enough to reach out into the otherworld and ask to speak to the first spirit to knock. She felt pity then for Marion and the others. To be taken in by such shenanigans. To have their hopes raised that they might communicate once again with those they loved and missed. She thought the merciful thing to do might be to put an end to the charade by turning the lights back on with a quick spell, but no sooner did she get the idea than the room chilled.

A second later the madame arched her back against her chair as if a seizure had overtaken her body. She twisted her neck from side to side, her mouth gaping in spasm, and then a voice not her own issued forth, seething with slippery, venomous praise.

"How lovely you've grown," said the voice as the head lolled. Marion gasped, though the noise she'd made was muffled, as if it had come from another room. "Like the lacy hemlock, you've adapted well to your non-native soil, tending the vine and crushing the grape." Then the madame's eyes opened, flat and dark and staring straight at Elena. "But blood will tell, blood will remember, and your true calling will lead you home."

Elena blinked back her bewilderment. Was this real? An elaborate trick? How could Madame Fontaine have gleaned such details about her mother? Fontaine didn't even know Elena would be attending, as she'd been RSVP'd as a guest of Madame Martel.

Eyes adjusting to the contrast of light and dark, Elena peered around the table looking for any sign of manipulation, a hint of a deceptive smile on the assistant's grim face. Did the woman work in the records office? Did she know about her mother? Her crime was well known, but it had happened over twenty years ago. Did people in the city still remember?

Or was it possible her dead mother was truly speaking through the medium?

"Who are you?" Elena asked. "Why are you here?" But no answer came as the connection seemed to fade, and when she looked again the medium sat normally as if nothing had happened. Instead of channeling her mother, Fontaine appeared to be speaking about Jean-Paul's father and how much he missed his dear wife.

"Astonishing," Marion said, her hand gripping tight to Elena's. "To think Philippe was here in this very room!"

Elena had no idea how to respond. Had she somehow slipped into the shadow world? It was the only plausible explanation, but she knew she hadn't. She'd been conscious of her location the entire time. And yet no one else in the room seemed to have heard what she had. The encounter left her feeling uneasy. Rattled. As if some unbidden magic had invaded her mind.

After two other guests had relatives speak to them through Madame Fontaine, she thanked the spirits for presenting themselves, then slipped out of her trance. Or rather she released her grip from those at the table, clapped her hands together twice, and welcomed in the light. The sconces burned brighter, the mood lifted, and everyone let out a much-needed sigh of relief that their psychic wings hadn't been burned by flying too close to the otherworld.

They were not the only ones relieved to have the light return.

"My dear, are you all right?" Marion asked. "You've gone pale."

"The spirits can be somewhat unsettling if you're unaccustomed to their strong presence," said the comté, trying to be helpful.

As Elena gathered her wits, Madame Chevalier remarked, "Don't despair. It's rare to have a spirit address you on your first night. It must have taken three visits for me to hear from my beloved Arturo."

Madame Fontaine agreed. "The spirits can be quite stingy about who they will and won't respond to until they are *sure* of your intentions."

Her intentions? Had she somehow conjured the voice of her mother because of her spoken desire? Was this mortal woman somehow a conduit for the spirit world despite her obvious lack of supernatural talents? Elena's flesh grew cold.

Blood will tell, blood will remember.

Hadn't Grand-Mère said as much? Always worrying about her mother Esmé's bloodline showing itself in her? As if the art of poison were a disease that could be passed on from one generation to the next. Maybe it was. Maybe that was the thing she'd felt swelling beneath her intentions.

Blood will tell, blood will remember.

Oh, Grand-Mère. She wished she could send the old woman a dove to express how deeply the regret and sorrow she felt still festered in her heart. But the channel to the spirit world had closed, sealing the fissure between this world and the next.

The comté and others continued to stare. To assuage their concern, she replied, "I'm fine, really."

Yet she was far from all right. Yvette might wear her scar on her face for all to see, but others carried them deep inside, where only their bearers knew the damage done.

CHAPTER ELEVEN

The sun had barely cleared the rooftops the next morning when clouds conspired to obscure it. Yvette opened the window to check for the smell of rain and discovered the mouthwatering scent of bread baking nearby instead. She was only three streets removed from the boulangerie she'd terrorized as a child, stealing croissants and macarons off the counter whenever Madame became preoccupied with watching her oven. Her stomach clenched at the scent, but she'd been punched by hunger before. She knew how to take the hit. What she couldn't take was waking up and not having a single cigarette to puff on. And neither the threat of rain nor the threat of incarceration was strong enough to keep her mind off her next cigarette.

The three centimes she'd found stacked atop the stove behind where Monsieur Whiskers slept ought to be enough. The cat had claimed the space for his own, and it was only after he'd trotted outside first thing in the morning that she noticed the money. Elena must have set the coins there before she left the day before, not mentioning the charity for fear it would have been rejected out of some stupid sense of pride. Not likely. Not from a girl born on the butte, where the line between survival and falling through the cracks to the netherworld was often no wider than the lifeline on an open palm.

Her fingers twitched again. No getting around it. She'd have to go out. Either that or gnaw all her fingernails off from the craving. Despite Elena's warning to stay inside, she thought walking the street in the morning ought to be safe enough. At night all the ghouls were out. Mornings were made for old women to sweep their sidewalks and see their husbands off to work at the mill or tannery.

After securing her updo with the pencil-thin handle of an old paintbrush, Yvette wrapped the stolen velvet over her head and scuttled down the stairs to the street. The smell of fresh bread assaulted her again the minute she turned the corner, as did the sight of the street urchins creeping about the perimeter of the boulangerie three streets later. She'd been able to spot the children watching from the ivy along the iron railing and from the recessed door of the tenant building across the street, because that's where she used to hide. They were young but had already learned an empty stomach was filled quickest when the sun came up and the trash went out.

For a spark of a second the old competitive instinct flared—dive for the bin, throw an elbow, stomp with a pointy-heeled boot and take, take, take and run, run, run to the other side of the butte. She extinguished the impulse with a deep, distancing breath, even as something else caught fire within her. Following an instinct, she waved one of the children over, a girl with a pair of mismatched pigtails tied up with butcher's string. The gap in the girl's smile from a missing front tooth suggested she was no more than seven or eight years old, though the sunken eyes and rip in her frock sleeve confirmed she'd already been at this game awhile.

Yvette knelt when the barefoot girl approached. "I used to wait for the bread too," she said.

The girl pointed matter-of-factly. "Your eyes are dirty."

Yvette rubbed the back of her hand under her eye and came away with a streak of kohl. She must look like a ghoul with her black eyes and frazzled hair, though she doubted she came close to the strangest creature the girl had ever encountered on the butte.

"Hold out your hand," she said.

"What for?"

"Because there's a magic coin in my pocket that keeps trying to jump out, and if I don't find a safe place for it soon, I'm afraid it might fly away."

The girl stuck her hand out. Yvette set one of her three coins in the girl's palm, then told her to watch it try and take off.

A butte-born skeptic, the girl stated the obvious. "It isn't doing anything."

"Voilà! The money must be happy right where it is." Yvette closed the girl's fingers over the coin, planting the first of what she hoped might be a magic seed. Even a witch without a mother knew the three-fold law: that which is cast out—either good or bad—will come back three times as powerful. And she had a storm of bad karma that needed to be blown out of her life. She shooed the girl toward the bakery to fill her stomach with soft, warm bread.

Yvette stood, achy from withdrawal and hunger. She wished she had a coin to give to each of *les enfants*, but her fortunes were as flimsy as rusted tin at the moment. Well, though her prospects were never much better than they were now, she had found *some* stability working the carnival. That was probably lost for good. And even if Elena could help her unravel the book's message, what then? She was still wanted for murder and escape. She'd have to leave the city for good. Perhaps the country. But if Sidra was telling the truth, she could do none of that until the wish was fulfilled. But what if it never was? How long could she live on the streets as a murderess on the run?

The children began to gather and stare, hoping for more money to come, so Yvette made for the next street over. Given her appearance, she decided her fate was best trusted to the familiar back lanes where one only stood out if they *weren't* oddly attired. A dirt road led to a handful of little hovels atop the butte where the windmills still ground wheat into flour alongside the derelict taverns and bistros.

The lane proved as grubby as it had always been as Yvette side-stepped a pile of horse manure. Under the eye of a gloomy morning sun, the ground reeked of emptied bladders and the rancid-grease smell of unwashed bodies. On reflection, she was feeling a little ripe herself, but in this end of the butte it only helped her blend in with the crude population of comers and goers. Yvette cut through the section of the street where the cabarets and drinking houses huddled hip to shoulder, including Le Rêve. She'd just crossed the road when a sallow man in a wrinkled frock coat and dirty spats stumbled into the back of a two-seater *fiacre*. Memory rippled through Yvette, riding her nerves like a bad hangover. Two doors down from where she stood was where the prelude to the murder occurred that sent her to witch's prison and a date with *la demi-lune*. The "gentleman" took notice of her standing on the corner. He whistled, wet and sloppy, for her to get in the coach and warm the seat beside him. She ignored his drunken proposition and marched forward with her head down, eyes on the pavement, even as he called after her, branding her a worthless whore for walking away.

Merde, she needed a smoke. There was a kiosk not too much farther up the lane. Or at least there used to be. She hadn't walked this side of the butte in years. She felt the coins rubbing together in her pocket and walked on, anxious to get her ciggies and get back to the room. No sooner did she have the thought when she got a funny feeling inside, a ruffle in her intuition, that told her to look up. Yes, there on her left, a rakish young man in a shabby brown corduroy coat approached from a narrow alley, something familiar about his walk. The way he carried a folder under his arm yet kept his hands in his pockets and his head up as if he had all day to admire his surroundings. She didn't know anyone that carefree in life, and certainly not at this hour of the morning, but what little witch instinct she possessed made her take notice.

Out of the corner of her eye she saw him stare straight at her as he emerged from the alley, then quickly turn his face away and walk in the opposite direction she was headed. She didn't know why exactly, but the young man's retreat left her disappointed. Before she was forced to conceal herself under a shabby velvet curtain, it sometimes happened that way with the left side of her face. She'd been told enough times she might be a real beauty if not for the odd scar that ran along her jaw-line. People clicked their tongues in that sad sort of way, as if the mark were an unfortunate scratch on a mahogany table or a blemish on an otherwise perfect peach. Strangers sometimes asked her outright about it, and almost always when they were drunk and had abandoned their manners. She made up various stories about its origin depending on her mood and level of annoyance—a mugging turned violent, a scratch from a leopard at the zoo when she'd ventured too near to the cage, or the result of a lightning bolt that had entered through the top of her head and exited through her toes. As long as there was astonishment in their eyes at the end of her story, Yvette was satisfied. The truth of how she got the scar, however, was as much a mystery to her as it was to anyone else. She remembered nights as a child trying to scrub it off with a washcloth, as if she could rub the skin raw enough to erase the mark.

The encounter with the young man, however minor, had left her jittery and unsettled so that she kept looking over her shoulder past the heads of the street sweepers and barrow men, but he was nowhere to be seen.

Even more desperate for the distraction of a smoke, she scanned the sidewalk for the news kiosk. Blessedly it was still in the same spot near the square, still run by the same old man who could barely straighten his back as he turned the pages of a newspaper. She felt the jingle of the only two coins she possessed and reconsidered spending them on something that was so easy to take. She ought not to test her luck—she really did want to avoid the lockup again—but she knew she could swipe a tin of ciggies easy enough. No harm done. And no old man to recognize her as she handed over her coins.

Mind made up, she leaned against the wall beside the kiosk to wait for the right distraction to come along. While she waited, the young man's reaction to her scar continued to bother her. Not that he'd been all that handsome. Well, he was—in an openhearted, wide-eyed, bright-smile sort of way—but those types were always more trouble than they were worth. And if she was going to go straight at the end of all this, she had to start thinking differently.

A raindrop struck her on the nose. At last the distraction she needed. The clouds had converged to form a thunderclap signaling an impending storm. The newspapers on top of the stacks began to ripple in the moistening air. The owner would have no choice but to come collect the stacks before they were ruined. Once he did, she could swipe the tin of ciggies behind the counter quick enough. She inched closer to the window to wait for her chance, keeping her eyes down as if scanning a headline in *Le Journal*.

As the newsprint came into focus, she did more than glance. On the front page, in bold letters, read the headline: Fugitive Murderess Still on the Run.

The paper seller stepped out of his kiosk to move the stacks in from the rain as predicted. Instead of grabbing the cigarettes from behind the counter, Yvette swiped the top copy of the newspaper and stuffed it under her wrap the moment he turned his back, then ran for the nearest doorway around the corner. Tucked safely away in the alcove, she opened the newspaper. Not only was there an article asking for the public's help in finding her, but the booking photo they'd taken at the prison was right there on the front page, the caption below noting her scar as the one identifying detail the public should watch out for.

Yvette plucked the paintbrush loose, letting her hair fall around her face. She pulled a few strands forward over her cheek, more self-conscious than ever. Why was she still front-page news? Twisting a strand of damp hair between her fingers, she read on, but there was no mention of Sidra, only her. "*Merde, merde, merde!*"

"That's a spot of bad luck, isn't it?"

Yvette snapped the newspaper shut and found the young man in the corduroy jacket standing in front of her. Blocking her escape, really. The biting scent of turpentine rose off his clothing.

"Are you often in the habit of accosting single women in the street and jabbering nonsense, monsieur?" she asked without looking at him, adopting an air of confidence that defied her racing heart.

"Nonsense?" The young man stuffed the leather folder under his jacket and pointed to the newspaper. "Knew it was you the minute I saw you." He took in her entire appearance, head to toe, in one quick glance. "Circled around to make sure and saw you casing that kiosk back there."

Damn it! Why had she left the room? She had the paintbrush, but stabbing someone with it would make a hell of a mess on a public street. She clutched the weapon in her fingers anyway. "What do you want? Money? I haven't got any."

The young man actually looked hurt. "I don't want . . ." He took a step back and removed his cap. "Don't you recognize me, Yvie?"

Yvie?

"It's me, Henri."

Underneath the foppish hair she slowly recognized the once famil-iar boyish face. Only now it was covered in stubble and a smudge of blue paint on the tip of his chin.

"Henri Perez?"

He'd filled out in some impressive places since their days of snatch-ing bread and oranges from the food carts in rue Colline. He and his two brothers had lived in the two-story apartment on the street behind Tante's place. The trio had grown up feral as cats, left on their own to discover the rancid underbelly of the city and all its vulgar beauty. They'd each ended up working the light-finger trade by the time they were ten years old, stealing a watch or a few loose coins to keep enough food in their stomachs so that they didn't wash down the sewer with the rest of the rats and ragamuffins.

"One and only." He grinned, and she thought of all the starry nights they'd run through the streets to hide behind rain barrels and spy on the men in top hats who'd journeyed up the hill to watch the cabaret dancers kick their skirts up over their heads, later seeking out courtesans once the lamplights dimmed.

He was all right, this one. At least he had been. Must be seven years since she last saw him, and that was a long time to measure whether someone was still a friend. People changed. "So, what now, Henri?"

Before he could reply, a middle-aged man in a black derby exited the building through the alcove. He "hmphed" disapprovingly at them, barging forward until they were forced to step into the street. Once he'd passed, they both noticed the police officer outfitted in a double-breasted uniform and flat-topped *kepi* speaking with the newspaper seller. He smoothed his bushy mustache with his fingers as the owner pointed first one way and then another.

Henri placed his hand on Yvette's elbow. She waited half a beat to see if he pushed or pulled, the grip on her paintbrush tightening.

She was not going back to prison.

When Henri pushed her toward the public square across the street, she ran beside him, the paintbrush still tightly poised in her grip. No one appeared to follow as they escaped down a narrow lane, past the restaurant with the pink walls, and into the vacant lot atop the butte. There they scrambled up the slope among the rubbish and weeds and tucked themselves under a corrugated sheet of tin fastened in place over the corner of a brick wall. Heavy drops of rain splattered at their feet as they caught their breath.

"I haven't run from *les flics* like that since we were kids." Henri laughed and shook the rain off his coat. When she didn't join in the amusement, his face grew more serious. "You didn't think I would turn you in back there, did you?"

Considering she'd only been back living on the butte for two days and had already had a run-in with a childhood acquaintance and a near miss with the police, she was more than a little skeptical of the coincidence. "You still living on the hill?"

"Can't afford anywhere else. Why?"

"What are you doing out this time of morning? Kind of funny running into you of all people. You still working the crowds?"

He shook his head and took a cigarette from his pocket. "Let's call it providence." He struck a match, lit a ciggie, took a puff, and then offered it to her. "Truth is, I was on my way to see a beautiful woman before we met."

"Oh?" She accepted the smoke and inhaled with the deep relief of the addicted.

A glint of devil-may-care mischief darted across Henri's eyes. "The *magnifique* Mademoiselle Delacourt." Met with Yvette's blank stare, he pulled a face and added, "She's Tulane's most famous model. He painted her many times. His masterpiece, *Bisou d'amour*, hangs in the Musée Couloir. I go nearly every week to study her. The way he captured the bend of her arm and the tone of her skin is his true genius."

"Oh! She's a painting?" There was more relief in her voice than she expected. "That's right. You always were an artist. That's why the, um, blue paint." She pointed to the smudge on his chin.

"I suppose that's been there all morning." He rubbed the spot sheepishly, then brought the shabby folder out from under his jacket, untying the leather string holding it closed. "Would you like to see?" She nodded, and a flutter of sketches—some marked on rectangles of canvas, others drawn on scraps of butcher's paper—fanned out. Many were of the same woman, presumably the Mademoiselle Delacourt, kneeling in a bed of flowers with a man standing beside her kissing her cheek. And a few were of a woman on a park bench, though each from a different angle, as if he'd observed her on more than one occasion. And one, a palm-size painting, was of a young woman with blonde hair who could have been a fairy-tale damsel from another age. She sat on *les escaliers* near the top of the butte as she gazed out over the city below. Yvette could almost believe it was her, if not for the flawless skin and happy expression on the model's face.

There was a true verve to his art, a passion that translated through the lines of charcoal and strokes of paint. Movement, imagination, and promise. At least to her inexperienced eye.

"They're wonderful," she said, and meant it. She could tell he was pleased.

"Anyway, that's what I've been doing with my days the last couple of years. Can't say I don't still hit the theater crowds at night now and then. A little cash here and there, or a pocket watch for when I can't pay the rent." He went silent then, long enough to make her think he was considering if they were still close enough for him to ask the big question. And then he did. "What about you, Yvie? Why'd you come back here? You must know how dangerous it is, what with your, you know"—he pointed to the newspaper tucked under her arm—"circumstances."

"You mean because I'm wanted for murder?"

Henri checked the direction they'd come. "Look, I've known you since I was old enough to climb that back wall, Yvie. I know what happened that night couldn't have been your fault. The authorities must've got it wrong. But you shouldn't have come back to the butte while things are still hot."

"Had to."

"Why? What's worth risking your neck on the guillotine?"

Yvette pretended to look at a scuff on her shoe. "I had to see her."

He bent his ear forward like he'd heard her wrong. "You can't be serious. You came back to see *her*? You know there've been men watching the front door for weeks."

"I snuck in through your mother's back courtyard." She allowed the corner of her mouth to curl up when he balked at her boldness. "Listen, Henri. I can't explain how, but I was given a second chance to come back and find some answers. Things I have to know to be . . . to be a . . ."

"To be what?"

She lifted her head and looked him straight in the eye. "The witch I was meant to be."

She'd said it to him before, once when they were kids, to see how he'd react. They'd stolen a pair of tarts from a bare-bones patisserie and ran to the construction site of the new basilica. It's where the gang of neighborhood kids gathered under the scaffolding after the workers had gone for the day. Another boy who'd overheard her say she was a witch had told her to prove it by turning a stray dog into a cat. When she said it didn't work that way, the boy had scoffed and called her a liar. But Henri hadn't. He merely bit into his tart and stared at her with eyes wide and believing. The same way he did now.

His boyish grin returned and he closed his portfolio, tying it back up. "Where are you holed up? I'll walk you back so you get in safe."

She hugged her knees as she thought about it. Henri had always been one of the good guys. But seven years was seven years, and she only had this one stolen wish to make things right. If she blew it now, she'd never get a chance to be who she wanted to be. But what if Henri's sudden appearance was also part of her fate? Part of the wish?

"I gotta go, Henri."

"Well, can we meet again? Maybe I could draw your picture sometime?"

She pressed her fingers to the ridge of scar along her cheek, then glanced at the leather folder held tight to his chest. What dreams did he hold inside? Did he think his sketches could transport him to a new and better life? She'd always thought of Henri Perez as a sweet boy born into a sour lot. But even he seemed to think a boy born on the top of the butte could be more than a street tough who stole bread and pocket watches to pay the rent. If he could believe it, why couldn't she?

As the rain stopped, she stuck her hand out and agreed to meet Henri for a coffee date, and then she let him escort her halfway home.

CHAPTER TWELVE

Henri couldn't believe she'd turned up in the street like that. It was Yvie, all right. Same tussle of blonde hair that wouldn't stay pinned in place; same green eyes smudged with black kohl that didn't miss a move. Couldn't be a coincidence. Leastwise, none of the regulars at Hell's Mouth would say it was anything but meant to be. Written in the stars, they'd say, and then point to a chart on the wall showing the cosmic path of one planet bumping up against another's, offering proof.

Yvie had clearly endured a rough few years. Word was she'd been hiding out on the carnival circuit. The harlequin tights peeking out under her skirt suggested it was true. But what Henri couldn't understand was why she'd come back. She was already in the wind, according to the papers. And no one returned to the butte for a second helping of abuse from Isadora. Sure, she said that same line about being a witch she'd been saying since she was a kid, but did she actually believe it? Probably. These days everyone in the city was convinced they had some special connection to the great beyond, with their Ouija boards and crystal balls.

Henri tucked his portfolio under his arm and began to dig through his pocket for the coins it would cost for both of them to take a *fiacre* to the top of the butte. But then he thought better of making the offer. He ought not go flashing too much money in front of someone as savvy as Yvie Lenoir, who could put two and two together faster than anyone he'd ever worked with. Plus the fewer straights who saw her the better, and not just because she was on the run from the police. But damn that reward. It was enough to set a man up in his own studio and start a career.

"Probably best if we walk," he said, leaving the coins in his pocket. "Take the side streets. Like the old days."

She grinned, impish and bold, and he longed to capture the expression with his charcoal before it was gone. Still, he could never forget the curve of her lip, not when she smiled at him like that.

"Let's take the back stairs," she said and pulled the tatty velvet curtain up around her face so only her eyes peered out. "If the streetlamps aren't already busted, we can always throw a few rocks at them."

That was Yvie, all right. She nudged her head, and he couldn't help but follow.

CHAPTER THIRTEEN

Elena sat on the single cot in Yvette's rented room and thumbed through the curious little book again, comparing the symbols written in gold with those in her grimoire. There were some similarities. The text could be a code based on the basic symbology of the astrological chart, or perhaps even ancient hieroglyphs. Centuries ago, before the covenant reformations, certain kings and queens relied on court occultists. Their magical work was disguised with codes to protect the throne from ridicule from those opposed to magic. So the precedent for a coded magical message was well established. But why go to the effort of disguising a book's contents, only to keep it from its intended recipient until she turned sixteen? What possible message required such a sophisticated level of coding? And for a girl who practically grew up on the streets?

Yvette, her hair sopping wet from a brown hair-dye concoction they'd applied, blew a stream of smoke out the window. "Anything?"

"I'm afraid not." Before crushing Yvette's hopes too much, she added, "As soon as the color takes, we'll visit the man I mentioned. He's an absolute wizard at this sort of thing."

Yvette wiped a brown drip away with a dirty paint rag. "Where did you get this stuff anyway? Smells awful."

Elena hadn't found the potent scent offensive. If anything, she wanted to break down the potion to see what else could be done with the ingredients if mixed in a slightly different order. It was a unique concoction, something not quite a poison, not quite a prescriptive. She was intrigued. Even more so if the inventor turned out to be a mortal, though she rather doubted this. Considering the combination of elements that would be required to alter a person's hair color permanently, she presumed there must be a spell bonded to the chemicals.

The cat mewed, and she caught herself thinking more about chemicals than she normally would. The revelation bothered her. Yes, she'd always had a curiosity about spells involving certain dangerous ingredients, but she was sinking into preoccupation.

"Hair coloring is all the rage in the shops on the boulevard," she answered. "At least if you believe the advertisements in the shop windows I pass on my way to and from the Metro. Seemed just the trick we needed to change your looks, so I induced a hair stylist to offer me the kit, saying I could do it myself."

"You mean you put a spell on him. Jiminy, I wish I could do that."

"I used a good old-fashioned bribe, actually. Now, let's see how well the color worked."

Yvette tossed her cigarette out the window, then bent her head over a bucket. Elena poured a pitcher of cool water through her tresses, thinking this new hair-coloring kit couldn't have hit the market at a better time. It was a shame to cover the girl's lustrous blonde hair with the artificial brown, but those golden locks were like a neon light drawing attention to her. Elena gave the hair a second rinse, then wrapped a towel around Yvette's head.

"Let's see how it took," she said and removed the towel.

The hair had turned a deep shade of chestnut. If the inventor wasn't a witch, he ought to be. There was obviously nothing to be done about the girl's scar, but the transformation was still impressive. Elena handed Yvette a hand mirror as the cat preened his fur with his tongue.

"Would you look at that." Yvette genuinely smiled, and a spark of radiance emanated from her aura for a split second.

"Do that again."

"What?"

"Look at yourself in the mirror and smile."

The young woman seemed to doubt the reasoning behind the request but obliged. She gazed at her reflection, smiled, and then stuck out her tongue. The aura didn't change. But something else did.

"Wait, there's something wrong." Yvette did a double take in the mirror. "The dye didn't work. My hair's changing back."

The brown dye receded right before their eyes, retreating from the roots and exposing Yvette's bright golden hair an inch at a time. The artificial color drained completely away, like water repelled by the oily feathers of an odd duck. Yvette stood once more with a head full of yellow locks.

"Why'd it do that?" Yvette reached for the empty bottle and took a sniff, as if the harsh smell might hold a clue. "What's in this stuff?"

This time, however, it was Elena who smiled. "Possibly the sign we've been looking for," she said, knowing her eyes hadn't deceived her. That was no trick brought about by chemistry. It was magic, pure and simple. And it had come from Yvette.

Now if they could only figure out what kind of magic it was.

⌘

"So, this wizard fellow is some kind of expert in weird things like my hair?"

Yvette adjusted the end of the head scarf over her cheek for the fifth time since they'd gone underground, repositioned the hatpin holding it in place over her hair, and hopped on the train running south. After checking on the progress of her portrait, Elena had borrowed a rather smart green silk dress and matching head scarf from Pedro's new live-in bohemian girlfriend. The fit was almost perfect on Yvette's lithe frame. On reflection, the young woman cut a striking figure once attired in properly fitted clothes. But she'd forgotten about shoes, so the girl was forced to continue padding around in her carnival footwear. In fact, she seemed to prefer them, walking lightly in her high-wire, pixie way.

"He's a shop owner interested in all kinds of phenomena," Elena whispered when she noticed an elderly woman across the aisle paying much too much attention to them. "I'm very curious to see what he has to say about you."

"Oh là là, if he tells me I'm a stub witch who can't control her own magic like everyone else did, I'm walking out."

"You've been examined before?"

"Just some old guy Tante hired to show me the basics. Gave up after a couple of weeks on account of me being a hopeless case. I think she was expecting me to bring in money for her by doing a few exotic spells or something."

Yvette turned her face to the window. It couldn't be easy for her, after the life she'd lived. Abandoned as a child, brought up in a cabaret by a mortal woman who cared little for her—is that where the scar had come from?—and then forced to go on the run after being accused of killing a man. Elena didn't know the details, but she found it hard to believe that the young woman she'd come to know was capable of cold-blooded murder.

Then again, the girl had never denied it.

The railroad car rocked steadily as it hurried down the tracks in the claustrophobic tunnels beneath the city. The old woman across the aisle from them continued to stare. And mutter. She seemed to be reciting something over and over again under her breath—possibly a spell of some sort—the intensity of her attentions going beyond acceptable curiosity in her fellow passengers. Elena stared back, ready to utter a spell of her own, when the woman stood, splashed the contents of a vial of presumed holy water at her feet, and spit out the accusation of "*venefica*" before relocating to a different car.

Yvette stood and flicked her fingers under her chin at the woman before she was able to get the carriage door shut. "Mind your own business, beldam!" The encounter seemed to pump the life back into the girl. She practically bounced on the seat next to Elena. "What the hell was that about? Why'd she call you that? Crazy old woman."

Elena looked down at her hands folded in her lap. Her fingers, normally stained red this time of year from cleaning the lees out of the vats, were as clean as freshly pressed linen. What spot of filth had the woman seen that she herself could not?

The train slowed as it approached the next station. "This is our stop," she said, letting Yvette's question go unanswered.

They emerged onto a busy street on the right bank of the river not far from the university. After turning left and left again, they found themselves in a narrow urban canyon on a lane as old as the city itself. Elena knew if she put a hand to any one of the stones beneath their feet, she would hear the roar of centuries gone past, to the time of kings and courtiers, peasants and tyrants. And witches who had plied their trade for as long as the walls had stood.

Up ahead Elena spotted the epicurean shop on the corner that specialized in ingredients she added to certain fragrant spells to ease winter's gray days, like dried bergamot, patchouli oil, and the shaved bark of the agar tree. They'd come to a part of the city where a witch on the prowl could find just about any requirement she needed for a spell. A craving inside her to find a pinch of dried hemlock or a sprig of nightshade spurred her to look through the glass of the market shop. She had no spell she used for those, but her heart told her she could devise one easily enough.

Blood will tell, blood will remember.

The thought startled her. She'd always had a talent for poison, yes, but her curiosity about the art had never risen inside her like a craving. And yet she could feel it tugging at her, pulling her down. Had the simple clerical act of revoking her status as a vine witch done that? Was it possible to change a person's constitution with the mere mark of a rubber stamp? Is that what the old woman on the train had sensed?

She stepped back and hooked her arm through Yvette's for courage, as much for herself and the strength to walk away as for the young woman and the precarious trust she had in Elena to do the right thing. With a sigh of relief, they came next to a little shop with a lock and key flanked by two crescent moons painted above the door. As they stood on the threshold of their destination, Elena made a silent plea to the All Knowing to repel the creeping seduction of poisons taking hold inside of her as thoroughly as Yvette's golden hair had rejected the bottle of dye.

CHAPTER FOURTEEN

"What is this place?" Yvette could see movement inside as dark silhouettes passed behind the exposed portion of the window beside the door.

"It's a curio shop. Mostly." Elena opened the door.

"It doesn't look like any shop I've ever seen." She'd been expecting more of a bookstore, something akin to the kiosks that set up shop by the river, only with walls and a door. Not a fancy gentleman's shop that appeared as if it required an invitation merely to walk inside. Of course, now she understood the change of clothes Elena had insisted on. Even in the silk dress and matching head scarf they'd found for her to wear, she'd still be a common pigeon among the sparrow hawks in a place like this. And she knew how their sharp eyes always kept a lookout for new prey.

"Trust me," Elena said, nudging her at the elbow. "The place isn't as fancy as it looks. It only pretends to cater to the city snobs on the outside."

Trust. Not a word she'd hang around most people's necks, but Elena was different. She was counting on it.

The scent of faded perfume and upholstery infused with lingering pipe smoke met Yvette's nose as she stepped inside. Though it proved a curio shop as Elena had said, there were a large number of books. Piles of them, really, scattered around the chairs and ottomans for sale. Several were titled in languages she didn't recognize. Others, their pages coming loose from their worn bindings, served merely as end tables on which to display a lantern, or gravy boat, or pair of snuff boxes, and in one case a walking cane with an onyx stone dragon affixed as a handle. On another pile rested a brass compass and a doctor's stethoscope. Above them a sign on the wall stated: ALL MERCHANDISE GUARANTEED.

Yvette pointed and asked Elena, "Guaranteed to do what?"

"Everything here has been enchanted in one fashion or another," she said. "But that doesn't mean the proprietor guarantees the functionality of any of the objects, only that they've been magicked at some point in the past. Buyer beware."

"Right," said Yvette, careful not to bump into anything too suspicious looking.

She had just picked up a small perfume bottle with a glass stopper, wondering how a bottle could be enchanted, when a short man in a black frock coat stepped through the curtains from the back room. A tiny moth fluttered out from beneath his lapel as he dabbed at the corners of his mouth with a napkin, as if he'd moments ago finished his midday meal.

"Ah, Mademoiselle Boureanu, is it not?" The man adjusted the pince-nez on the bridge of his nose to get a better look. "It's been a long time since we've seen you in this end of the city."

"I'd been away for a while, Monsieur Olmos."

Yvette thought Elena was uncharacteristically nervous, the way she fiddled with the marble chess pieces assembled on top of the front counter. He was just a frumpy old man who ate alone, for goodness sake.

"Eh, curses. They're the worst infestation of the soul, are they not?"

Elena blanched as Yvette questioned the remark with a pointed look and raised eyebrow.

"Fortunately, there is a remedy for those lucky enough to find it," Elena said.

"Ah, love. Indeed, it is the best antidote to be had for the price."

Pleasantries out of the way, Olmos turned his attention to Yvette. She'd seen that look before. The one all shop owners gave her when she entered their store. By the way his eye searched her hands, his nose lifted to better see her down the length of it, and his lip tightened in disapproval, she knew he took her for a thief straightaway. Good instincts, she supposed, but offensive all the same. Nonetheless, he struck the pose of one ready to serve by folding his hands behind his back.

"As perceptive as always, Alexandre. Which is why I'd like to introduce you to Yvette Lenoir."

"*Enchanté*, mademoiselle." The shopkeeper's gaze overshot the top of her head by a good six inches, as if he were watching a shadow floating above her; then it settled again at eye level.

"If you are a friend of Elena's, you are most welcome in my little shop of books and intrigues." The man blinked through his lenses at Yvette. "Yes, most welcome, although I must inform you that particular perfume bottle is not for sale," he said and took it carefully from her, setting the object behind the counter. She thought then how smart she'd been to leave Sidra's bottle in the little apartment tucked behind the plaster in the wall. It was way nicer than the one this man was worried about.

Yvette felt her center tilt a little off-kilter at the way the man kept checking her aura, but she remembered what Elena had said about him being some sort of expert in strange stuff, so she ignored his attentions and managed a respectable nod in return. "Intrigues?" she asked, feeling the need to take a second glance at the shelves around her.

Alexandre gestured toward the room. "For the uninitiated we're mostly regarded as an occult bookshop." The man took a slim volume off the nearest shelf and flayed the pages open for her to see. "This is one of my best sellers among the city's housewives. An encyclopedia of sorts. Descriptions, terms, and illustrations to give the reader a sense of how to execute a few harmless incantations. All rather droll but, as I said, the mortal women in the city can't seem to buy enough of them."

He snapped the book shut. "Very popular. You see, its small size makes it convenient to tuck behind a cushion or ditch in the empty flour tin in the event the disapproving mother-in-law arrives and you'd rather she didn't know you're dabbling in the supernatural arts." Alexandre presented the book for inspection. "I must sell half a dozen a week."

"Oh, I want to do more than dabble. I should have learned this stuff ages ago."

Yvette took the book when offered and thumbed through the opening pages. She didn't see any incantations she recognized from her days at the carnival. Professor Rackham, a witch who'd made his living working as a carny psychic, had always had a spare moment between shows to tutor her in basic tarot and potions. Well, when he wasn't otherwise diving into her cleavage with his eyes.

Alexandre tapped a finger against his lips as his eyes studied the space over Yvette's head yet again. "But, of course, that's not why she's here, is it?" he said to Elena.

"No." Elena walked to the front door and turned the sign so it read Closed to anyone passing by. "We have a situation I believe only you can help with," she said and locked the door.

"In addition to the young woman's stagnated aura?"

Stagnated?

"I believe they are related," Elena said, signaling Yvette to present the leather-bound book. "Her mother left this for her sixteenth birthday, though she only recently received it. Is it a spell book of some kind? There are patterns and codes, but none that will reveal themselves to me."

Alexandre looked over the book with interest, holding it so that only the tips of his fingers touched the edges as he moved closer to the shop window to better study the pages in the light. He adjusted his pince-nez and squinted at the neatly lined symbols, turning each page slowly as if absorbing the information in tolerable small doses. He checked again that the front door was locked. Satisfied, he went to a shelf at the back of the store, one with several decrepit old books propped up by a pair of candlesticks. There he removed a book with a red leather binding, flipped it open to a middle section written in similar gold lettering, and did a side-by-side comparison with Yvette's book. After a grumble or two he shut the book and replaced it on the shelf, only to retrieve a different one from beneath a woman's hatbox. This one proved more promising, drawing a pursed lip followed by a muttered "possibly" from the witch.

He seemed then to get an idea. Alexandre closed the book and gazed again at Yvette, scrutinizing her aura for anything he might have missed. "The radiation is broad yet weak. And there are sections that fade altogether."

Elena agreed. "Most notably near her face."

He moved in closer to study the scar running along Yvette's jaw. "How long have you had that unfortunate mark?" he asked abruptly, staring but not touching, seemingly unaware of the impropriety of asking such a personal question.

"All my life," she said, and she swore she felt her cheek begin to tingle.

Whether it was the atmosphere of the enchanted shop or the tension wire of secrecy with which they went about their talk, Yvette's limited intuition pricked its ears. An uncomfortable twinge within her chest followed.

A revelation was about to devour her.

"Not all your life, I'd wager."

"What is it? What do you see?" Elena swung around so that she stood behind the shop owner's right shoulder.

Alexandre sorted quickly through the items atop the display table beside him. "Ah, this will do, if memory serves," he said, picking up the stethoscope. He hooked the earpieces around his neck and aimed the bell end at Yvette's face. Oddly enough, a purple light shone out of its enchanted end.

Elena gasped and covered her mouth. "It's shimmering under the ultraviolet light."

"Shimmering?" Yvette rubbed her hand against her jaw and looked at her fingers. Nothing. "You mean like glitter?"

"More like those pulsating electric lights on that monstrosity of a tower." Alexandre rummaged through a third source of books stashed within a picnic basket. He pulled loose a black leather tome with seven brass stars embedded in its cover. "I suspect your scar was not caused by any childhood injury but by magic. Now, let's see if we can sort out what kind and, if we're lucky, perhaps even why."

"You keep a copy of *The Book of the Seven Stars* in a picnic basket?" Elena asked.

"Safest place for it." He shrugged and began scanning the pages for the information he was after.

Yvette ran to an ornate mirror hanging above an umbrella stand, desperate to see what they were talking about, but the antique's unfortunate enchantment reflected back the face of a horse. "*Merde*, what's happening in this place?"

Alexandre traced his finger over the sentences in the book until he slowed and tapped on a single satisfying word. "Ah, yes, an *étouffer*, mademoiselle, that is what is happening."

Yvette looked to Elena for an explanation. "Is that bad? If it's in that book, it's bad, right?"

"Don't worry," Elena said. "It's not a curse or hex or anything. An *étouffer* merely means someone has muzzled your magic. Your scar may prove to be the place where they sealed the spell. Like a stopper in a bottle. Honestly, I could kick myself. I should have seen it from the start, the way the magic can't seem to find a proper way out of you."

"Muzzled?" Yvette collapsed in an overstuffed chair. "So, I really am a witch?"

"Without question you come from a magical bloodline." Alexandre rubbed an itch above his bushy eyebrow. "Though there is something peculiar about the way your energy swims within your humors. It's trapped because of the *étouffer*, yes, but the flow is . . . erratic, to say the least."

"But I'm a witch." Yvette perked up. "So, is that my spell book? Is it my mother's grimoire? Can I start learning spells?"

"Ah, yes, the book. That I cannot say. Not yet." He returned to the coded pages, giving them another glance. "One has to ask, if this were a mere family spell book, why hide the incantations? Why make a daughter wait until she turned sixteen? And why has your magic been muted?"

"Is it malefaction?" Elena asked with a look Yvette had seen before when they'd faced off against a three-hundred-year-old demon-loving witch in the depth of a creepy wine cellar.

"I cannot honestly say. There seems to be a confusing haze in the room on that topic," he said pointedly at Elena, to which she demurred. Then choosing to hunt down his own line of thought, he asked Yvette, "Why didn't you receive the book when you were sixteen? You are beyond that age, I presume."

"I . . ." Yvette exchanged a glance with Elena, who nodded, despite her face going pale as if she might be sick. "I had to leave the city before I got the chance."

"On account of?"

"On account of killing a man so he wouldn't kill me. Only the law sees it one way. Murder. So, I got the hell out. Don't you read the newspapers?"

Alexandre ignored her question. "Did this by any chance occur near your sixteenth birthday?"

"Night of. How'd you guess?"

Alexandre moved closer, his eyes squinting behind the pince-nez. "Tell me, what did this man do? How did he approach you?"

"He . . . I don't know, he paid, you know, to go to my room at Le Rêve." Yvette reached for the ashtray on the table beside her. "Can I smoke?"

"Absolutely not."

Mon Dieu, these straights and their rules.

"What do you mean he paid?"

Elena interceded. "She grew up in a cabaret that apparently doubled as a brothel."

"Ah. Go on, then."

"I did the usual stuff, took his hat, offered him a drink, and then, I don't know, he went nuts. Pushed me down on the bed, but instead of coming after me he starts tearing through my vanity table and wardrobe. Figured he was a white-powder fiend or maybe chasing the green fairy for the first time and he thought I had money stashed in the room. I don't know many spells, but Rings—he's a thief who works the right bank—"

"Yes, yes, I'm aware of who he is."

"Someone taught him a spell to open locks that for some reason always worked for me and no one else, so I tried writing a few spells of my own. When this guy didn't find what he was looking for, he came at me again, demanding I tell him where I had it hidden or he'd kill me."

"Did he name the thing he was after?"

Yvette had always thought the attack strange but chalked it up to the man's drug habit. "He kept yelling at me for the map. What map? Where was I going to go? I told him I didn't have one, but he started hitting me again." Yvette wiped a tear from her cheek. "That's when I fell on the floor. While he ripped everything out of the wardrobe, I recited the words to a spell I'd made up. Next thing I know, a pair of scissors from the vanity go flying at him, pointed end first. Stabbed him right in the neck. The blood went everywhere, so I ran."

"She was also attacked two days ago," Elena added.

"The day after Tante gave me the book."

"That man demanded a key from her. At the time we thought it a random mugging, but it couldn't be a coincidence."

"A key? You're certain?"

Yvette and Elena both confirmed it with a nod.

"A key. A map." Alexandre held his hand over the journal, as if trying to read its energy. "Certainly, appropriate words to describe a book of ciphers. But for what purpose? If it is a key, then what does it open? How does one find the matching lock? If it's a map, where does it lead? And how does one get there?"

The front door rattled, making Yvette jump out of her chair. A customer in a black shawl peered through the glass and frowned before reading the sign and moving on. The interruption shook the shop's owner out of his reverie, and he slid the book back to its owner. He scrutinized her jawline once more, this time daring to touch the scar tissue.

"There is a method for removing the *étouffer*," he said, as if daring Yvette's curiosity. "We could do it now, if you like."

"Would that be wise before we know her lineage?" Elena asked. "I checked her lifecycle record. Her birth is written down, but she was never officially registered as any type of witch. And, strangely, her parents' names have been erased. There's no way of knowing what type of magic we would be setting free."

"One can't run from whom they were meant to be," he said, as if peering at some hidden location inside Elena. "The transformation, the struggle between light and dark, that is what propels life forward. That metamorphosis is one's purpose for existing." His eyes scanned the space above Elena's head as if he were reading newsprint. "It can feel like one is trapped or been sent into the murky water never to swim free," he added, "but there is a place to rise and see clearly again."

"Wait, are we still talking about me?" Yvette asked. "Because if this muzzle thing on my jaw is blocking my magic, I definitely want it removed. Just tell me how."

"The one spell she's mastered killed a man. Do you really want to uncork her powers and let them fly without any hint of which direction the magic will go? I've seen malevolent magic at work, monsieur. I do not wish to revisit it again."

"Oh là là, Elena. You think I'm going to be as mad as that old demon-loving bat in the cellar? Thanks *so* much."

"Of course not. But it would be reckless to ignore the Pandora-esque danger of not knowing the history of your bloodline first."

"But I don't even know who my parents were," Yvette pleaded.

"And neither does Alexandre. Which means there's something strange going on. Something someone tried very hard to hide, which makes me wonder why."

"You're correct; I cannot detect her lineage until the magic is free," Alexandre interjected. "Which is why I suggest we remove the *étouffer* and have a look."

"I second the motion," Yvette said, eagerly sitting forward.

Thief, gutter rat, prostitute, murderer—she'd heard it all. Absorbed it, lived it, become it. But for the first time in her life she was filled with the sense that she was worth more. This moment had value greater than gold, she could feel it, and so she thrust out her jaw with the conviction of the recently converted. "Do it," she said.

"We'll need candles." Alexandre reached in a drawer behind the counter while Elena closed the drapes in the front window and then cleared a space in the middle of the shop floor by pushing a pair of tables and an ottoman out of the way.

"What should I do?" Yvette asked.

"Stand here." Elena directed her to the center of an invisible circle on the floor that she'd paced out by walking fully around the open space. Alexandre returned bearing four candles, each with a different colored ribbon tied around it, and a blonde-haired porcelain doll in full dress and petticoat. Elena lifted a wicker basket and removed a silver letter opener with a questioning glance aimed at the shopkeeper. When he nodded, she adopted it as her athame. With the tool she directed the flow of energy in the circle in a counterclockwise motion while

Alexandre entered and began placing the candles on the floor, one for each cardinal direction.

The way the witch and wizard worked together without speaking, simply knowing what needed to be done next from a lifetime of experience, sent a snaking vine of envy slithering over Yvette's heart. But soon she would be able to do that magic too. She just knew it.

Alexandre asked Yvette to take the doll and draw a line on its face with a smear of blood to represent her scar.

"Where do I get that from?"

"I presume it runs in your veins?"

Yvette gulped. "You mean cut myself?" She eyed Elena's letter opener, but the witch shook her head and placed the blade on the makeshift altar inside the circle.

It seemed a harsh request to draw one's own blood, but magic had its own logic—always had. Yvette pulled the hatpin loose from her head scarf and used it to prick her finger. The blood quickly pooled in a bright red spot on the tip, which she used to draw a line on the doll's face. She blew on the wet blood to get it to dry, then held the poppet to her chest.

Alexandre struck a match and lit the first candle, the one with the gold ribbon. "Turn north, my dear." He gently turned Yvette's shoulders square to the back of the shop. "You too," he said to Elena, who stood behind them both, her hands already held in the sacred pose to honor the All Knowing.

The wick flared and he stood the candle up on the wood floor at the north edge of the circle. "Earth," he said and bent to draw an inverted triangle with a horizontal line through it, using a stick of charcoal on the floor. He made a quarter turn to his left and lit the green candle, placing it on the western point. There he drew a second inverted triangle, this one without a line. "Water," he said and circled behind the women. There he lay his match against the red candle directly south and outlined a right-side-up triangle, announcing, "Fire." He came around, moving spritely for an old man, and bent to light the blue candle on the eastern side and marking it with a triangle. "Air," he said and blew out the match.

After checking his pockets, he returned to the north position to stand beside Yvette. "There ought to be flowers or gemstones as an offering, but we'll make do. The masculine and feminine energy contained in the circle should serve us well enough for the task. Ready?"

She felt a flutter of hesitancy, the fear of the unknown whispering in her ear. Yvette nodded before she lost her nerve, knowing it was go forward and realize her wish or stay locked in the city and its own form of limbo as a prisoner forever. "Ready," she said and took a deep breath.

"Let us call the beneficial elementals to our side, then." Alexandre began to chant, raising his hands in the sacred pose as Elena had done. "Earth, air, water, fire. Your presence here we doth desire. Air, water, fire, earth. Ye advocates of frolic and mirth. Water, fire, earth, air. Thou spirit bright and spirit fair. Fire, earth, air, and water. Cast your blessings on this daughter."

After a brief moment of calm the air stirred inside the circle. The candles flickered. The wood beams creaked beneath their feet. Yvette's armpits grew damp with sweat.

"They're here." Alexandre held his hand out for the doll. "They can be a little unpredictable. Best if they get to know your representative first, to be safe," he said and held the poppet over his head.

The air swirled inside the circle, faster and faster until the women's hair whipped up over their heads. There was something terrifying yet beautiful in the way the magic swept around them. Such power. Such ferocity. Forceful yet benevolent. Yvette felt more than saw them as they whipped past her body, though she was certain four distinct embodiments of the elements were present. They circled her, evaluating, prodding, considering. Alexandre licked his thumb and wiped the blood from the doll's face, as if to communicate his intention to the faceless energy swirling overhead. A whoosh of energy went through her, and Yvette felt the lightest fingertip touch against her cheek. Her skin tingled, and the scent of burning cedar invaded her nostrils.

Elena, her hair thrashing wildly about her face, inspected the site of the scar, then raised a hand and thanked the elementals for their intervention. The spirits whirled and swooped over their heads, doused the candles one by one, but then paused on the southern point where Elena stood. They spun slowly around her, as if curiously sniffing out a wrong scent. Their momentum built, encircling her in an ever faster whirlwind, until she raised her hands in the sacred pose. The elementals ended their frenzy. As suddenly as they'd appeared, they dissipated like smoke through a stovepipe, flying back to whatever ethereal realm they'd descended from.

The circle still hummed with the vigor of their passing when Elena picked up the letter opener and cut a gap for a door by slicing the air, releasing the energy of the spell. There was a brief flicker, like moonlight passing through a skylight, and then the shop was quiet except for the sharp intake of breath from its owner.

"Remarkable." Alexandre smoothed his hair back in place as he stared at Yvette's face. "How do you feel?"

"Not sure," she said, swaying on her feet and blinking as though a steam engine had just whooshed in front of her at top speed. "A little buzzy feeling, but otherwise okay." But it was more than a slight tingling under her skin. Her veins felt like they'd been connected to a wire full of electricity. Plugged in like one of those light bulbs with the wiry filaments that sparked and sizzled as it glowed to life. Was that what it felt like to be a witch? To have the touch of magic crackle like static beneath your fingertips?

"Is it gone?" Yvette ran to the mirror, forgetting the glass was charmed to give a false image. A halo of incandescent light shone back at her, albeit around the face of a toffee-colored mare.

Elena forced the mirror to behave with a cleansing spell. "Not only is the scar gone, but you seem to be emitting a low-frequency energy, something with a bit of a shimmer to it." No sooner had she said it than the initial blossom of radiance diminished.

"Would you look at that!" Yvette turned her face from cheek to cheek, then leaned closer to the mirror. "What do I do now? Am I a witch?"

"Do you feel anything in your hands? Any tingling or itch?"

Yvette wiggled her fingers. "It feels like quicksilver sliding through my fingers."

"Try to create a little fire on your fingertips," Elena said.

Alexandre balked. "In my shop? I think not. I may not carry luxury goods, but I'd like to protect the merchandise, all the same."

"Right, good point. We still don't know what we're dealing with." Elena eyed the doll Alexandre was holding. "What about a simple charm? I learned to curl my doll's hair when I was a child using an elementary enchantment."

Elena handed her the doll and told her what to say. Yvette wrapped a strand of doll hair around her finger and repeated the words, concentrating for all she was worth. "With a twirl or with a swirl, every girl should wear a curl."

The doll responded by sprouting a vine with curling tendrils that trailed down its back.

"Not quite there yet," Elena said, but she encouraged Yvette by observing that *some* kind of magic had come through.

"It is odd, though, isn't it?" Alexandre studied the doll's leafy hair. "For the charm to have turned the way it did." He set the doll on a bookshelf. "At any rate, it's no misfit in this shop."

"But I still am," Yvette said with obvious disappointment.

"You simply need a little training. To learn how to control the flow of energy."

"Maybe that's what the book is for." Yvette brightened and retrieved her mother's book before handing it over to Alexandre. "Will you keep trying to figure out what it says?"

He seemed at first to want to say no, then gingerly accepted the book and the challenge. "It may take some time," he warned. "Days, a week, a month."

Yvette began to have second thoughts, but if this eccentric old man could keep a copy of *The Book of the Seven Stars* safe in a picnic basket, he ought to be able to protect her little book of spells.

CHAPTER FIFTEEN

Henri had been in the curio shop once or twice before. Bunch of junk, really. Nothing in there ever seemed to work the way it was supposed to. So, what was Yvie and that other one doing in there? And why was Yvie hanging out with her anyway? Unless they were partners. Two women working together could steal the shirt off a man on the boulevard before he knew what was up. They could maybe get a few coins for a busted pocket watch in a shop like that, though he never heard any rumors about the old man being very generous. And the woman Yvie was with didn't look like she needed the money either. Of course, that could be part of the con.

"What are you up to, Yvie?" Henri whispered the question to himself as he smudged a charcoal line to soften the angle of her jaw. He'd drawn her a hundred times in his sketchbook. Sometimes from afar, most often from memory, once when she'd sat still for him with the spring sun shining in her hair, and again at night under the soft glow of October moonlight. She inspired his artistic eye like no other. Not even the Mademoiselle Delacourt from the museum excited him the way Yvie did. Which made what he had to do next rise like turpentine in his throat.

Henri looked over his drawing, added a final detail to her head scarf, then closed the sketchbook. He'd finish it later when he was alone.

After he sobered up from the alcohol he knew he'd numb himself with later.

The shades went down inside the store, and even Henri didn't miss the irony of the moment. Something shady was going on behind the shop door. Yvie had gotten herself into a powerful mess to have the sort of people interested in finding her. As soon as news hit she'd escaped prison, there was word of a reward from a private source. Not just for her, though. There was some book too. No deal without the book. Henri couldn't imagine any book being as valuable as the money being offered. Worth a year's earnings or more working the high end of the street near the theaters. Or maybe ten paintings when he was famous. *If* he could ever sell one to anyone besides his mother. "Christ, Yvie, where'd you ever steal a book like that from? Is that what you're doing in there? Trying to sell it?" She'd be better off turning herself in to the boss. Well, money-wise anyway.

Henri packed his sketchbook and charcoal away and gave up his position outside the door to the epicurean shop. And good riddance. The entire street gave him the shivers with all the palm readers, and painted wagons advertising amulets, and animal feet and tails for sale as good luck charms. People acting like all that occult stuff was normal fascination. Whole city had gone twitchy. If they wanted a real scare, they ought to follow him to the basement in Hell's Mouth. One trip there would cure them of their need for a morbid thrill. Of course, half of them probably already frequented the damn place on the regular.

The courtyard clock struck the hour. He was late. Worth it, though, to get a glimpse of Yvie in that dress and get to draw her one more time. The wind shifted and he nearly gagged on the nearby stench from the *abattoirs*, where the slaughter of horses for their meat continued day and night to keep up with the city's demand. With the reek of blood and excrement caught in the back of his throat, he jumped on the first omnibus going north and took it as far as the base of the butte where the five streets converged in the infamous cabaret district. From there he ducked down an alley most would pass by, thinking it a dead end where only stray cats gathered to screech and howl. But if you walked all the way to the back, turned left, and squeezed around the drainpipe coming off the back of the building—*le trou du cul du diable*, the devil's asshole, as the gang called it—you ended up in a second alley that emptied out at the back side of the butte's graveyard. It also led directly to the back door of Hell's Mouth.

Henri entered using the key he'd been given five years after his initiation. The churned earth scent of mold that rose out of the basement always made him think of the bodies planted in the next street over. Good reminder about which side of the dirt he preferred to be in, and one he always took with him into the meeting room. More moldering earth breath hit his face as he descended the rickety stairwell. At the end of the basement hall, beneath the glare of an oil lamp, an armed guard stood watch outside a door. Henri was late, but they wouldn't start without him.

"Jean-Baptiste le sauvage," he said, naming the notorious pirate who terrorized the high seas two centuries earlier and this week's password. The guard let him pass, and he stepped into the room.

At night the morbid space served as the Underworld room of Hell's Mouth, the three-tiered cabaret catering to the demons-and-angels trend the occult-obsessed city couldn't get enough of. Upstairs were the semichic Heaven and Hell, but the basement was for the truly dispossessed. Bats and bones and coffins—he didn't like any of it, but he couldn't deny the crowds. People clamored to get into the nightclub and rub up against a little sin and madness.

"Glad you could join us, Perez." Rings, a burly man with a twice-busted nose and a pencil-thin mustache, made sure the expression on his face contrasted his words.

On the wall behind Henri's boss hung a skull and crossbones with a scarf tied over the skull's nose and mouth like a bandit. A gesture of comedy and tragedy in one ghastly combination. A reminder that their purpose on the streets was to act as plundering pirates, albeit ones set sail on a sea of hapless marks.

Four other young men watched Henri as he took the last stool. The man on his right showed more curiosity than he should have as Henri set his satchel on the floor. That was the problem of working with thieves: you couldn't trust anyone.

"Right, loot on the table, men."

A clattering of metal hit the tabletop as everyone emptied their pouches. Gold chains, pocket watches, rings, medals, ashtrays, and a silver hatpin with a jewel-encrusted bee formed a display worthy of a shop jeweler. Well, one who sold on the rue de Misère anyway. Rings sorted through each man's offering, grunting neither approval nor disgust, as Henri had come to expect. Rings was all business. Profit his only companion, money his only lover.

"Two of you seemed to have come up short."

Henri being one. He'd spent too much time sketching Yvie and hadn't left enough time to pick his afternoon round of pockets.

"Out of your pay." Rings scooped the assorted valuables into a leather duffel bag, items which he would later sell for twice what he paid his crew to fetch. "Now, on to other business," he said, tightening the drawstring on the bag with one hard tug. "Seems our Yvette is still out there somewhere on the run." He held his right hand up, each finger ringed by a silver or gold band. "I know some of the gang felt we ought to protect her. Take her in, if we found her, seeing how she used to be one of us. But I've had word her price has gone up. Seems she was spotted on the butte by a gent selling newspapers, near abouts where you live, Henri. Client's getting anxious."

Rings let his gaze fall on Henri for an extra-long, suspicious-feeling beat. The look made the vein in his neck start to pulse so hard he worried someone might see it jumping under his collar.

"And don't ask me why, but this client is still demanding the book," Rings said. "Worth a fortune, apparently, and our girl has got it. So, find the pair of 'em, and this crew will be eating frog legs and swishing champagne up on the boulevard with the bougie suckers for the next six months."

"We'll find her." Theo was like a predator catching the scent of prey. "How hard could it be? She's hiding on the butte somewhere. But then what? Who do we turn her over to?"

"Leave that to me." Rings tapped his fingers on the table. "Just find her and I'll get her in the right hands." He made a rude grabbing gesture with his hands that made the men laugh, all but Henri.

"How do we know what the right book is?" he asked. An obvious question, but the rest of the room looked at Henri like he'd replaced their gin with water.

Rings leaned forward on his elbows. "Now, now, it's a good question. Thing is, and I really shouldn't tell you this part, but there's supposed to be some gold lettering inside. Rumor is the book is a kind of treasure map." He pointed a ringed finger at his crew. "But not one of you good-for-nothings better go getting any ideas. It's protected with codes and shit, so just get the girl, get the book, and bring 'em both here. Got it?"

Henry got it, all right. Rings knew exactly what he was doing when he mentioned the word "treasure." Yvie had the price of gold on her head, and now *les flics* and his gang of thieves would be tearing up the streets of heaven and hell to find her.

CHAPTER SIXTEEN

Elena stood on the terrace of her soon-to-be mother-in-law's second-story apartment, mixing a salve and contemplating the painful effect of adding a little salt for protection. The back of her neck still stung from the burn she'd received in the magic circle an hour earlier. She should have known better. Participating in an invitation to the elementals while in a state of flux was a foolish, foolish thing to do. They'd sensed her uncertainty the moment they entered the circle. Of course they had. Teasing her. Testing her. Tempting her while she was pinned in the liminal space between positive and negative energy, light and dark emotions. The inconsistency and doubt over her future as a witch weighing her down. Had they also sniffed out her fear? She'd lain awake the past two nights worrying over what would become of her if she could no longer work the vineyard, if she could no longer place her hands on the canes to commune with the thread of life running through the vines or shape the growth and coax the grapes to the perfect fullness to make the wine. A part of her would rather give up magic than risk sinking into the devious art of poison her mother had followed. That, she believed, was the reason for the swipe.

Elena delicately probed the burned flesh on the back of her neck and decided against the salt.

She had considered relinquishing her magic shortly after Grand-Mère had passed. While in the throes of grief and new love, she'd flirted with the idea of walking the path of the mortal beside Jean-Paul to live a simpler life. But the vines had beckoned her back from the brink of such thoughts, and for that she thanked the All Knowing. Yet now she found herself once again in the midst of a terrible choice: give up the vine or give up Yvette.

Oh, but the girl had transformed. The illumination that had flared briefly when she smiled at herself in the mirror had bloomed into a full corona. The light oozed out of her as soft as moon glow from beneath her skin. Such perfectly smooth, radiant skin. Not a trace of the scar showed, and yet her magic had remained stymied. Yvette still could produce no fire, conjure no wind, nor breathe life into even the simplest incantation. But there was something supernatural residing within her. Celestial almost. Something that had been forced to remain dormant by the *étouffer*.

Elena crushed a pinch of thyme along with a spoonful of honey, both stolen from the kitchen pantry while the cook was busy preparing his bouillabaisse. She'd also swiped a sprig of lavender from a side-board vase of dried flowers. She stripped the petals from the stem and crumbled them into her mixture with the thyme and honey. She hadn't thought to bring any of her own salve in her travel valise, but even this simple recipe should soothe the burn and seal the skin with a protective spell against the wrath of the chastising elementals.

Jean-Paul called for her three times before finding her on the terrace.

"There you are," he said and eyed the honey mixture she was working on with some skepticism. "And that's for?"

Her first instinct was always to shield him from her world, though she knew she couldn't. Or perhaps shouldn't. He'd asked her to marry him, to share her life with him. The good *and* the complicated. She'd said yes, of course, but what if this feeling was just naive optimism by a couple too drunk on love to recognize their vast differences? There were mornings she thought he watched her too closely, studying her as if she were one of his specimens under glass. Then he'd hold her and whisper that she was the most exquisite creature he'd ever seen.

She would wonder, on occasion, if it were true.

"It's only a minor burn." She pointed to the back of her neck, where the three-inch fire claw had grazed her skin. "Would you mind dabbing a layer of honey over it?"

"Christ, Elena, what happened?"

"A run-in with a southern fire elemental. It was merely a warning." Though one that could have been so much worse had she been any deeper in the midst of her own confusion.

"Warning? Against what?"

"My own intentions." She leaned her neck to the side to make it easier for him to work the salve. "Did you find anything useful at the library today?"

Jean-Paul fumed as he applied the mixture, knowing he'd been shut out until she better understood the thing nagging at her intuition. "Nothing that would hold up against the order," he said. "Not yet."

The sting on the back of her neck went away almost immediately, once he affixed a piece of gauze over the honey. She let her hair down to cover the injury, then faced Jean-Paul with a smile. "Much better. Thank you."

He touched her cheek with the back of his hand. She allowed it briefly before stepping out of reach so that he might not kiss her. If he did that, she might lose her nerve.

"What is it you're not telling me?" Jean-Paul glanced toward the french doors leading to the main salon. "Where is—"

"She's dressing for dinner."

He led Elena by the arm to the opposite edge of the terrace. "Tell me what's wrong," he said, lowering his voice. "You've not been yourself since we arrived in the city. You're worried about the court order, I know, but you must have faith. Everything will be fine."

"Will it?" She could barely meet his eye. She'd been brooding in insecurity for days, wondering how a mother she never knew could have brought her so much grief right when she'd been on the verge of reclaiming nearly everything she'd lost from the curse. It wasn't just that she would lose her position as a vine witch. Something inside her was changing, adapting, as if her magic was metamorphosing to fit the mold of the new title they'd forced upon her. *Venefica.* The name had tasted of bitter herbs and vinegar when she'd first been told the truth of her bloodline, but for days now it had begun to round out in her mouth, taking on the pleasant bite of a sweet plum, one to sample over and over again. Oh, the things she could do with her instincts!

And yet those ripening instincts also terrified her.

"Durant at the records office may have just been following orders," she said, "but he was right about one thing. You cannot own the vineyard at Château Renard and be married to a registered witch of poisons. No one would ever trust the wine again. If we cannot find relief from the law, how can we marry?"

"Elena, what are you saying? You no longer wish to marry me?"

"Of course I do. But the vineyard—"

"Damn the vineyard. We'll sell it, if it comes to that. Travel the continent in a covered wagon if we must. I'm not giving you up for all the wine in the world."

She let him embrace her, smooth her hair back from her face, and kiss her softly on the mouth. She wanted so much to believe him. When he withdrew he held her by the shoulders. "There's always the direct solution," he said. "I know you feel affection for the girl, but if it comes to it, can you truly put her freedom and happiness above our own?"

She resented having to choose, having no control over her circumstances. He was right, of course; they were only beginning their life together. To ask him to abandon all their plans for their future for the sake of a hotheaded, brash young woman who would probably end up in prison again anyway was a fool's errand. And yet how could one betray a person who'd saved their life and then live with the consequences?

⟞⟝

Elena wore her burgundy travel suit yet again the next morning, thinking it the most practical choice among her meager ensemble. But the color also reminded her of home and the wine hopefully waiting for her in the barrels, so she wore it like a charm, an amulet to fend off the creeping doubt over her future. Jean-Paul's words still buzzed in her mind as she ascended the steps of Le Maison Chavirée and entered the hallway of the artist flophouse, with its pungent mix of chemical and human musk. She'd promised Marion she would have a progress report on the portrait at dinner, and since the woman had given her ample space to pursue the project on her own, she made a quick check on the artist before seeking out Yvette.

She found Pedro in his apartment staring at the canvas, a wet paintbrush clamped between his teeth, his thumb and eye doing a sort of balancing act with his line of vision. He was clearly flummoxed. Best to check on the photograph and spell and make sure everything was still functioning as it should.

"Hello," she said after knocking on his open door. "May I see?"

Pedro looked from his painting to the photograph propped on the chair, then to the woman standing in the door. He smiled and shook his head, as if he finally understood the obvious link that had eluded him until that moment. He removed the paintbrush from his teeth. "No, señorita, she is not finished yet. But I begin to see how I have come to this new point of view." He ignored her then and went back to his work, dabbing a bit of blue on the canvas as he tilted his head to evaluate the placement. "But next I paint the other one, eh?"

"The other one?"

"With the hair like gold. If Tulane had ever seen a girl like that when he was alive . . ." He kissed his fingertips as though he'd just tasted some divine delicacy. "There would not have been enough gold paint to fill his brush."

Apparently, the spell continued to work as it should, but his last remark concerned her. With some trepidation, she left the artist and went down to the end of the hall where Yvette's room was located. After a quick knock she opened the door to find the girl dancing on her toes to a song she hummed with unusual delight. The cat was there, too, sitting atop the stove with his front leg dangling over the side, a look of boredom in his eyes. Behind him, on a windowsill, sat three empty bottles of wine, a bowl of grapes and oranges, and a loaf of crusty bread, as well as a small portrait of a beautiful blonde woman in a green dress hastily painted but with obvious enthusiasm for the subject.

"What's going on here?" Elena picked up one of the bottles of wine and sniffed. Cheap plonk from the market down the street, but sturdy enough to get drunk on.

"*Bonjour!* Isn't it a lovely day?"

"Have you been drinking?"

Yvette did a final pirouette and stopped her humming. "Don't be ridiculous. But we did have a wonderful party last night. Then this morning I woke up feeling lighter than air with the sun shining through the window. Isn't it the loveliest day?"

"You said that already." Elena picked up the portrait. Definitely Yvette. The paint was still fragrant with the scent of linseed oil and pigments. "Who did this?"

"Oh, that would be Claude from down the hall. He's an artist. Everyone here is an artist, except me, but I plan to do something about that starting today."

"You let a man in here to paint your picture?"

Yvette, seemingly beaming with the elixir of life, smiled and shrugged. "They all came over last night. Impromptu, you might say, to welcome me. Artists are full of joie de vivre, living in the moment. Celebration is the food of life."

The young woman was like a bottle of champagne, bursting open and spilling everywhere.

"I know what you're thinking," Yvette said coyly. "I shouldn't have had people over when I'm supposed to be in hiding. But they adore me. They would never do anything to hurt me."

"Yvette, you just met them. Do they know who you are?" Elena lowered her voice, though it still came out overly harsh. "Or that you're wanted by the police?"

Yvette shook her head, then picked up a bunch of grapes from the bowl and began eating them one at a time, as if she'd lost all her problems in the back alley between yesterday and today. "They don't care. All they're worried about is producing art for art's sake, and I applaud them. Pedro has asked to paint me *déshabillée*. I'm thinking of saying yes. Well, I'm thinking of saying yes to everything, if you must know."

Elena collapsed on the bed in frustration. What kind of witch had they unleashed? She knew it was a mistake to undo the *étouffer* without knowing what would result, and now she was witnessing the proof of her better instincts. She hated to think it, but maybe Jean-Paul was right. Was she putting this self-centered child's well-being above her own?

Yvette danced over, humming that song of hers, and kissed Elena on top of her head. "You've been such a good friend to me," Yvette said. She smiled, and Elena swore she felt the sun's warmth against her cheek.

Did the All Knowing favor this girl? The radiance under her skin from the day before seemed to have only grown.

"What are you feeling? Inside. Can you describe the course of the energy?"

"It's all aflutter. I feel like a dandelion floating on the breeze."

"That's not normal, Yvette. You need to find your center and harness that energy so that it knows you wield the direction of flow."

"I don't want to hold it back. I've never felt so . . . *merveilleux!*"

She was clearly aligning with the light, whereas Elena feared her own luminosity was quietly sinking into the bog of a bleak future creating poisons for housewives dealing with rat infestations and schoolmasters needing to rid their student populations of head lice.

She'd meant to walk Yvette through some basic tutoring to try and tap into her magic now that it was freely flowing, but she no longer had the stomach to deal with such optimistic buoyancy. And so she left, despite the cat clawing at her hem, begging her to stay, and Yvette promising they could sip wine and nibble cheese on the rooftop. Elena closed the door behind her as the girl began to sing once again.

Outside, with only the buzzing bees and flutter of leaves to guide her thoughts, Elena strolled the old cobblestone lanes of the butte to recalibrate her mood. The hilltop village wasn't a place she had explored much on previous excursions to the city, except for two occasions with Grand-Mère when they'd been after some rare ingredient advertised as being effective against leaf rot or fruit mold when stirred into a potion under the right combination of moonrise and cloud cover. Sometimes the mixtures worked, sometimes they knew they'd been taken in by a hoax perpetuated by false advertising. The Charlatan sisters and their ilk came to mind. Grand-Mère had always warned the butte was full of hucksters. But then Elena's own family had haunted the back lanes of the village too. She'd been too young then to remember much beyond the feel of the wagon rocking back and forth over the uneven lanes and the tincture bottles filled with cures and poisons clinking against each other in their wooden crates. The difference, of course, was that her parents were no sham potions artists. Their poisonous goods delivered as promised, and there were three dead mortals as proof.

A breeze blew from the west, so Elena turned east down a winding lane no wider than a mule cart. A witch's lane. There, a single black door wedged between two larger buildings caught her attention. Written across the glass insert in an arc of scripted gold read ESSENCE DE FLEURS. Beneath the letters rested a single fleur-de-lis that glimmered with a pale opalescence when the sun hit it. The effect was hypnotizing.

Entering the shop, Elena caused the bell above the door to jingle. Still, no one came out to greet her right away, so she had a casual look around. The main counter exhibited a decorative ebony finish with a white marble top, while lace curtains hung in swags above the windows in a cheerful, sparse presentation. Despite the name, it was not a shop for perfume or flowers, though the remains of blooms were evident in the multiple bins of rose hips and dried potpourri mixes on display. A bowl of dragon flower seedpods sat on the counter, promising a remedy for inflammation. Elena picked up one of the tiny skull-like pods and shook it gently. The seeds rattled inside, still trapped within the skull's tiny brain cavity by a holding spell.

"Tokens." A woman in a black dress with a scarf draped over her head backed down a wrought-iron spiral staircase tucked in the back of the shop. An attic perhaps, where she kept her stores. "I give them away with each purchase. Take one if you like."

"Thank you." Elena did not take one, but she did find herself interested in several of the shop's other offerings. She let her fingers sift through a metal bin brimming with nightshade seeds. A dozen belladonna potions came to mind. Combinations that could stop a ticking heart, inflame a fatty liver, or put a halo around a man's sight so he only saw a crystalline version of the world before him.

"Careful with those; they're likely to send you flying out the window if you pay them too much hands-on attention."

"Or send me nose first against the floorboards." It was a small jest among witches, none of whom could fly with or without the aid of herbal concoctions. Astral projection, on the other hand, was entirely possible and advantageous for those with the gift of seeing in the shadow world. Still, the feel of the poison on her fingertips gave her a pleasant tingling sensation.

Elena brushed off her hands and inspected a wicker basket half filled with tufts of dried chrysanthemum flowers. She sniffed them for potency and found them to be exceedingly fresh. Crushed and mixed with a little water, one could distill a powerful poison for insects. But such flowers she could grow for herself.

"Is there anything in particular you're looking for?"

A solution to life's problems would be a start. "I suppose I'm in the mood to browse and let the right substance come to me."

"A shrewd strategy, that. I do hate to see people try and force things in spells they aren't well adapted to."

The shopkeeper had kept her back turned while she unloaded a small crate packed with straw behind the counter. But there was a mirror, a shop owner's trick to keep an eye on customers even when they couldn't face forward. In it, Elena saw the face of a middle-aged woman wearing a pair of round glasses with jade-green lenses. Blind? Light sensitive? Or simply the latest chic trend among city folk?

"I don't generally like to gossip," the woman said, "but I had a gentleman come in two weeks ago who was insistent on taking home a jar of white baneberry. Thought he knew a spell that allowed him to substitute it for imported cerbera." The shopkeeper finally turned from her unpacking, shaking her head as she set down a brass urn of dried poppy seeds. "Poor fellow, he'll damage his reputation by diluting the potency, but the baneberry is half the cost, so . . ."

It was then Elena let her eye travel over the entire store and found it wasn't merely a shop for dried botanicals. All the bins and baskets were topped up with nature's deadliest offerings—laburnum, larkspur, foxglove, and even satin gift bags stuffed with dried death-cap mushrooms. She'd heard of the city's *apothicaires toxiques*, but Grand-Mère had never allowed her to go near one—for fear her parents' toxic blood would surface while in proximity to so many deadly ingredients, no doubt. And perhaps Grand-Mère had been right. Her blood did swim faster through her veins the longer she perused the shop's offerings.

"Any particular plant you specialize in?" the woman asked.

Elena hardly knew how to answer. A week ago, she would have claimed to know the grapevine as well as or better than anyone, but now she fumbled for how to answer. "I . . . I've always had an affinity with wolfsbane," she said, and a rush of adrenaline flooded her limbs.

The woman smiled. "Very practical. Though I've been overexposed to it myself, working in the shop as I do," she said, gesturing to the sunglasses. "Permanently dilated my pupils from so much handling. A hazard of the work. May I wrap up a bundle for you?"

Without thinking, Elena agreed to a small packet wrapped in waxed paper and threw in three small red feathers kept in a sealed jar on the counter, which the shopkeeper retrieved with a pair of tweezers and a stiff warning. Elena set down her coins, then shoved the purchase in her purse beside Minister Durant's bruised business card.

"Don't forget your dragon flower skull." The woman slipped one into Elena's palm. "A little curative with every poison, my store motto," she said and wished Elena a nice day.

A little poison with every cure it seems as well, Elena thought as the sting on her neck flared again. She'd let herself succumb to the energy calling her to this place, but it was answered with the equal energy of resistance. The prospect of so many ingredients colliding into powerful yet deadly elixirs thrilled her. She couldn't deny it. Poison had always intrigued her, but it was not—*could not*—be her calling in this life. It simply couldn't.

CHAPTER SEVENTEEN

For so long Yvette had clung to the shadows, lingered in the dark, and tucked herself under the eaves. Out of sight, out of trouble, and out of jail. But today, wearing her borrowed jade-green dress and head scarf—and Sidra's bottle tucked just between her breasts for safekeeping now that so many artists freely wandered in and out of her room—she stepped out of the dank hallway and into the afternoon sun that filtered through the trees. Nearly weeping at the lightness of her being, she felt like a frilly yellow flower bouncing on a tall green stem as she skipped over the flowing wastewater that dribbled down the lane from the boardinghouse at the top of the hill. Whatever magic this was oozing through her, making her feel light and free, she wanted more of it.

To think that single jagged scar had been cursing her all her life, denying her this brilliant effervescence. If she ever learned who had put that cork in her magic, she'd be highly tempted to scratch their eyes out. A man passed her on the sidewalk and tipped his straw hat, as if she were a proper lady worthy of sincere attention. She forgot her pique after the exchange. Gone in a wisp. Replaced with a buzzy sort of curiosity about how it would feel to be kissed by the hatted stranger. But then she reminded herself of her purpose in crossing the courtyard in broad daylight. She smiled and turned the corner, passing one of those rag-and-bone man wagons led by a single straggly horse, eager to sit with Henri in the café and share a coffee. Oh, and a lemon tart! She had such a craving for the custardy filling with a sprinkle of sugar on top, she swore she could almost smell the scent of the flaky crust floating on the air. She still had the two coins she'd saved from the day before, and now she planned to splurge.

She saw him then, sitting at the corner table, his hair hanging slightly in his eyes as he guided a stick of charcoal over the page of a notebook while he waited. With a sudden pang of longing, Yvette wanted desperately to be the subject of Henri's art. She straightened her head scarf, pressed her lips together to bring on some color, and managed to take three steps toward the café before she was yanked off her feet. A clammy hand cupped tight over her mouth, gagging her with a rag doused in something sickeningly sweet. She fought for breath as her head became woozy, and the next thing she knew she was being dragged into the back of a wagon. A halo of stars painted themselves across the insides of her eyelids just as she was buried beneath a blanket.

CHAPTER EIGHTEEN

A rag-and-bone man led an old nag and wagon down the narrow lane, lugging his heap of goods out for sale. Shutting the door to the *apothicaire toxique* behind her, Elena followed him a little way, noting with curiosity the many rings on his fingers, until her eye drifted to an idle dove perched under the eaves of the building across the lane. It cooed at her, making her stop in her tracks. She had the minister's address. It was there on the business card. All she had to do was call the bird to her and send it on its way. She'd be free of her dilemma by dinnertime. Free of Yvette. Free of this affair of poison and the cunning inclinations running rampant through her blood.

She eyed the bird as it preened its feathers. Tentatively she lifted her hand to call it down, imagining the words she would whisper in its ear—*she's there in Le Maison Chavirée, dancing and singing as if she hadn't a care in the world*—when something in the lane pricked her instinct. The whiff of incense and coffee. The brass ting of a finger cymbal.

Following the impulse, she let her hand fall at her side and headed up the hill, skirting the great domed basilica looming over the top of the butte. She was sick of doubt and misjudgment and so she called on all her senses to home in on the thing pulling at her, wanting to feel certain she was after something that mattered. A few steps later her nose caught the scent of leaves in the seasonal process of losing their chlorophyll. But not just any leaves—grape leaves.

There, on a slope filled with rubbish, a single grapevine sagged against a retaining wall, its canes still laden with withering fruit. She'd nearly forgotten about the small vineyards that were once scattered across the butte until the spread of blight from the witch Celadine's phylloxera curse took them a decade earlier. To discover this single survivor, an anomaly among the hodgepodge buildings, gaslights, and muddy lanes, seemed a near miracle. Elena gripped the hardened cane of the vine and closed her eyes, tapping into the energy of the plant even as the flow was retreating down to the roots after a summer of growth. She needed to feel that vibrancy and be reminded of her power again. But as hard as she tried, she could find no history in the vine, no memory, no trace of reciprocation between the roots and the soil, the leaf and sun. It was like the vine had simply materialized out of thin air. Perhaps it had.

Elena released the vine and opened her eyes. A smoky cloud heavy with the scent of frankincense wafted over the wall.

"Hello, Sidra."

"*As-salaam-alaykum.*" Sidra reanimated and nodded her head in greeting. "Follow me," she said, more as an order than an invitation.

The jinni's robe billowed out behind her as she led Elena to the other end of the retaining wall to where a scarlet tent sat with its front flaps rolled open. A café table and two chairs had been centered on a woven rug. An offering of fist-size dates sat in a blue bowl atop the table. Sidra invited Elena to sit across from her. As she did, a waiter wearing a brown hooded robe seemed to appear from the ether to bring them coffee. He poured the light-brown blend from a brass *dallah*. Unlike any Elena had seen, the coffeepot had a long crescent-shaped spout like the bill of a shorebird. The server filled two decorative demitasse cups halfway. Sidra called the cups *finjan* and instructed Elena to drink but not drain the coffee inside.

"Your ruse worked like a charm," Elena said, picking up her cup. "I was fully taken in by the rare appearance of the vine."

"You were looking for a sign to guide you." Sidra teased Elena with a knowing smile. "But I assure you it is real. I'm pleased to leave the vine where it is as a gift, if you think it wise." Sidra pushed the plate of dates toward Elena. "Please, you will find the fruit is the best to be had."

The tent, and everything in it, had to be a mirage, and yet it was real enough that Elena could taste the cardamom in the coffee and feel the leathery, sweet texture of the dates with her teeth.

"I've been suffering from a bit of doubt lately," Elena said and set her cup down.

"It is the girl. She has always been trouble, that one." Sidra took Elena's nearly empty cup and swirled the dregs at the bottom around three times before covering it with the saucer and flipping it over. "She stole a wish, and now she's affected the fate of those around her."

Elena felt a tinge of guilt at the way she'd walked out on Yvette. It was true the girl was difficult at times. Ignorant, headstrong, impulsive. But she was also brave and resourceful and openhearted. And in the midst of transformation. They both were.

"Yvette mentioned you hadn't meant to return to the city, that you're possibly trapped here?"

"I swore never to return to this stinking place." The light in Sidra's eyes turned ominous as she glanced over her shoulder to scout the lane for threats. "That is what I mean. That girl, she compelled us here, and now all our fates are caught in the dog's teeth of her wish." Sidra tapped the overturned cup with her finger. "It seems we were all linked to the same chain of fate for good or ill in that prison. But this does not mean one may tug the chain in only the direction they wish to go."

"The authorities have threatened to take away my status as a vine witch if I don't turn Yvette in to them. But how can I?"

"You find this a difficult choice?" Sidra gave Elena's saucer a quarter turn.

"She hasn't had a chance at life yet, at least not the one she was supposed to have. Someone stifled her magic when she was a mere child. Yvette doesn't even know what kind of powers she has. How can I take her future away from her?"

"But you can condemn your own future to save a murderer?"

"Apparently I'm being compelled by some jinni's convoluted desert magic."

Seemingly pleased with the logic, Sidra grinned, revealing her gold-inlay teeth. She turned Elena's empty cup right side up again. The fine sediment that had settled in the bottom after Elena drank the coffee clung to the insides of the cup, forming a pattern. A pair of butterfly wings, symmetrically defined with a central body, revealed itself in the dregs.

The jinni was conducting a form of coffee tasseomancy, the same fortune-telling ritual the witches of the Chanceaux Valley sometimes practiced with wine sediment left in glasses.

"You have dormant skills waiting to emerge," the jinni said. "You were in that shop of seeds and poisons because they call to you." Sidra gestured to the lane with a glance, then back at the cup. "This place remembers you as a daughter."

Elena stared at her hands, still feeling the tingle of the poison's energy on her fingertips. "I think I was born here."

"Yes, but you are a twice born. Two mothers, two fathers. The past and future each claim you as their child." The jinni gazed at the cup, turning it in her hand to see it from all angles. Then she asked pointedly, "What are you if not a winemaker?"

"Nothing," Elena said before she had time to consider.

Sidra confirmed it with a nod. "Confusing your fate with the girl's is making too much mess. It is true the wish must be granted, taking whatever twisted path the magic requires. Whatever pain it causes, whatever injury it inflicts, that is how the alchemy of wish magic works. But one should not forfeit their free will, even *if* compelled by a superior form of sorcery. One must learn to sway the influence instead, as if maneuvering on the wind, to truly transition between past and future, the born self and the created self."

As Sidra spoke, the winged shape sitting at the bottom of the cup came alive, turning into a spotted-brown butterfly that fluttered into the air.

"Was it prophesied somewhere that all must suffer the agony of uncertainty before finding their way to safe harbor?"

"That is knowledge as old as the oldest stones."

"Then I am grateful to have finally been trusted with the lesson," Elena said, holding her hands up in the sacred pose to honor the All Knowing.

"*As-salaam-alaykum*," Sidra answered.

The butterfly circled Elena's head in a final gesture before dispersing into a cloud of coffee aroma. The tent vanished, the *dallah* and *finjan* cups evaporated, and the jinni dissipated into a cloud that mingled with the cook smoke lifting over the rooftops.

When the mist cleared, Elena sat alone at a café table, a bowl of dates in front of her. She popped one in her mouth, shrugged at the young man with his sketchbook and charcoal gawping at her from the table on the other end of the sidewalk, and then hurried down the hill toward Yvette's flat.

CHAPTER NINETEEN

What was *she* doing here? Was this some kind of setup? And where was Yvie? She was supposed to meet him at the café thirty minutes ago. If she and that other woman were working together, then why wasn't Yvie with her? Couldn't be coincidence that she showed up and Yvie didn't. Had he been followed? Damn it. He was never good at recognizing a tail. That was always Yvie's best talent. Aside from picking locks. He never saw anyone as good as Yvie at picking locks.

Henri had to find her before anyone else, but he had no idea where Yvie had been hiding out these past few days. A handful of people on the butte had seen someone who could have been her near Tante's place a couple of nights ago, but nothing since the day he saw her at the newspaper stand. His only lead was this meeting today. If she didn't show up soon, he'd have no choice but to approach the mademoiselle in the burgundy suit. The one talking to herself.

Mon Dieu, Yvie, why do you always get attached to the weird ones?

Henri put away his charcoal and paper. The woman in burgundy was leaving. And in a hurry. He decided to risk following her.

He knew it was a dumb idea, having Yvie meet him in a public café. But it was the butte. No one here would turn her in. No one who was born here. But maybe she got spooked. Didn't trust the neighborhood anymore. Or maybe she didn't trust him.

Henri swallowed the doubt rising in his throat and ducked around the café corner to watch where the woman was headed. There was something different about her. She had eyes like a cat's, amber colored and full of unspoken thoughts. He wasn't sure, as an artist, if he had the skill with the brush yet to capture the odd glint he'd seen reflected in them. She crossed the courtyard and headed straight for Le Maison Chavirée, the squalid apartments every artist he met at the tavern seemed to return to at night. Was it possible she modeled for Pedro or Claude? Had they already figured out the right mix of pigments to re-create those eyes on canvas?

Henri didn't want to confront her. Not yet. But he needed to get a closer look, if only to satisfy his curiosity about the woman Yvie had befriended and find out which side she was really on. He crept along the wall downhill from the apartments, trying to stay in the shadows the way he'd been taught by Rings. Invisible. Out of sight, out of trouble, out of jail. He kept his eye on the front door as the woman entered. A mistake, because if he'd been paying more attention to the shadow behind him, he might have seen the knife before it was jabbed against his ribs.

"Date stand you up, did she?"

Theo's bad breath hit the back of Henri's neck. The thief nudged him in the ribs again with the point of the knife, only this time he pierced skin. A warm trickle of blood ran down Henri's side, pooling along his waistband.

"This way, Romeo."

They'd followed him to the café. Which meant they knew he'd been lying about Yvie. Which meant he was a dead man.

CHAPTER TWENTY

Elena knocked three times before opening the door. A scattering of energy from Yvette's ultraradiant aura lingered in the room, but the young woman wasn't there. After a quick peek, she learned Yvette wasn't in the water closet down the hall either. Elena had no intention of knocking on every artist's door in the building to find her, having no wish to discover the young woman in a state of undress. And yet she had the distinct feeling she wouldn't find her in the building. The cat was gone too. The animal had grown too fond of Yvette to leave her sight, which meant she must truly have gone out. What was that fool of a girl thinking?

Elena returned outside with the hope of tracking Yvette's aura. To her horror, she found blood instead. One rust-colored dot followed by another on the street until the blood, fresh enough to still have a shine, turned into a steady trail. Yvette's? Her heartbeat jumped into a staccato rhythm at the thought of the young woman in pain. And all because she'd walked out on her. Elena reached in her purse to take a quick inventory of her herbs and vials to see what she had for an emergency, then followed the crimson trail into a narrow passageway with a gate to a private courtyard at the back end. Two men stood at the gate. One of them, the young man from the café with the sketchbook, pressed a hand against his damp shirt. The other, the one with the bad teeth and stained trousers, wielded a knife. So not Yvette's blood after all.

"One more step, mademoiselle, and I'll cut both your throats."

She had no doubt the ruffian holding the knife would do exactly that. Given the shadows in the narrow passageway, the lack of windows in the buildings on either side, and abundance of barrels in which to dump a body, she grudgingly gave him credit for choosing an ideal location for a murder. Where he went wrong, of course, was in assuming she'd turn and run.

Elena opened her purse. Wolfsbane or snapdragon? On a whim she removed the dragon flower skull she'd been given at the *apothicaire toxique*. The man warned her again to leave, then raised the knife against the poor artist's throat as if to make clear he was not bluffing. Elena simply crushed the skull between her fingers and scattered the seeds on the ground.

"From small seeds a dragon grows, hit the ground and strike your pose."

A stout lizard the size of a large dog lumbered out from behind her skirt. Its tail swept back and forth against the alley's bricks as it sniffed the air with its tongue, a carnivorous dragon baring its teeth in preparation to attack.

"Charge the gate and do not pause, let them feel the weight of your claws."

Both men stared wide-eyed, backing up as far as they could against the metal gate. The one with the knife forgot all about committing murder, while the other recovered from his wound with amazing agility, climbing atop the barrel she presumed he was soon meant to occupy.

"Wait, wait," begged the young man with his hands held up in surrender. "I'm a friend of Yvie's. Call it off!"

Yvie?

A friend of Yvette's? It couldn't be a coincidence. Did he know where she was or if she was in some kind of danger? Best to get him out of there. Elena beckoned the young man, still bleeding slightly from his side, to follow her. For a brief second, he seemed to consider who was more dangerous, Elena or the dragon, before jumping over the giant lizard and staggering out of the passageway. The knife-wielding assailant, his wide eyes giving away his panic, tried to make the same move, but the beast lunged and snapped its jaw, cutting him off. The long-tailed lizard was only an illusion, the best she could conjure based on the photograph Jean-Paul had shown her in his geographic society magazine, but the animal did seem to display the required ferocity. The would-be murderer gave up trying to leap over the creature's head and hugged the metal bars of the gate, working frantically to open the lock and get free before a leg or arm was bitten off.

Walking quickly so as to be out of sight when the ruffian finally realized there was no real threat, Elena headed up the hill before ducking behind a ramshackle shed in the dirt. Behind it the arms of a windmill slowly rotated, grinding bushels of freshly harvested wheat into flour. The young man, wary but still on his feet, staggered in behind her, short of breath.

"What was that thing back there?" The terror had not drained from his eyes.

"Nothing but a shadow. Now who are you? And where is Yvette? Is she hurt? In danger?" Elena took a menacing step toward the young man. "Answer me."

He backed up until he hit the shed wall. "I'm Henri. Yvie and I grew up together." He gripped his satchel tight to his chest, as if it were the most valuable thing he owned. "She was supposed to meet me for coffee but never showed."

"Impossible. She was told not to leave the room." Elena realized too late she never actually put a spell on the girl to make her stay put. She had, however, seen the young man waiting restlessly for someone who never joined him, making it likely he was telling the truth. But then, where was she?

"Weren't *les flics* who got her," he said and winced as he pulled his sticky, wet shirt away from his side.

"Someone *took* her?"

Looking pale and shock-worn, Henri slid down the shack wall, landing on the ground with a grunt. He lifted his shirt and probed the narrow knife slit in his side. His fingers came away with blood, and he nearly fell over sideways. It'd be no use getting information out of him while he was distracted by the pain, so Elena dug in her purse, beneath the bundle of wolfsbane, and found the pot of salve she'd made for herself. She opened the lid and passed it to him. "Dab a generous amount over the cut. I'll do the rest."

"What is it?" He sniffed at the pot.

"A healing balm."

"I suppose you think you're a witch like all the rest?"

"Yes."

He licked his lips and nodded. "I think I believe you," he said and lifted his shirt again.

The wound wasn't life-threatening, though it was a good thing she showed up when she did or the next one surely would have been. He applied the balm as she spoke a quick healing spell that seemed to make him flinch more than the medicine.

"Now, tell me where Yvette is."

"Don't know where they took her. I only know they've been looking for her."

"*They*, Henri?"

He gently pressed his palm to his side, then touched it again as if surprised the wound no longer bled or, presumably, hurt. She snapped her fingers to get his attention back on track.

"The man who tried to kill me is one of them. And the boss who told him to come after me too. They've been watching for Yvie ever since she escaped prison." He blinked and pointed at Elena. "Wait, you're one of the women she ran away with. I remember seeing your picture in the paper next to hers. You murdered some winemaker."

"I was cleared of those charges, thank you. Now, tell me who this boss is and what he wants with Yvette."

Henri went silent, his eyes checking the muddy road in either direction to see who might be watching. He bore the same emotional wall around him as Yvette, built up from living on the streets and learning from necessity how to deflect danger.

"Henri, if you don't tell me what you know, we'll never be able to help Yvette, so speak up." Elena conjured a prickly ball of energy in her palm, the light snapping and hissing at the young man in a suitably menacing manner. "Maybe you aren't a friend of hers after all."

"Okay! I sometimes do work for a guy named Rings."

"Yes, I've heard of him. A thief."

"Yeah, well, he got wind that someone important was looking for Yvie and offering a reward. Said if we spread out and kept our eyes open, we'd be able to find her before anyone else did, on account she used to run with the gang."

"What important person?"

"I don't know, but he's obsessed. I think she stole a rare book from him. Must have been real old or something, because that was part of the deal. Get the girl and the book."

So, just as they had suspected, the attack on Yvette when they'd first reunited hadn't been a random mugging on the street. They'd tried to get to her before, which meant the code in the book had to be hiding something of great worth.

The wheel on the flour mill behind them began to creak and turn, grinding on, reminding Elena of the time they'd already lost.

"Were you planning on abducting her too? Is that why you were waiting for her?"

"*Me?* I could've grabbed Yvie a dozen times if I'd wanted and turned her in. I was trying to protect her. That's why I got jumped.

Rings must have figured out I already knew where she was and didn't tell no one."

"Why not?"

Henri sheepishly reached in his satchel and removed his portfolio of sketches. Half were of Yvette. And they were quite good, the evidence of a young man's infatuation.

"I couldn't hurt Yvie that way. Maybe I thought about turning her in when I first heard about the money, sure. Who wouldn't? But she's my Mademoiselle Delacourt."

Elena did a double take. "Your what?"

"My muse, my inspiration. She's why I paint. Someday I hope to actually capture how beautiful she is on canvas. Like Monsieur Tulane did with his paintings."

Elena looked closer. Yvette was delicately drawn with freckles and filament-thin eyelashes and blue veins under translucent skin. He was a decent artist, she supposed. But on second glance she noticed, too, the intimacy of the details in the sketches, the obvious voyeurism, the near worship of Yvette's unique beauty.

He was in love with her. Or obsessed.

"Do you know where they took her?" Elena asked. "You must know something about this man who ordered her abduction."

Henri shook his head. "Rings is the only one who knows his identity, and he didn't tell any of us the rest of the plan. Probably wouldn't have split the money, either."

"What will they do to Yvette if they have her but not the book?"

Henri shrugged. "Don't know. Rings said the buyer was dead set on it being both, though, so they'll find a way to make her tell them where it is."

"And you truly don't know where they took her?"

"No, mademoiselle."

She would have accused him of lying, except the boy had sincerity written all over his face. He truly did care about Yvette, which got her thinking again about the strange magic they'd unleashed in the girl. She was undeniably imbued with a supernatural energy. Yvette *and* the book.

Yes, whatever the book was meant to do, it wouldn't, or perhaps couldn't, do it without Yvette. Their magic was tied, one to the other.

Elena began to walk with purpose toward a tree-lined embankment that overlooked the city. There the great tower—wizard-made, if the rumors were true—loomed above the glitter and squalor below. Using it as her compass point, she followed the river to the left with her eye.

Henri closed up his portfolio and ran after her. "What are you doing?"

"It's safer and more reliable than sending a telegraph," she said, stopping beside the tallest tree she could find. A pair of mourning doves cooed on a branch above. She called them down and whispered her message as they walked in a circle at her feet, their heads bobbing in all seriousness as they listened to her detailed instructions.

"I don't . . . I don't understand."

"I imagine not, Henri. But the birds do, and that's all that matters."

The doves flapped their wings and off they flew, soaring over the rooftops, heading for the heart of the city.

CHAPTER
TWENTY-ONE

Yvette opened her eyes. Orange flames from a single torch flickered in the darkness. The air was cool and musty like a cellar, but there were no casks of wine. A cave or tunnel, then? She sat up. Her head pounded and her tongue furred in her mouth for want of water. She'd been knocked out, and good. The lightness that had nearly lifted her off her feet had dimmed. Her limbs felt heavy as lead, but at least her hands and feet were free. She squinted into the dark to see if she was alone. That's when she spotted the first bones—ribs and femurs piled up as dry and weathered as stacked driftwood, with the occasional skull stuffed between to form a wall. Oh *la vache*, that sick son of a bitch dragged her into the Maze of the Dead? It had to be, though in some faraway corner. The bones were not so neatly stacked here as they were at the entrance where the tourists gawked at the two-hundred-year-old skeletons of plague victims. No wonder she wasn't tied up. She could wander for days in the abandoned tunnels and never find her way out.

Panic punched her in the throat, stifling her scream so it came out as a muffled squeal. The noise she'd made was enough to attract attention. A figure approached from farther down the tunnel. As he stepped into the circle of light, she saw he was a middle-aged man with a pointed beard and mustache that curled up at the ends. His suit looked expensive, though the hems on the trousers were beginning to fray. His shoes, too, might have cost more than a few coins when new, but they'd been buffed so many times the leather was wearing thin. Following behind was an obvious flunky wearing a flat cap and a pair of baggy trousers, a small iron hoop slung over his arm. The same rotten fellow who had tried to mug her on the butte a few days earlier.

"Hello, Yvette." The middle-aged man lit a cigarette. "May I call you Yvette, or do you prefer Mademoiselle Lenoir?"

"What the hell is this?"

He raised a brow at her swearing. "Don't be vulgar. You are in the Maze of the Dead. A forgotten section of it at least. Show the dead the respect they deserve."

Yvette didn't yet trust her legs to hold her up, so she wrapped her arms around her knees protectively as she took in her surroundings with new understanding. "You aren't *les flics*, so what do you want with me?"

"You possess something I've been waiting a very long time to see." He casually slipped one hand in his pocket and blew out a long stream of smoke rings, a move too smooth for a stiff like him. This man wasn't a typical street thug. Not quite one of the *bon chic* with those worn shoes, but a well-to-do straight all the same. So what was he doing mugging and kidnapping young women on the butte?

"I don't have anything you could possibly want," she answered, but she knew her eyes betrayed her.

"The book, Yvette. I want the book with the gold lettering," the man said. He knelt in front of her, moving slowly like a predator watching for the slightest hint of flight. "So, I'm going to ask you nicely this one time. Where did you hide it?"

"I didn't steal the book. It's mine. My mother gave it to me."

Yvette swore the bone pile rattled as the man's nose flared and the muscles in his jaw clenched. "Your mother doesn't *give* anything. She only takes. Or perhaps you hadn't noticed how she stole your life from you, abandoning you to live like a common mortal."

"You knew her?"

The jaw clenched again. "Unfortunately, she's my wife."

The breath went out of Yvette.

This pompous ass was married to her mother? But then . . .

"Wait, are you saying you're my *father*?"

"Blessedly, I am not." The man stood and checked his pocket watch. His mustache twitched in response to the time.

Thank the All Knowing, she thought. But then what was this about? "Look, I don't know how much you know, but that book is a bunch of gibberish. Makes no sense to anyone."

He snapped the pocket watch shut. "The degree of your ignorance is astounding. But one shouldn't be surprised given your upbringing and dubious mongrel bloodline." He stared at her with eyes devoid of sympathy, tracing the features of her face as if hoping to recognize something he once found interesting. He pivoted away in disgust, but then something made him stop and turn. He bent and viciously gripped her jaw in his hand. "Your scar is gone." He twisted around and glared up at the flunky. "You didn't notice that?"

"Sorry, boss. It was dark when we got here."

"So that's how she hid you."

He released her jaw with a jerk and stood. Yvette stretched her mouth wide. How did *he* know about her scar?

"I imagine you're not feeling so light and airy down here in the gloom and damp, are you?" he said. He stubbed out his cigarette and removed a small tin from his trouser pocket. She thought he might offer her a ciggie, but instead he dug a fingernail into the tin and raised it to his nose, inhaling a white powder. "One of the weaknesses of your kind," he said. "Luckily I know how to take advantage of it."

Her kind?

The drug hit his bloodstream quick. His eyes took on a menacing sheen as he scrutinized her a second time, paying close attention to the aura space above her head. He put the tin away and snapped his fingers. A blaze of light shone down on her from the palm of his hand. "So, was it the vine witch who removed the scar?" he asked, aiming the light at her jaw.

Jiminy, how long had they been watching her? Did they know about Alexandre too? She was deep in the shit, but she was going to have to keep paddling. Yvette nodded, pretending it was a great cost to admit. "Yes, it was Elena who figured it out. She's the smartest witch I know."

The man scoffed. "Do remind me to send her a thank-you note. Removing the *étouffer* has only made my work that much easier. You should be flattered by such loyalty. Even I was surprised by how far Mademoiselle Boureanu was willing to go to protect you. But of course, that's the flaw of the virtuous. You can always rely on them to do the right thing."

"You're mad," she said, but at least he didn't know about Alexandre or he would have called her bluff about the removal spell.

"If self-preservation is a madness, I confess my guilt. Now, one more time. Where is the book?"

"Why are you doing this?" she yelled. "It's just a book my mother made me. It doesn't mean anything to you."

"My dear girl, it means *everything* to me," he said. He nodded to the flunky. "Find out where she hid it." Then he snapped his fingers and used the light that formed in his palm to guide him out of the maze, leaving her alone with the man in the flat cap as he grinned and swung the iron hoop toward her.

CHAPTER
TWENTY-TWO

Elena and Henri had returned to Le Maison Chavirée, where they waited in uncomfortable silence for the inevitable tap at the door. When at last the sound came, Elena eagerly answered.

"Alexandre, thank the All Knowing you got my message."

"Good heavens, people actually live in this bohemian flophouse?" He wiped his shoes off on the carpet in the hall, then entered the squalid apartment where Yvette had been hiding the last three days. He poked the tip of his birchwood cane against the stove and it came alive with a cozy fire. "It's a good thing you sent the dove when you did. I had just enough time to put a protection spell around the shop before I left."

"I still don't know where they've taken Yvette, but apparently it's the book they really want," Elena said.

The old witch removed his black derby hat and nodded at Henri, who stood in the corner staring wide-eyed at the flames in the stove. "You must be the young man assisting in this mischief."

"Uh, how?" Henri merely pointed at the stove.

Alexandre's eyebrow quirked. "It's only a fire, boy."

"Right. Perfectly normal."

"Were you able to learn anything more about the writing in the book?" Elena asked. "It's likely only a matter of time before they figure out we have the blasted thing."

"Ah, yes." Alexandre retrieved a folded piece of paper from his left breast pocket. "Something interesting finally revealed itself."

"What? What is it?"

"I had a look through the clarinet, and it appears the symbols themselves tell a small but perhaps important tale." He paused to acknowledge Henri's obvious confusion. "It simply functions like a microscope, my boy," he said, waving his hand to encourage the young man to go along with the anomaly. "The paint used in the book contains traces of pure gold, as we suspected. But there's also evidence of citrine and quartz!" he said in triumph. "And a bit of marula oil mixed in with the pigments."

Elena shook her head waiting for the translation. "Which means?"

"Wait, did you say gold and quartz?" Henri asked. "But that was Tulane's preferred mixture. He's famous for it."

"Is he? Perhaps the process has become common, then. Nonetheless, the paint used on the book's pages proved unsurprisingly enchanted. Which, I presume, is the function of the crystals."

"Christ, is everyone around here a witch?"

"You'd be surprised," Elena said as Alexandre spread his paper out on the rickety table. "Were you able to determine the spell?"

"Oh, yes. A common concealment charm."

"But I tried to make the symbols reveal themselves to me and they didn't respond."

"Or perhaps they did and you simply didn't notice." Alexandre tapped on the paper. "I didn't want to risk carrying the book on my person, but I managed to copy a single page using a mirror spell. The code is backwards so it's of little use for transcription. However . . ." He pointed to the first line highlighted in gold. "Beneath the concealment the symbols appear nearly identical to how they originally presented themselves. Only now take a gander at them using a magnifying glass." Alexandre patted his pockets until he found the glass cake knife he'd brought with him.

"Another piece of dodgy merchandise from the shop?" Elena took the knife with a sigh and held the blade over the symbols. To her amazement, the lines of the symbols weren't solid veins of paint at all. Under magnification they appeared as strings of smaller symbols, possibly sentences, but so small the human eye could never read them. Most were vine-like in shape, with romantic flourishes ending in curlicues. The way the text interwove in places reminded her of intricate metal filigree work. Alas, though beautiful, whatever message they contained remained just as unreadable to Elena as it had before.

"Is it some kind of foreign language or magical symbolism?" she asked.

Alexandre held his hands palms up. "That is the reigning mystery. I've cross-referenced it against all the literature at my disposal, including *The Book of the Seven Stars*. Oddly, none of these, what I presume are letters invented for the purpose of communication, show up in any of the resource material."

While they spoke, Henri hovered over Elena's shoulder. The glass knife still rested over a small section of the page, magnifying a few of the microscopic symbols. He pressed in closer, encroaching on Elena's aura space.

"What is it?" she asked.

"I've seen that one before," he said, pointing.

"Henri, that's highly unlikely."

"That one too, maybe." Henri opened his satchel and spread his portfolio on the table next to the paper. He shuffled through his drawings until he found one of a woman kneeling in a bed of flowers and a man standing beside her, kissing her cheek. "This is a rough sketch I did for practice, trying to copy Tulane's style. But look here." He tapped on the lower right-hand corner of the drawing. "He's put these types of symbols on most of his later work. I always figured they were decorative. Embellishments. Like a signature or something. They're fun to draw, you know."

Elena compared the crude drawing to the magnified markings. They truly were similar. Alexandre evidently thought so too.

"I think we need to find this Tulane and have a chat with him," the old witch said.

"You can't," Henri said. "He died. Years ago. That's why his art is worth so much now. They've got three of them hanging in the Musée Couloir."

Elena collapsed onto the cot. "Our first real breakthrough and we hit a literal dead end."

"Not necessarily," Alexandre said. "As I recall, there may yet be someone who can shed some light on the book's mysterious past."

Elena sat up. "The woman who raised her. Of course."

"I think at this juncture it would be prudent for us to drop in on the proprietor of the—what was it? Le Rêve?—and get information about the girl's family relations."

"Tante Isadora?" Henri pulled a face. "Have you met her? You'd have better luck trying to charm a snake to dance in your hand."

"I have not had the pleasure of her acquaintance," Alexandre said, "but now that I know you are familiar with the madame, I can depend on you to introduce us properly. Gather your belongings, Henri. Off we go." Alexandre put his hat back on. "And by the way, getting a snake to dance in your palm is child's play for most witches," he said, giving his derby a pat.

With firm resolve, the trio set out on the five-minute trek across the butte. Elena and Alexandre followed at a distant pace behind Henri to absolve anyone of the idea they were together.

Alexandre cleared his throat and took Elena's arm in his so they might talk quietly. "How fares your neck?"

"You saw that, did you?"

"Difficult to miss an elemental taking a swipe at one of three people inside an arcane circle." His cane tapped steadily along the sidewalk, tip-tap. "It wouldn't have anything to do with the bifurcation in your aura, would it?"

"I didn't realize my predicament was so obvious."

"The rift has grown wider, even in the time since yesterday. The elementals must have sensed the tension in your aura. One can be at peace within one's own chaos, but not in another's, which this business with the young woman is turning out to be. That swipe may have been their way of saying you're risking imbalance. Whatever it is that's causing the split, they're letting you know you must eventually relinquish one side or the other before irreparable harm is done to your aura and power."

Elena hadn't quite understood what was happening to her at first. But she knew now what he said was true. Her family bloodline was demanding she return within its fold, tugging against the vine magic she'd been given by proxy through Grand-Mère and Grand-Père. She could feel both sides pulling her energy in two.

Ahead, Henri walked to the top of the hill, lit a cigarette as prearranged, and turned right down a side street.

"Ah, here we are," she said as they strolled up to the corner where Le Rêve stood at the top of a steep incline. In the glare of daylight, the partially rural setting and whitewash exterior did little to enforce its reputation as a bawdy cabaret. However, the overwhelming odor of alcohol infused within the wood, plaster, and dirty cobblestones did. The place reeked of nightly drunken abandon even before they'd entered.

Two men playing poker at a sidewalk table under a nearby tree set their cards down when Alexandre and Elena approached the door. One glanced over his shoulder at them, his bushy mustache highlighting a grim expression. Police? One of the men tried to catch her eye, so Elena ducked inside the cabaret behind Alexandre, hoping they hadn't recognized her.

The main room of Le Rêve was empty and dimly lit, except for the corona of sunlight seeping in around two small shuttered windows in the front and a pair of gaslit sconces hung over the bar in the back. Elena's eyes generally adjusted quickly to the dark, but Alexandre, whose sensitive vision allowed him to read auras, asked for a moment so that he might not trip on the unseen step or obstacle before his pupils dilated properly.

"We're not serving yet," said a woman's voice from somewhere beyond the glow of the gas lamps. "Come back this evening." The sound of shifting bottles followed.

"We're looking for Isadora Lenoir, the owner of the establishment," Elena said. "We'd like a word with her, if she's available."

A pale face topped with a bird's nest of red hair showed itself in the lamplight. A cigarette dangled from the woman's bottom lip as she spoke. "What about?"

"Yvette Lenoir."

"What about her?"

"Are you Madame Lenoir?"

The woman exhaled. "What's Yvette done now? I assume since those men outside are still watching the place, she's not back in jail yet."

"My name is Elena Boureanu, and this is Monsieur Alexandre Olmos. Please, may we sit? We'd like to ask you a few questions about her family."

"It's all right, Tante, they're with me." Henri entered from a back room he'd somehow managed to access from behind. "They need to ask you some questions about when Yvette first came here. She's in trouble. Serious kind this time."

"What's new." Tante smirked before going back to her work. "There's nothing to say. The girl was abandoned as a child. I took her in out of the goodness of my heart. She decided to bite the hand that fed her, and now she's an escaped murderer. Haven't seen her in years.

But if you do, remind her she owes me money. Now if you'll excuse me, Henri, take your friends out. I have work to do."

Elena removed her gloves and laid them on the bar. "That's not quite true, though, is it?" she said. "Yvette was here four nights ago and left with a rather unusual little book, which you'd been saving for her until her sixteenth birthday."

There was a long pause; the silence of a woman's mind calculating risk.

"Louise? Get the lights."

"Allow me." Elena rubbed her hands together and blew the heat from her palms into the air. A moment later the room filled with the smoky yellow glow from the gas lamps affixed to the walls and center chandelier. In the brightness, the red wall behind the bar came alive with a painted scene of a golden cherub shooting a tiny arrow at a pair of lovers in recline. It also revealed the dark-blue half-moon bruise under Isadora's left eye.

"That's real convincing," she said. "You ought to work the séance rooms."

Her reaction to the magic appeared muted for a typical mortal, thought Elena.

"That's because we're witches." Alexandre raised his walking cane, which functioned as an oversize wand, and pointed it in a manner some might interpret as threatening. "Witches in need of some answers," he further explained and locked the doors with a manipulation spell to prevent interruption.

Isadora peered at them with the narrowed gaze of a woman who'd had her share of run-ins with troublemakers before and come out victorious every time. Except, perhaps, during whatever incident had caused that nasty black eye.

"In that case, be my guests." Isadora gestured to the barstools while still holding a bottle of gin in her hand.

Elena took a peek over the bar as she sat and discovered the source of the clanking bottles she'd heard when they entered. The woman had been funneling less expensive alcohol into fancier bottles that could be sold to customers at a higher price.

"I'll tell you what I told the others," Isadora said, picking up the funnel again. "I have no idea what the book is for, and I don't know where it is. I don't know where the girl is, either, and I don't care."

"Others?" Alexandre asked.

The woman exhaled loudly. "You think you're the first to come by my establishment looking for Yvette and that damn book?"

"Did someone else use force to get answers about Yvette?" Elena pointed indelicately at the woman's bruise.

Isadora eyed the cheap gin as it trickled into the olive-green bottle with the exclusive label. She ignored the question.

Elena was about to ask her question again when Alexandre rested a hand on her arm. Had he sensed something in the woman's dull aura? Pain? Deception? There were a few mortal emotions that registered on the astral plane for someone as sensitive as Monsieur Olmos.

"Madame, if I may ask," he began humbly. "Why did you agree to take the girl in? She couldn't have been more than a babe. Were you friends with her mother?"

Ah, perhaps he'd seen evidence of a maternal instinct. Some piece of her heart must have flared in his sight despite her facade of not caring about Yvette. She stopped pouring the gin briefly, as if recalling the moment she'd decided to take in another woman's child. It was an extraordinary commitment, even if the only thing she'd wanted was free labor out of the girl. But no, Alexandre's tone suggested he was of the belief she'd done it for a more altruistic reason.

"I tried with Yvette. I did. I thought that maybe . . ." She looked at Henri and set the bottle of gin aside. "She's supposed to be like the two of you. And yet . . . she's different. Broken. She couldn't do any of the tricks you do. I thought I could use her talent in the show—something unique, exotic, to get the crowd going. But there's something about that girl that doesn't work right. Never did. And yet her mother . . ."

"What about her mother?" Alexandre leaned in on both elbows, as if listening to the confession of a friend.

The woman made a show of having said too much, but after another soft nudge from Alexandre, she relented. "Her mother was grace itself. A dancer. A model. And now dead for all I know. And probably for the best she never had to see what became of that girl."

Elena had to restrain herself from pointing out the less than ideal conditions Yvette had grown up in, raised in a cabaret that catered to lustful drunkards.

"And her mother was a witch?" Alexandre asked. "I apologize for being so straightforward, madame, but why would she leave Yvette in the care of a mortal?"

The woman's face shifted. The eyes tightened, the jaw clamped tight, and the lips puckered slightly so that the deep lines around her mouth grew even more exaggerated. "No one else would take the child in. It was as simple as that."

Alexandre folded his hands over his cane's handle. "And yet, madame, everything about your spectral energy says you're lying."

Isadora stuffed the cork back in the gin bottle. "I dare you to accuse me of that again," she warned.

"You are deliberately misleading us, madame. For what purpose, I don't know, but you're hiding something."

"You're right. I am." Isadora reached under the bar and produced a silver handgun with pearl handles just small enough for a woman to tuck in her purse. "I think it's time for you to leave," she said, raising the barrel so that it was level with Alexandre's nose.

"Here we go," Henri said, shaking his head as if he'd seen it all before.

"Perhaps we should leave," Elena said, knowing the answers they sought weren't worth possible bloodshed. Besides, the woman wasn't giving them the information they needed.

Alexandre merely tapped his cane twice against the floor. The old witch rose from his stool and crossed behind the bar to where Isadora stood trembling, as though confused at the gun in her hand. "You don't want to hurt anyone," he said with a calm yet authoritative tone, using what Elena recognized as a mild hypnotic spell to put her at ease until she lowered her arm a few inches. He took the weapon and patted her hand. "That's better. Now, madame, I need to know the truth about the girl's mother and father."

"No, I can't. I won't," she said, pleading. "I promised."

"Yes, tell me about that promise."

She shook her head, resisting, fretting more and more like a trapped bird in a cage rather than the fierce tiger that had wanted to shoot them moments ago.

Isadora shoved her refilled bottles under the bar. She attempted to storm out, her will stronger than Alexandre had likely counted on, but the door to the back hallway was still locked by his magic. "Louise, open this door."

"I can't," said Louise from the other side. "His spell is stronger than mine."

Isadora banged her head against the door once before turning around and marching straight for Alexandre and Elena. "You've interfered in things you know nothing about," she hissed, jamming her finger into the old man's chest. "Private family matters," she yelled at Elena. But once she got the initial heat of rebellion out of her system, her rational mind seemed to respond. She exhaled loudly through her nose. "What's happened to her? Where is she?"

"She was taken off the street," Elena said before glancing at Henri. "Possibly by the same person who gave you that black eye."

Henri confirmed it with a nod.

Tante Isadora absorbed the news as if it were the worst they could have delivered. Her eyes glossed over from genuine concern. "If he's found her, then she truly is in danger." She clapped a worried hand over her mouth, as if rattled by the heavy sound of consequences hitting the floor. "You have to find her. You have to help her."

"That, madame, is why we're here."

Tante Isadora nodded, then relented before pouring a round of cheap gin and sitting at one of the cabaret tables. Her body slumped into the chair as if the burden of standing had become more than she could bear. "I'll tell you," she said. "I'll tell you everything, and then you have to promise me you'll get that girl back."

CHAPTER
TWENTY-THREE

Logically Yvette knew the metal was cool to the touch, yet every time she moved, the hoop they'd slipped around her body burned her arms as if it had been stoked in an open flame. Unlike the carefully crafted rune cuffs they used in the witch's prison, with their glowing blue energy that severed prisoners from the source of their magic, this damn thing was made of common mortal iron. The band shouldn't be hurting her, but already she could feel the blisters rise on her skin.

"For the tenth time. Where is the book?" The thug in the flat cap gave Yvette a kick in the backside as a punctuation to his question.

"I lost it. Threw it in the river. Set the damn thing on fire." She tried to put as much defiance in her words as she could muster, but she'd fallen over onto her side, too tired from fighting pain to hold herself upright anymore. She could barely lift her head once a strange, offbeat vibration had begun humming inside her body.

Flat cap came around and squatted in front of her. His face looked like someone had molded it out of a block of clay and then shoved their fist into the botched result when it disappointed—nose squished to one side, droopy eyelids, and a mouth shaped like a knife slit. And this one had to be a *real* charmer with the ladies with that body odor of his.

The man smacked Yvette on top of the head. "Where is it?"

What had his boss said about the dank and dark and "her kind"? Did he know something about her magic she didn't? She'd been so completely filled with the light of life, it had practically shone out of the top of her head when she'd left the flat to find Henri at the café. But that was hours ago, and now that energy had been drained away, siphoned off by the darkness and fear.

She tried uttering a spell, the same one that had saved her once before. "Scissors, knife, or broken sword. Fly to my aid, heed my word." Yvette strained to see if the man was still hovering over her or if he'd actually keeled over from a sharp object embedding itself in his throat. But no, he was still there, sucking food from his teeth with his tongue. The vibration rattled through her body again, making her wilt like a flower out of water. Drooping, dying, burning.

Her abuser stood. He turned on his heel and paced in front of her face with his thick-soled boots. She'd give them the book. She knew she would. If he asked her one more time, she would tell him. Anything to be done with this pain of withdrawal. From what substance she did not know, but it was possible she'd had a taste of her true magic and now it was gone and she would never have it back again.

The shudder ended, and she knew it was coming. The question. The kick. The squat and wait. But then a light flickered in the dark. Someone was coming. The boss. The man married to her mother but not her father. Cuckolded, she thought, and managed a dim smile as he shone the light in her face.

The man stood over her. A second thug toting an iron chain flanked him on his side. Come to take the second shift of kicking a helpless young woman in the dark?

"Nothing?"

Flat cap shook his head.

The boss knelt. He set his palm-light on the ground near Yvette's head. She could feel herself curling toward it, craving the radiance. "You should know I'm a very patient man," he said, stroking her cheek as he pushed aside a limp strand of her damp-with-sweat hair. "My patience will outlast your resistance. I don't think your mother ever fully appreciated how persistent I truly am. Don't make the same mistake she did."

She grabbed his trouser leg when he began to stand. "Wait. Tell me something about her. Something real. Something I can keep. And then I'll give you the book."

He shook loose of her weak grip. After straightening, he stood in silence, breathing, thinking. And then he ordered his thugs out. Obeying, flat cap and his disappointed partner fumbled through the darkened tunnel, disturbing what sounded like a pile of bones. When they were gone, the boss gazed down at Yvette.

"You're nothing like her, you know."

"No, I don't know. The only thing I ever had of her was the book. And now you want to take it from me, and you won't even tell me why."

"Very well," he said and took a sniff of powder from his tin. "I first saw her on a Sunday. She was standing on the steps of the Palais Opéra under a halo of sunshine. She'd just been made principal dancer. *Sleeping Beauty* was to be her showcase performance. She was the epitome of poise the moment she stepped onto the stage. I knew then I would become her *abonné*. A patron to help guide her career and maturity."

"Wrong. My mother was a cabaret dancer."

"Is that what that woman told you?" he asked, followed by a cynical laugh. "I suppose there's some poetic justice in the great Cleo Marchand being remembered by her only daughter as a high-kick girl," he said with a smirk.

Cleo Marchand?

"The famous ballet dancer who used to be on all the posters? You think she's my mother?" Yvette laughed as well, even though it caused the pain to swell inside her. "You've got the wrong girl," she said. "Which means you've got the wrong book."

The man knelt and spitefully doused his palm-light so all that remained again was the flicker of the distant torch. Yvette writhed on the ground. That small ball of light had been sustaining her, but only just. The tremor returned, shaking her body from her bones to her skin.

"No, I don't think so." He narrowed his eyes and leaned in. "Do you even know what you are, Yvette? Why you're in such pain?"

"You drugged me."

He shook his head. "Merely a chloroform-based spell. The effect is temporary." He held his hand out and cast a new palm-light. The radiance immediately eased her craving.

"How'd you do that?"

"I didn't. Your magic merely responds rather predictably to luminescence. Your mother was the same." He tossed the ball of light in his hand, turning it into a plaything. Much like her life at the moment.

The trembling stopped. She endured the burn of the metal as she asked, "What kind of witch am I?"

"Tell me where the book is," he demanded and tossed the light so that her heart soared and fell with it.

"The book's hidden in the Palace Cinema," she said, desperate for the answer. "There's a catwalk above the balcony. They store old junk on the landing outside the projection room. It's there, hidden in a movie-reel case. The one for *Le Voyage dans la Lune*. Now tell me."

"That wasn't so hard, was it?" He bounced the light in his hand one last time before crushing it in his fist and walking out, leaving Yvette alone once again without answers.

CHAPTER TWENTY-FOUR

"Her mother and I were both students at the *École de danse de l'Opéra*," Isadora explained. "Back then we were girls still giggling behind our hands. *Petits rats*. But even then she was a flower among the weeds. Anyone could see she would rise above the rest."

The hardness had receded from Tante Isadora's face, softened by pleasant memories of girlhood. Elena believed it was possible both women had met at the ballet school. Young girls from all areas of the city entered the school each year, each ultimately vying for a coveted paid position in the corps. Even now she could see Isadora had the figure and bearing of a trained dancer as her back straightened in her chair, her body also remembering the past.

"It was a difficult life. Few of us had food enough to keep us alive, let alone to perform the rigorous dance combinations demanded of us over and over again, day after day. But you did what you had to do to stay." She gave a little shrug as she traced a circle on the table with her finger. "After we were promoted, Yvette's mother met a man backstage one evening. It was where the gentlemen came to watch the girls warm up before the performance. The *abonnés*. Many were the last of the nobles, men with titles and money. To them we were like racehorses at auction. They put their cash on the table and did their shopping, evaluating the sturdiness of our legs, the straightness of our backs, and all the while their hands measuring the trimness of the waist and the plumpness of the breast."

Elena had heard stories about the girls at *l'Opéra*. How they were sometimes deliberately put in the position of having to offer sexual favors to wealthy men, often men much older than they, in exchange for a patronage—someone to pay for their costumes, their evening meals, and maybe provide them with enough coin for a decent dress so they could say yes to a career-advancing invitation to dinner. For many it was simply an economic choice. A strategy for survival. Even a witch with all the talent in the world still needed a dry place to live and bread to fill her stomach.

"Cleo eventually married her *abonné*. I don't think she was ever in love with him, but he kept her in silks. At least at first."

Alexandre interrupted. "Pardon, madame, but you can't mean Cleo *Marchand*, the grand ballerina of the Palais Opéra?"

"*Oui*, but of course."

Alexandre's gaze casually drifted above the woman's head as if to check the veracity of her aura. "You're saying Cleo Marchand is Yvette's mother?"

Isadora's eyes teared up, and she bit her lip as though in awe of her own power of resistance. "I have kept that secret for eighteen years," she said and let out a breath.

"But what happened to her?" he asked, incredulous. "She was in all the newspapers. Did grand performances. She toured three continents as a prima ballerina. She was at the height of her fame when she vanished from the scene."

"She fell in love with an artist," Isadora said, as if it explained everything.

Henri affirmed it with a knock on the table. "You mean Tulane."

"The same artist who mixed the crystals in with his paint?" Elena was beginning to see how the pieces fell together.

"Yes, I'm sure of it," Henri said. "His favorite subject was a dancer who was rumored to be married, only he called her Mademoiselle Delacourt." He turned to Tante Isadora. "I'm right, aren't I?"

Isadora nodded. "They were inseparable. She admired him, his art, his intellect. And he cherished her, her talent, and her compassion. But," she said, holding up a warning finger, "she was still married."

"And I'll wager she was carrying a child inside her that was not her husband's," Elena intuited. "Which I can only imagine created harmful repercussions at home."

"If you mean the husband was ready to murder Cleo, you are correct. He nearly did kill her when he found out the child wasn't his. I don't know what he did to her, but he left her permanently disfigured. Her forearms, just below the elbows, were badly burned. Scarred." Isadora rubbed the skin on her arms as if reliving the sight of her friend's injury. "She was forced to wear long gloves every day after that."

"Was her husband a mortal?" Elena asked.

Isadora shook her head vigorously. "*Non*, one of yours. I only met him once. Early on. Backstage. He was from an old family, as I recall. Old nobility. Proud. But Cleo mentioned once his father had lost all the family's money in some bad investment. But you'd never know it the way that man looked down on everyone. He made it very well known to those in his circle he believed he was superior because he had witch blood running through him. If that was the case, why didn't he magic himself more money? Poof. Rich."

"It's not allowed," Elena said. "Covenant law."

"Instead, Cleo told me they lived from one job to another, mostly on the money she made off her fame, all the time trying to keep up appearances amongst the socialite crowd. One evening she came to a performance with tar and straw holding the bottom of her shoe together. And her a prima ballerina!" Isadora took out her cigarette case and allowed Alexandre to light a cigarette for her. "Thank you," she said, maintaining eye contact with him for an extra beat before continuing. "But then something happened. Something big. Cleo wouldn't tell me what it was, but she came alive again. With her, you could see the sun shining inside her when she was happy." Isadora swirled the remaining inch of gin in her glass, then swallowed it down. "I'm certain that's when she decided to leave him for Tulane."

Alexandre removed his pince-nez to give them a wipe with a handkerchief. "But how did Yvette come to live with you? Did her mother not want her? Perhaps Tulane made her give up the child?"

"Of course she wanted the girl. She adored that child. They both did." Isadora looked away, and her brow tightened in thought. "But wherever they were going, something happened at the last minute. They could no longer take the child with them. And yet Cleo was terrified of her husband finding Yvette and taking her away. They were both distraught when they came to me. Begged me to take her. To raise her. To keep her safe. They gave me a little money and made me promise I'd save the book for when the girl was old enough to understand."

"I'm sorry, madame, but were there no relatives they could take her to?"

"None that she talked about. And anyway, he would have tracked the child down if there had. I may not look to you like the ideal mother," she said, pointing her finger against the table in fierce self-defense, "but he never found the girl here in all those years."

As bad as things might have been for Yvette under this woman's wing, an overpopulated city orphanage would have proved worse. Elena sympathized with the mother's odd choice a little better now. "But Cleo never told you what the book was for? Or what the symbols meant?"

"*Non*, only that the girl would know what to do with the book once it was in her hands," she said with a roll of her eyes. "As if that girl ever had any instinct for magic."

"But how could she know? Yvette never had a mentor, never learned what kind of witch she was meant to be."

"No, she was taught more important lessons, like how to survive in a world that didn't know what to do with her." Isadora shifted in her seat, twisting her torso to face Elena. "Maybe it's time you tell me why you're all so interested in Yvette and this book. Why, exactly, are you helping her?"

It was impossible to explain the magic whirlwind she'd been sucked into when Yvette stole the wish. But aside from that, the truth was Elena wanted to help her.

"I owe it to her," Elena said. "She's a brave young woman who just needs a little karmic nudge in the right direction so she can find the wings to fly on her own."

They exchanged a brief look, each assessing the motives of the other before Isadora replied. "I think Cleo knew she would never see Yvette again. I always thought the little book was like a diary, something she wrote about her life, her family maybe. That's where they were headed, I believe. Home. But for obvious reasons maybe she couldn't return with an illegitimate child."

But there had to be more to the story than that. A man had kidnapped Yvette off the street to get his hands on the book, having twice sent thugs to steal it. And Yvette had gone to prison for murdering a man who tried to take the treasure from her. She supposed a mother's shame could explain the concealment, but then why bother to record the story for Yvette in the first place?

"Could Cleo have shared something important, something incriminating about the husband?" Elena paused. "Who did you say she was married to?"

Alexandre cleared his throat. "If I'm not mistaken, it was Ferdinand Marchand, the Comté-du-Lac du Nord."

"The comté? But I was introduced to him the other day by my fiancé's mother."

"He's here? In the city?" The panic in Isadora's voice was unmistakable.

Elena's instinct recognized the preposterous coincidence of having recently met the very man they discussed. "Is it possible he could still be looking for Yvette after all this time?"

Alexandre wasn't buying it. "He's a well-respected member of the *noblesse*. What could Cleo have possibly written in the book that could affect a man like him so many years later?"

"I don't know, but I think we can safely assume Yvette is in immediate and grave danger if he's found her. Maybe even more so because of her ignorance of magic."

Henri let out a helpless breath, summing up exactly how they all felt.

CHAPTER
TWENTY-FIVE

Whenever Yvette had found the courage as a child to ask Tante about her mother, it was always the same answer—she was a dancer, like all the other women who came and went at the cabaret. But none of the women there ever said they knew her. Now she knew why, if that powder-sniffing stuffed shirt was to be believed. It gave her a shiver, like gold dust shimmering in her veins, to think her mother might have been the extraordinary Cleo Marchand, even if the notion was absurd.

Despite the iron burning her arms, the cold and dark seeped under her skin. She'd survived more than a month in a filthy prison with nothing but straw and a thin wool blanket to keep her warm, but she'd had the daytime sun, meager food, and the company of smart women to sustain her. Though she'd tried to fight the impulse at first, thoughts of dying in the Maze of the Dead had a morbid beauty to it she decided, until she realized her body wouldn't be found this deep in the catacombs for a year or ten or never.

Yvette rolled over onto her back, groaning from the effort of expending so much energy. He'd soon figure out she lied about the book. Then what? Come back and torture her some more? She wouldn't last through another round of kicks in the dark. But if she did give him the book, he'd have no need of her anymore, and then what? How would he kill her? Quick with a knife? A killing spell might attract too much attention, even in a place that might as well serve as the threshold to hell's basement. But what if he decided to leave her there on the floor without food or water in complete darkness, once the torch went out? She would actually, truly die, slowly and with a whimper.

What if he'd already left her?

Panic was as good as a dagger when it struck the mind in one sharp blow. Yvette lifted her head and measured the flame of the torch with her eyes. Had it gone down? Was it nearly out? She would have cried at her miserable fate, but a weird twitch in her instinct told her she was no longer alone. There was no sound, no voice, and yet she was certain someone was there outside the pale glow of the torch.

"Hello?" No answer, but a faint scent of fish and cheese surfaced. And fur. "Monsieur Whiskers, is that you?"

The black cat stepped out of the shadows. Covered in dust, he sat two feet in front of her and licked his paws.

"But how did you find me?" It didn't matter. Seeing the cat gave her hope, even if he was the last living thing she would ever see before the torch, and her life, went out.

The cat froze mid-lick, listening. Someone was coming. So, she hadn't been abandoned yet to contribute her bones to the Maze of the Dead's macabre decor. A scurry of footsteps approached. But unlike the hard boot sounds of the thug in the flat cap, these were quick and nimble, scuttling over the path in the dark that led straight to her. The cat arched his back, then casually walked toward Yvette, swishing his tail before sitting squarely in front of her. She was forced to lift her heavy head to see over the cat's ears.

Tiny halos of light approached, like fireflies floating on an ocean of dark water. Behind the lights appeared a half dozen small people, two foot tall at most. Their heads were large for their bodies, their arms long for their torsos. One was dressed in greasy deerskins while the others wore workaday woolens covered in the same dust as the cat. The little goblin men, for she was sure that's who they were, toted picks and shovels over their shoulders while their free hands held up the tiny lanterns casting the firefly-like lights. All wore baggy knitted caps that allowed their long, pointed ears to poke through. Their swarthy faces were incredulous at the sight of her, apparently unaccustomed to meeting young women bound in iron bands on an everyday basis.

"What is it?" asked one of the little men in wool.

Yvette lay back down, hoping the cat might obscure her face from view. But it was no use. The little men moved closer. She was going to be murdered by a gang of pickax-wielding goblins.

"It's moving," said another, lowering his shovel.

The cat mewed, and six grotesque heads tilted at once to look at him.

"I weren't going to smash the frilly thing," the goblin said in his defense. "I just want a closer look. Never saw one with all its skin still on. We only ever see their brittle insides down here."

"They're called bones, you numbskull." The goblin in the deerskins gestured for the others to put down their pointy tools.

"What's that band going around her for, Gustave?"

The goblin in deerskins, presumably their leader, scrunched up his bulbous nose. "I reckon that's iron they put on her." He took in a deep breath. "Has the smell of it, like blood. Seen it used before. Not gonna kill her type, but it's got to smart some."

"My type?" Yvette asked, too weakened by circumstances to be afraid of the little men and their curious looks any longer.

"No offense, mademoiselle, but you do have the look of the topsiders," Gustave said. He held up his lantern and approached with his chest puffed out, as if to show he wasn't afraid if she weren't.

Topsiders?

"But what does—"

"Hush." Gustave frowned as he inspected the iron ring fastened around Yvette's body and the burn marks it had left on her arms. He glanced sidelong at the cat. "That's a right dirty trick they done, all right."

Monsieur Whiskers twitched an ear.

"Can you get it off?" Yvette pleaded. "With your little tools?"

The goblin scratched his chin. "How much you got on you?"

"Oh là là," Yvette whimpered, barely able to keep her eyes open. "You want money at a time like this?"

"Wouldn't be fair to work for nothing," he said, and the others snickered behind him, confirming their terms.

Yvette closed her eyes, ready to die. If she couldn't find mercy from a group of tunnel-dwelling goblins carrying everything they needed to help her, then there was no hope.

The cat sauntered in front of Yvette, swishing his tail. When he sat again on the other side of her head, there were three gold coins lying on the ground where he'd been. The goblin swiped them up, bit on one between his granite teeth, and nodded.

"Now that's the stuff to get the blood pumping," he said and showed her a pirate smile full of crooked teeth.

"So it was you all along." The cat nudged up against Yvette's neck. "Just what kind of cat are you, monsieur?" she asked as he half closed his eyes and purred into her ear. It was enough to calm her down and forget about the burning metal and her impending death, if only briefly.

Gustave motioned to a fellow goblin. The malformed manling in wool hefted a pick and hammer over his shoulder and ambled forward.

"If we hit her here and here, it might pop off," Gustave said. "Mind, that's witch magic binding it to her."

The second goblin squinted as he ran a gnarled finger over the iron band, feeling for the soft spots. After touching the metal for himself, he nodded his approval, lowered his knit cap over his eyes, and hefted his hammer over his head. Yvette would have been more afraid of the strike, but seeing as the hammer wasn't much bigger than a steak knife, she didn't think it would do much damage. Still, she braced for the blow, squeezing her eyes shut with what felt like her last ounce of energy. The hammer connected, smashing one side of the band in a violent blue flash that pierced her eyelids.

She wanted to scream as she hunkered down for the second strike. The hammer hit. The flash exploded. Yvette opened her eyes. The relief of being released from the fire of the metal rushed over her body like a cool stream. But it wasn't enough to revive her as she rolled onto her back, too weak to revel in her freedom.

The cat arched and hissed at the goblins.

"All right, put your back down." Gustave waved at his men, and they gathered around her. One by one they set their lanterns down so that she was surrounded by a chain of lights. Gustave knelt and blew gently on the flame in front of him until it glowed bright and yellow. The others followed his lead, until the coved space was bathed in golden light from a half dozen goblin lanterns.

The manlings, with their misshapen bodies and grotesque faces, lifted their feet to dance. They moved slowly at first, awkward and unwieldy, stepping sideways a few tentative inches at a time until they found their rhythm. Soon a soft glow formed at their feet, conjured out of the dust and darkness. As the light grew, their leather-shod feet moved faster and surer, stomping and leaping in a raucous circle around Yvette's curled-up body. After three times around, the glow grew strong enough to penetrate her skin. Yvette roused as it slipped through her pores and slid into her veins. Her head filled with thoughts of sunflowers and lemon tarts, and her body practically rippled with the pulsating energy of a star. Revived, she sat up, ravenous for a plate of soft cheese and warm bread with a glass of red wine. The goblins stopped and patted their sweaty brows.

"I thought I was a goner," she said.

"Sometimes all you topsiders need is a little light and a little dancing," Gustave said and handed her a corner of flat bread he'd saved in his back pocket.

Yvette wasn't sure if she should accept food from a goblin, but refusing seemed the more dangerous option, outnumbered as she was by so many grotesque faces. "Thank you."

The little men picked up their shovels and pickaxes and hoisted them over their shoulders. They bowed to the girl and the cat and gathered their lanterns.

"Wait, where are you going? Can't I come with you?"

"*Non*, your kind belongs up top in the air," Gustave said.

"But how do I get there?"

"You've got your glamour back, haven't you?"

"My *glamour*?" Yvette looked at her scuffed and dirty dress, burned arms, and filthy shoes.

The goblins shook their heads as if she were teasing them. Ignoring her question, they walked back out the way they'd come. Yvette got to her feet and followed their trail of light in the dark, stumbling occasionally on the odd bone or stone in her path as she called after them. "What glamour?"

The cat trotted nimbly at her heel as the little men got farther and farther ahead until they came to a small hole chiseled in the wall where they disappeared altogether. Yvette knelt, trying to squeeze through the opening, but it proved only big enough for a single-file line of goblins or a scrawny black cat. As the trail of lights disappeared, leaving her in the tunnel without the aid of a lantern or torch, Yvette hugged her knees to her chest, terrified of the dark and the dead around her.

She was doomed.

CHAPTER
TWENTY-SIX

It was most inconvenient that Alexandre had not brought Yvette's book with him. He'd chosen instead to entrust its safety to the chaos of his shop and the protection spell cast around the perimeter. Now they had to travel halfway across the city on a crowded, overheated underground train so they might return to the shop, decode the as yet understood language, find Yvette, and attempt to barter the book's contents to secure her release from her captors. If, indeed, they could figure out who had taken her. On top of that, Elena was expected for dinner with Jean-Paul and her future mother-in-law at Maurice's at seven thirty sharp. She crossed her arms and slumped in her wooden bench seat, wishing she knew of a spell that could turn back time.

"Could it be written in some ancient dead language?" Alexandre pondered aloud, pulling out the paper he'd copied of the symbols. "Or something runic? Musical notes perhaps?"

Elena had considered those possibilities as well. But there was something distinct yet familiar about the scroll-like writing they'd discovered in the symbols, something that chafed at her instinct. He handed her the paper and cake knife so she might attempt to decipher it one more time.

Try as she might, her mind would not stay focused on the cipher. She kept thinking about the coincidence of meeting Ferdinand Marchand that same week in the séance room and him being an acquaintance of Jean-Paul's family, no less. Elena stared at her reflection in the window, thinking back to their introduction. Yes, Marion Martel knew the man as a client of her late husband's, but there was something else there in the undercurrent. The whiff of rumor or uncertainty about the man. She made a mental note to ask Jean-Paul about him later at dinner.

Unable to concentrate, she handed the cake knife and paper to Henri to see if he recognized anything else. In the meantime, she let the train ride lull her into a shallow meditation, all the while thinking about Marchand and Cleo, Cleo and Tulane. She couldn't get the image of the comté licking his finger and turning the page of his newspaper out of her head. Had they also been brought together by the whirlwind of a girl's wish? As the train trundled down the track, Elena's eyelids drooped and she felt herself go under, her mind off to wander the shadow world in search of answers.

She soon found herself on a grassy slope with lavender and daisies growing nearby. The perfume from the flowers floated on the air as a slim young woman in a gauzy dress walked barefoot through the field. Her laughter rose and fell in song like some incantation in a secret language that aroused bees and crickets, butterflies and birds, to dance with her. Elena looked to her left when a man cleared his throat. He sat on a rock under a pair of trees with a sketchbook and stick of charcoal in his hands. He turned to Elena and lifted his hand as if to wave hello, but then he kept reaching until his hand found a cord running between the trees. He pulled it and a bell rang. A voice spoke: rue de Marchandes.

"This is our stop," Alexandre said for what Elena guessed was perhaps the second time as she reeled back into consciousness. The train pulled into the underground station. The cross streets were announced, and they exited the carriage with Henri following close behind.

Elena held the vision of the couple tight in her mind as Alexandre led them up the stairs back to street level. With quick steps they rounded the corner to the curio shop, thankful to find the protection spell still holding the place together. The old conjurer removed his athame from his suit pocket and cut the invisible seal binding the spell to the perimeter. Once the energy dissipated, they entered the shop and bolted the door behind them. Henri wiped a sleeve over his face, presumably to rid himself of the sensation of having walked through spiderwebs.

"I saw them," she said to Alexandre. "With my shadow vision. Yvette's parents, I'm certain."

"Good heavens, where?"

Elena bit her lip, forgetting that would be relevant. "I'm not sure. My instinct was more interested in who they were. Cleo, and Yvette for that matter, are unlike any witches I've encountered before. There's all this ethereal, radiant energy, as if *that's* their power." She waited for Alexandre to retrieve the book from a picnic basket buried beneath a life-size taxidermy fox with half its tail eaten away by moths. "Surely you must have been able to detect something unique about her peculiar aura when you saw her?"

"I thought at first Yvette's odd glow was merely a natural effect of having all that stoppered magic released in a furious burst. I'm no longer convinced that's the case. She's a witch, but her energy is scattered rather than concentrated."

"Do you think they'll hurt her?"

Alexandre stopped turning pages. "Her kidnappers? Depends on how desperate they are and what's at stake."

"Henri?"

His doleful eyes looked up from the clock he'd been studying. "Yeah, they will. Yvie can be brash, but if she doesn't give them what they want, they'll do what it takes to get the information out of her. Her mouth won't help her any, either."

But if it was Marchand, what could be motivating him after so much time? Enough to kidnap, injure, and perhaps even murder? Money and pride were the likely motivators. Simple hate would have long extinguished itself, or at least disarmed the instinct to act on the need for revenge. Elena knew from personal experience the desire for revenge was unsustainable on its own after so much time. But a lust for money . . . now that was a motivator that could easily stay burning for nearly two decades, greed being the gas that feeds the eternal flame of desire, as it were.

Even as she continued to wonder about the comté and the apparent money troubles Isadora had described during his early marriage to Cleo, the blissful image of the man and woman on the grassy hill wouldn't leave her thoughts. It was as if they were smiling at her, encouraging her to find them, perhaps so she could find Yvette.

"Would you mind if I took another look at your *Book of the Seven Stars*?" Elena asked, following a hunch.

Alexandre pointed her toward the picnic basket beside the copper fire extinguisher on the floor. Well, at least the book might be one of the first things to be saved by fire, she mused, if the nearby extinguisher weren't enchanted to shoot chocolate mousse or whatever other at-odds purpose it had been given.

Four books rested inside the basket. She pulled them all out, surprised to find the first was a blue book with an image of a witch on the cover. But not any witch she recognized. This one was wearing a pointed hat and riding a broom. Above her rose the full moon. Elena "hmphed" and was ready to toss the book aside when she read the title. A shiver coiled up and struck at the base of her neck. A fairy-tale book. There was a blue one, a red one, and another with a green cover. The cover of the green book depicted a fairy wearing a gauzy dress with dragonfly wings on her back. Rays of light shone out behind her.

No, they radiated from within.

"Where did you get these books?"

Alexandre snugged his glasses higher on his nose to better see. "I have no idea. I don't recall buying them. Complete nonsense on the covers, though I've heard they're rather popular with the mortal readers."

It wasn't a coincidence. Couldn't be. Three books about fairies buried in a picnic basket with *The Book of the Seven Stars*? Elena sat down and opened the latter, scanning for any mention of the fair ones. Meanwhile Alexandre showed Henri the rest of the symbols contained in Yvette's book, hoping he might be able to contribute something else about Tulane's paintings. As they weighed the merit of one curlicue's meaning over another, Elena struck gold.

"Listen to this," she said, gripping the book with near violent enthusiasm. "The *Fée* descend from an ancient magical pedigree of unknown origins. Understood to be creatures capable of traversing between this world and the realm of the Other, they are often endowed with powers ranging from spellcasting to charismatic magnetism, occasionally accompanied by a radiant aura." Elena looked up to gauge the men's reactions. Their impassive stares disappointed her, so she read on. "Due to their secretive nature, general disdain for the modern human world, and sometimes fickle nature, their various populations have been difficult to categorize and/or study with any regularity post antiquity. And yet they are known to observe a rigid court life with specific hierarchies of power in the world of the Other. On this side of the veil they enjoy mingling among common mortals, drawn to the extreme displays of awe with which they are received and also to the variety of food, drink, and sexual proclivities associated with mortals. Because of the nature of this attraction, the *Fée* are considered exceedingly hedonistic and narcissistic creatures by other races. Approach with reserve and caution, as their behavior can be unpredictable."

Elena added it all up. "That's Yvette."

"You think our foulmouthed girl with the kohl eyeliner is one of these otherworldly creatures?" Alexandre shook his head, doubtful. "I find that highly unlikely. Besides, as the book states, the *Fée* abandoned this part of the world centuries ago."

"But some are still drawn to this side of the veil. It says so right here. What if her mother was one as well?"

"There you go. Cleo Marchand lived her entire life in the city until her disappearance."

"We only know that's true while she was a dancer. But when she disappeared, it was because she went *home*, according to Isadora."

Henri looked up as though an idea had grown too large to keep to himself inside that curious mortal head of his. "But that's it. Don't you see? That's why Tulane called her Mademoiselle Delacourt."

"I don't follow, young man."

Henri pointed to the book in Elena's hand. "What she read about the *Fée*, about how they live. Their fancy court. It could be a private joke between Tulane and Cleo, or maybe a secret lover's language. He calls her his mademoiselle *de la court*."

"Oh, Henri, that's well done," Elena said, clapping a hand over her mouth at the obvious reference.

Alexandre squinted through his pince-nez and had a look at *The Book of the Seven Stars* for himself. He read the same exact passage Elena had read out loud and then turned the page. "If one wishes to communicate with the *Fée*, it is generally advised to do so psychically, considering the convoluted nature of their native language.

"Good heavens, could it be?" Alexandre hurried to the back of his shop and opened a freestanding wardrobe with double doors and a price tag that would set most workers back a month's wages.

"What is it?"

The proprietor tossed the contents out of the closet, digging past the women's parasols, buckle shoes, and feathered hats to find what he was looking for at the bottom. Elena wondered if he might have remembered there was a secret portal in the back or some other enchanted nonsense. Instead, he reemerged red-faced and triumphant. "This, mademoiselle," he said and held up a paper scroll wrapped with gold cord. "It's merely an odd souvenir piece I picked up at a witch's trunk sale, however . . ."

The old man stretched the parchment out on the front desk, using the clock Henri had been fiddling with, a pair of candlesticks, and a leather boot to hold down each of the four corners. Once opened, the scroll revealed itself to be a rather old yet detailed map of the night sky. Elena easily recognized the various constellations—Andromeda, Lyra, Cygnus, the families of the zodiac, and of course *la grand ourse*—only this star chart was not identified by the familiar names one learned in school. The constellations were instead individually labeled with the same filigree-style symbols found in Yvette's book.

"Astonishing," Elena said. "The style is almost identical."

"The man I bought it from assured me it was genuine pixie contraband. I bought it for a laugh, thinking someone might pick it up in the store for a novelty gift or some such."

"Pixie contraband?" Henri, mouth agape, hugged his satchel and sank in the same overstuffed chair Yvette had previously fallen into.

"So, it could be a fairy language?" And even as Elena uttered the words, a tingle rushed up the back of her neck, assuring her it must be true. She traced her finger over the map, beginning with the seven stars she knew for an absolute fact were part of the constellation of Ursa Major. The symbol hovering over it in black ink showed a set of consecutive swirls and dots. "Do you think it's possible to translate these symbols so that we can read them, based on the names we already know for the constellations?"

"Certainly not letter for letter I wouldn't think. But perhaps there's a way to distinguish certain words based on sounds or pronunciations. And based on a few assumptions, of course."

"You mean, substitute this symbol here for the letters in the Big Dipper?" Henri said, setting his satchel aside to stand and look at the map.

"Hmm, or do we call it Ursa Major?" Alexandre asked. "Or Ursa Minor, or the Cart and Plow, or the Dead Man's Coffin? Given how many names there are for that particular constellation, perhaps that wouldn't serve as the best word-for-word comparison for translation. But another might do. Yes, indeed, it just might."

Elena's hopes wilted. Given the scope of navigating the intersection of languages, it would be like trying to sail the open sea without a compass. Still, the book itself would be a bargaining chip if and when Yvette's captor decided to come out of the shadows and make his demands.

While Henri and Alexandre continued looking for something useful on the pixie map to use in translation, Elena picked up the book, consciously testing how the pages felt under her fingertips as she turned them, how the paint had bled into the paper before drying. Yes, she thought, her instinct tingling, it may yet prove the perfect bargaining chip after all.

Several hours later, the most Alexandre and Henri had to show for their translation effort was a single consistent symbol they were almost certain represented the letter combination of *Aq*. Or was it *Ar*?

As Alexandre argued the linguistic sense of a symbol against Henri's artistic interpretation of it, the clock they'd used to hold down the northeast corner of the star map chimed seven. Elena asked if the time was accurate, then nearly panicked when Alexandre confirmed it with a glance at his pocket watch.

"I'm late," she said, explaining she was expected for dinner at Maurice's sharply at seven thirty. "Right when we're making progress. I'm sorry, but I must leave."

Elena slipped her burgundy travel jacket back on. Both men gave her outfit a withering stare as she buttoned it up. "What is it? Did I miss a button?"

The men glanced at each other.

"It's your attire, my dear." Alexandre adjusted his pince-nez.

"What's wrong with it?" Elena scanned the skirt for dust or a snag in the hem.

Henri chewed his lip, avoiding eye contact. "It's just that Maurice's is . . ."

"What?"

"Exclusive," Alexandre said. "It is the territory of the *bon chic*, the affluent. One does not wear a wool travel suit to dine on white linen tablecloths and drink from crystal glassware."

Elena exhaled, though it felt more like the air had been knocked out of her. "I haven't time to change. Is my attire really that bad?"

"Maurice's is more than a restaurant," Henri said. "It's like going to a show, only everyone is both audience and actor. Me and my, er, associates could sum up a household's wealth based on the cut of a dress alone. Yvie always went for the madames in beaded gowns and feathered hats."

"So, one should dress to appease the taste of the pickpockets. I see."

Elena had a dress she'd planned to wear. Nothing extravagant, but passable for the fiancée of a former lawyer. Or so she'd thought. But there was no time to retrieve even a mediocre dress now.

"If it's not too presumptuous," Alexandre said, returning to the wardrobe where he'd found the map earlier, "I may be able to accommodate a more acceptable look for the evening."

Exhausted and in no mood for another struggle, Elena relented. After sorting through a few items hanging on the rack, Alexandre presented her with an evening gown any woman would be proud to stroll the boulevard in. It was made of an unusual seafoam-colored silk with an overlay of silver metallic tulle on the shoulders. The plunging neckline had been embellished with tiny sea pearls and silver sequins in a fetching scalloped pattern that sparkled even under the shop's greasy lamplight. And on the skirt, embroidered blades of grass rose up from the hem to regale sequined butterflies and neon-green dragonflies sewn just below the bodice.

"This is absolutely beautiful. Wherever did you get it?"

"In trade. For a favor. It's not worth knowing the details, but the gown ought to be suitable for the evening. You may change in the back room if you like," he said, gesturing to the curtain behind the front desk. "As I recall there are matching shoes and a hat somewhere. I'll rummage around for them while you change."

While the sensible half of her instincts told her there was something not quite right about his explanation—or even the prospect of enjoying herself at a fashionable dinner while Yvette was still out there somewhere being held against her will—her daring half longed to greet Jean-Paul while wearing such an elegant gown. And it did fit. Perfectly, without need of a corset, which was a comfortable bonus.

The hat and shoes were waiting for her inside the curtain as she emerged from behind the large filing cabinet she'd changed behind for privacy. The hat was like some divine dessert from a pastry shop, with its broad pleated silk brim to match the dress, graceful tail of metallic tulle trailing off the back, and jeweled hatpin secured to the band. The pin reminded her instantly of Yvette and her penchant for using her accessories as weapons of self-defense. She poked the hatpin through the crown of the silk cream puff, securing it in place, then slipped on the satin shoes. The effect of the ensemble was evident in the men's dumbfounded reaction as she stepped out from behind the curtain.

"Fashionable enough to have my pocketbook stolen on the boulevard?" she asked Henri.

"Oh, yes, mademoiselle." He smiled and stood. "In fact, I'd better escort you there just in case."

Elena was perfectly capable of getting herself to the restaurant safely, but the young man looked like he could use the break. She glanced once more at the map and the progress they'd made on the translation of the fairy language, but before she could say anything about the work yet to do, Alexandre assured her he would stay and continue the effort as long as he could. With that assurance, she left the old man in the curio shop and headed to Maurice's in her borrowed dress with a lovesick thief for an escort.

CHAPTER
TWENTY-SEVEN

Being abandoned in total darkness was as scary as Yvette had always assumed it would be. At least at first. But for someone whose magic had recently been unleashed by elementals, drained by thugs, and then restored once again by a band of goblins, there was an inkling of hope. Once the eyes adjusted, gradient shades of light could be found even in the abandoned tunnels of the Maze of the Dead, though, admittedly, the light seemed to be emanating from somewhere beneath her skin. The more her fear diminished the brighter the glow, until she was nearly as radiant as a firefly.

"But what now, Monsieur Whiskers?" She poked her head through the hole in the tunnel wall. And though she could see a short distance in either direction, she did not know which way was out and which way led deeper into the catacombs. She was still just as trapped as when she was left alone in the dark.

The cat twitched his whiskers and leaped through the opening.

"Yes, fine for you. You're small enough to escape." She knew if Elena had been in her position, the vine witch would have the perfect spell on the tip of her tongue to make the cat go get help. He would have spoken in full sentences to the first policeman he found. But, of course, that was not the type of help Yvette needed, only to be tossed out of one pot of trouble and dumped into another that involved handcuffs and locked cells and sharpened guillotine blades. "Well, go on, then," she said to the cat. "May as well save yourself."

The light radiating from within her was no brighter than a glow-worm, but she could have sworn the cat had rolled his eyes at her. Monsieur Whiskers then mewed and paced and tossed his head, as though encouraging her to follow. But how?

What had the little goblin said about her powers? She did seem to be shining. That must be worth something. And there was a sort of fizziness bubbling up inside her. She'd taken it for hunger or panic, but maybe it was something else entirely. What was Elena always saying? That intent was the force behind any magic spell?

"Right, then let's get the hell out of here," she said to the cat.

Concentrating on the size of her body and the size of the all too small opening in the wall—and the only exit she had any hint of how to find—she closed her eyes and focused on getting through the narrow space and onto the other side. She didn't know if she needed words, but as they'd never served her well in the past, she decided to squeeze her eyes tight and make herself heard by the All Knowing with the strongest intention she could muster.

She may have overdone it.

An explosion burst in the tunnel. Yvette felt as if her being had frag-mented into a million particles of spangled light. Yet she hadn't blown apart; she was simply lighter than air. Her body, or rather the substance of it—her limbs, heart, muscles, bones, and veins—had become some-how malleable. Shifting. Changeable. Flowing. She could have taken on any shape she wanted, she was sure of it, as she oozed through the gap in the wall like a gust of glitter blown out of a child's palm.

The cat backed up, darting his paws out of the way. But then he waited, watching, circling with pent-up energy, as if he wanted to run. Yvette concentrated, pulling herself together. Reforming, reshaping.

The fizziness remained under her skin, but there was a solidness too. The radiance around her dimmed, and her feet planted themselves lightly on the ground.

She'd done it. She'd passed through the opening three sizes too small for her body, and she'd done it like Elena said, using will and intent. For the first time in her life she'd wielded true, forceful magic of her own, unlike anything she'd ever experienced before.

"What do you think of that, Monsieur Whiskers?"

The cat mewed and flicked his tail, and she swore he smiled at her. But there was little time for congratulations. Her abductors could return at any moment to demand the book yet again. The cat trotted off, his sleek black coat disappearing in the dark. She held her hand out and willed her inner light to illuminate the path before her. When her body and her magic responded, she hesitantly laughed at the absurdity of her being good at anything to do with magic. It was a new sensation, but one she seized with her entire being before chasing after the cat and what she knew would be the way out.

CHAPTER
TWENTY-EIGHT

The city was alight with the garish white glow of the electric streetlamps strung along the boulevard. The bridges, buildings, and parks were all lit up, too, as if taking orders from the looming tower, with its finger pointing at an electrified future. Elena supposed the tower was beautiful in its own way, sparkling and full of innovation, as Jean-Paul liked to describe it, but there was no denying she longed for the soft lamplight of the countryside and evening walks in the vineyard. But would she be able to return there again? To tend the vines? Coax the wine? Confer with the bees, crickets, and moon on when best to harvest?

The cab stopped in front of a parade of men and women, each outlandishly dressed for their evening strut, just as Henri had described.

"Delivered safe and sound as promised, mademoiselle." Henri doffed an invisible hat at her.

"And you as well," she said. "You'll be safe at Alexandre's. It's a good place to hide for the night. Please assure me you'll return there at once."

Henri looked away, and she feared the worst, that he'd head out in the city to shake his sources to find Yvette. A dangerous move, given someone had already tried to kill him once. She reached in her purse, and he began to argue.

"*Non*, mademoiselle, you owe me nothing."

Elena wasn't offering money but a piece of amethyst crystal she carried for emergencies. She didn't have time to impart a personal inscription in the crystal for him, but if the young man didn't have the sense to return to the shop and stay away from trouble, at least it would offer him some semblance of protection against the forces wishing to do him harm.

Henri took the stone, weighing it in his hand and admiring the color. She realized then he'd likely imitate his hero Tulane and crush the thing up to add to his pigments, but either way it was done. She thanked him, and they parted ways.

Elena joined the spectacle of patrons assembling outside the restaurants, theaters, and salon parties along the boulevard. She spotted Jean-Paul in the crowd standing in front of the famous Maurice's restaurant looking dapper in a black tuxedo and crisp white shirt. He shook hands vigorously with another man, as if reminiscing about a shared memory from their youth. A ghost of a thought passed through Elena at the sight of him surrounded by the trappings of his former life, smiling and enjoying the excitement of the nightlife. She wondered then, after being back home, if a part of him regretted ever leaving the city for the vineyard and abandoning the privileged life he'd once led. Here under the bright lights there was no digging in the limestone soil, no trudging a horse and plow through a rocky vine row or battling the constant threat of disaster, whether from fungus, a gathering storm, or a mischievous hex from a neighboring vigneron and his vine witch.

Then again, he was not under any influence from her or any other magic she was aware of. The wishing string she'd once used on him to allow her to reclaim her right as vine witch at Château Renard had surely run its course. So, if returning to this glittering life of tuxedos and tall hats, fast cars and five-course dinners, was something he wanted, he was in full possession of his free will.

And yet . . . if her position as a vine witch was truly revoked, could she bring herself to live among these feathered and sequined creatures with him, doling out herbal concoctions as a *venefica* to cure whatever urban ailments they suffered from?

The buoyancy she'd felt after first trying on the dress had deflated like an underdone soufflé as she felt a hand at her elbow.

"Elena, my dear, I've been worried sick about you." Marion Martel hooked her arm fully around Elena's as if she meant to never let her out of her sight again. "You know it's one thing for a woman to be independent and go off and do things on her own. I'm a firm believer in equal rights for woman, as you know. *Les femmes veulent voter!* But, my dear, I think you've taken things much too far, don't you, being gone so many hours a day? Now, come. Let's join Jean-Paul, who has been waiting patiently for you to arrive."

"Of course," Elena said, her mind still troubled by uncertainty and doubt. But then Jean-Paul met her eye, and her heart vaulted, sprung to life by the desire to feel him next to her again and be restored. He dropped his conversation with the gentleman and greeted her with a tender kiss. Afterward he held her in a brief embrace and pressed his lips to her ear.

"I got your message. Thank you for using the old-fashioned method of writing it down."

She'd sent him a dove at the same time she'd contacted Alexandre earlier, only she'd known better than to expect a mortal to speak to a bird. Instead she'd sent the dove via a transcriber. There was a more than competent word witch who ran a translation business off the roof of the famous arc leading to *le jardin*. One simply needed to send a little praise along with the original message and the witch was said to feed off the compliment for a week.

They reluctantly parted, then Jean-Paul escorted the two women into the grand dining room of the infamous Maurice's. The vision of grace and architectural beauty that met Elena's eye upon entering the room was as enthralling as any magic she had studied or practiced. Overhead, the ceiling hung in a great arching dome of pale-green glass that immediately put one in mind of sitting inside a sunny solarium on a summer afternoon. An artist had even painted fruit-heavy grapevines on the glass to add a Dionysian mural. Jean-Paul smiled when he saw Elena staring up at the grand dome. She gave him the satisfaction of knowing it pleased her as he held her chair out for her. Once seated, she took a moment to admire the other extraordinary features—tables topped in white linen, stained-glass panels backlit by the glow of soft candlelight, and nine painted panels flanked by peacock feathers that surrounded the room, each depicting one of the nine mythological Muses of ancient Greece. Elena could no longer name them all, but their dedication to beauty and art inspired, nonetheless.

"The first time inside always steals one's breath away," Marion said with a lift of her chin, though Elena noticed she did not deign to look up at the scene she spoke of, presumably so she might not be mistaken for a dining room *débutante*.

Jean-Paul squeezed Elena's hand under the table and leaned over. "You're breathtaking," he said, and she swallowed the compliment whole. A moment later an attentive waiter dressed in a black jacket, a bow tie, and a white apron tied around his waist approached the table, offering expensive suggestions to create the perfect epicurean experience. Marion said yes to it all.

As they sat sipping their wine and tasting their first course of *foie gras poilé*, discussing the latest gossip from the psychic world of Madame Fontaine, a flutter of activity near the kitchen entrance caught their attention. Mild shrieks of amusement from patrons seated near the door turned to groans of disgust as a small grayish green bird flapped its wings over the feathered heads of some of society's shiniest couples. The tiny bird flew to the high metal rafters of the domed glass ceiling, where it perched to catch its breath among the painted vines. Not three seconds later its white-rimmed eye found Elena. It chirped and jumped off its perch, swooping down until it landed on the white tablecloth beside the plate of half-eaten duck liver. There it hopped back and forth, chirping and pecking at the silverware in obvious distress.

"One of yours?" Jean-Paul asked, scooting his chair back.

"Believe it or not, I think it's a stray." Elena leaned forward for a closer look and noted no shadow of spellwork in its eyes. "We don't generally use songbirds like the ortolan. Too unreliable."

Marion held her napkin over her face as if afraid of catching a disease from the poor ruffled thing. "Unreliable how, dear?"

"As dinner companions," she said and placed her hand on the table. She encouraged the bird with a trusting look, and it hopped up to perch on her offered finger.

"Oh, but they're a delicacy," Marion said before checking the menu.

Elena excused herself, and with everyone in the place watching her with open faces of astonishment, she walked the bird outside.

She had just finished listening to the ortolan hyperventilate about its escape from the kitchen moments before being plucked and dunked in a vat of *armagnac* to be served whole to customers when the *maître d'hôtel* approached her on the sidewalk. She nearly incinerated him to the ground after hearing the bird's side of things but stopped short when he announced there was a telephone call for her.

"Telephone? For me?"

"You are Mademoiselle Boureanu? The woman in the dragonfly dress, yes?" he asked.

"Yes, I suppose I am," she said and released the bird.

The *maître d'hôtel* escorted her back inside the restaurant to a small wooden phone booth beside his station. She hardly knew what to do with the thing, but she'd seen people lift the receiver to their ears before, so that's what she did. As if by magic, Alexandre's voice spoke to her from inside the odd contraption as soon as she said, "Hello?"

"We have a problem," he said. "The book is gone."

"Gone? How?" Elena asked, raising her voice slightly to make sure the sound would carry through the wires to the other end.

"Stolen by that duplicitous thief Henri, that's how. I do hate to interrupt your evening, but I thought you'd want to know right away."

Elena felt a headache coming on. "He's going to try and bargain for Yvette. He must have lied about knowing where they're keeping her, or at least how to get in touch with her captors."

"Would these be the same people who tried to kill him earlier?"

"Almost certainly."

"Then good riddance."

"You don't mean that," Elena said and turned her back to the *maître d'hôtel* when it became obvious he was listening in on her conversation. "That scamp, pretending to escort me safely to dinner when instead he'd meant all along to steal the book and march straight into the lion's den."

"Shall we hex him?"

The thought was tempting. Instead she sighed into the receiver, feeling the effect of the jinni's wish still churning in the ether around her, compelling her to act. "He cannot hand over that book. Not yet," she said, shutting her eyes in defeat. "I'm coming back to the shop. There may be a way to find him and, I presume, Yvette, if fate decides we've been played for fools long enough."

"Ah, good luck with that," he said. "I'll leave the lamp burning in the window."

Elena returned to her table and broke the bad news to Jean-Paul and his mother. With the eyes of the restaurant already keen to watch for more signs of disruption from the trio, there was little room for an open argument. Elena apologized and stood. Jean-Paul, as she expected, excused himself and followed, but then Marion did the same with a broad gesture of mea culpa to her dining peers before doing a quick-step to catch up with the couple on the sidewalk.

"What in heaven's name was that about?" she asked, showing her temper as she stamped her foot on the pavement.

"*Maman*, I'm so sorry. Please, go back inside and finish your meal."

Her head turned, zeroing in on her son. "And further humiliate myself by eating alone? As it is, I won't be able to return for a month." Then she pursed her lips and took aim at Elena. "And please enlighten me about what could be so important that you would walk out on your fiancé and his mother during a celebration dinner? Honestly, the two of you have been up to something all week long, and I demand to know what it is."

Jean-Paul opened his mouth to speak but seemingly found himself without a defense. Elena stepped forward, lowering her voice when she spotted the *maître d'hôtel* once again hovering suspiciously near the doorway.

It was time for the truth.

"My ability to remain a winemaker has been called into question this week." She held up a hand when Jean-Paul moved to interrupt. "In a sense, I'm being blackmailed by the Ministry of Lineages and Licenses to turn over a fugitive, a woman with whom I escaped prison when I was wrongly arrested for murder. They would like to have her back in custody, and if I don't help them do so, they are going to ruin my career and the reputation of Château Renard."

"But there is no such thing as a Ministry of Lineages and Licenses."

"There is if you're a witch."

"I beg your pardon."

"A witch. Which I am. And now I must return to the curiosity shop where I've spent my day so that I might locate a stolen book, most likely one belonging to one of the *Fée*."

"A what?" Jean-Paul asked.

"A fairy. Yes, I'm convinced that's what Yvette is. But she's in trouble, and so I really must go."

Jean-Paul and his mother exchanged glances as the downpour of supernatural information rained on them. And yet, a second later

Marion nodded, pulled up her gloves, and stuck out her hand to call her carriage.

"Well, what are we waiting for? It would be unconscionable to abandon a friend, let alone one of the *Fée*, if one knows they're in trouble," she said with the heart of a believer, and the three of them clambered into the cabriolet and headed for Alexandre's shop.

CHAPTER TWENTY-NINE

Henri had the cab drop him off at the intersection across from Hell's Mouth. At the foot of the butte the streetlamps were spaced far enough apart that he had a fifty-fifty chance of slipping through the alley without being recognized. Rings would know by now he wasn't dead, of course. A pity, given the obvious advantage of surprise at being a walking dead man.

He double-checked the weight of the book in his jacket pocket, then darted across the street, dodging the cars and *fiacres* racing to and from the city center. Already he could tell by the mood of the gathering crowd the money would be flowing like a stream through the streets tonight.

Squeezing past the downspout at the end of the alley, he paused before entering the back door. The book hadn't been the only thing he'd stolen from the old man's shop. He pulled the revolver out of his waistband to inspect the chamber for bullets. There were only three, so he lined the cylinder up so it'd be ready to fire. Just in case. His gang had already proved they were willing to kill him. It was only fair he returned the favor.

There'd be a man in the hallway. Henri could take the chance he wouldn't know him. Unlikely, though, given how many times he'd frequented Hell's Mouth in his life. Or he could force his way in by knocking the man out. Maybe with the butt of the pistol. But then what? Drag the man's limp body outside? Or down the hallway to an empty room? Forget it.

Thinking about his options, he glanced up to where a window sash was slightly raised in a darkened room. He *could* pull an Yvie and climb up the downspout, but he'd already wasted enough time. He had the book; they had Yvie. It was time to strike the deal, so he swung the door open and marched in as if he had every right to be there on business.

"Boss man here?" he asked, strolling up to the street thief standing guard. Upstairs the music from a four-piece band played a timely tune about a bird in a gilded cage.

The boy eyed him with a frown. "Thought they said you were on the outs."

"Not likely. What would Rings do without his best thief, eh? Besides, I light-fingered a little something for him he's really going to like." Henri patted his pocket so that the shape of the book showed through the fabric.

"Password?"

Merde. Given Rings's lack of imagination, he took a gamble it hadn't changed yet. "Jean-Baptiste le sauvage?"

The guard gave him the once-over again, staring at the shape of the book under his jacket. "Yeah, all right. They're all in there pissed on gin and toasting to skeletons," the boy said, pointing to the back room in the cabaret's maze. "Supposed to be your skeleton."

Henri laughed it off in front of the guard, then approached the crypt room with a face of stone. He hated going in there with its tables made to look like coffins, bones propped up in wooden boxes, and the gas lights on the walls that dimmed and flared to imitate the presence of ghosts. But this time too because, true to its name, it was a dead end with no back exit.

Henri stood in the darkened foyer and glimpsed through the curtain to the cavern-like room inside. There'd be a show on the stage later, an optical illusion to make the skeletons in the caskets appear to dance. The spectacle would bring in a crowd, always did, but for now the room was abandoned except for the cussing and laughing and constant sound of empty glasses being refilled by Rings and his crew. A special privilege of the in-house ring of thieves to have the place to themselves before the real crowds showed up.

Henri checked the revolver one more time. He cocked the hammer, took a breath, and, for good measure, gave the amethyst crystal the witch had given him a squeeze. Then he pushed back the curtain and entered the room.

"*Bonjour, mon frères voleurs,*" he said and pointed the gun straight at Rings. "It's time we had a little chat."

CHAPTER THIRTY

The path taken was not the way out. Or at least not yet. The tunnel had come to an abrupt end, with the final insult being a locked metal gate. On the other side of the bars appeared to be the basement storage area of a shop or warehouse. There was a single street-level window letting in light and a shelf filled with small decorative perfume bottles. Yvette could hear a woman speaking at the top of a stairwell about bergamot and musk oil needing to be mixed in the proper proportions for the scent to chemically adhere to the skin.

A perfumery?

"Not bad, Monsieur Whiskers." Yvette leaned closer to get a whiff. "Is this how you knew your way? By following the heavenly scent?"

The cat slipped through the bars and trotted to the bottom of the stairs. Green eyes stared back at Yvette, expectant.

"Right," she said, taking a step back to size up the opening she'd need to fit through. Confident she knew what to do, she willed herself to transform as she had before. The fizziness bubbled, stirring inside her. Her body became feather light. She approached the bars, expecting to slip through as easily as the cat. Instead, her body was thrown back, repelled as if she and the gate were magnets with the same polarity.

Yvette settled into solid physical form again and stared at the bars. Some force of magic was preventing her from passing through. Miffed, she pressed her hand against the lock to use her burglar's charm instead. There wasn't a lock in the city she couldn't open. And yet, as soon as her skin came in contact with the metal, her arm weakened and fell at her side. Her palm burned with the same heat as when that lowlife had put the iron band around her arms.

"I can't get through," she pleaded to the cat.

But there was nothing he could do. What little magic Monsieur Whiskers possessed she'd long suspected had more to do with luck and fortune than saving young women from their own stupidity.

She could call out. The woman upstairs might hear her and come down. But how would she explain being trapped outside the woman's cellar? And what if, thinking her a thief, she called *les flics*? She'd go from one set of bars back to another. No thank you.

Life tingled its way back into her arm, but she kept her distance from the metal all the same. Back in the shadow where her skin glowed softly, radiating in sync with the beat of her heart, she thought over her choices. If she couldn't go forward, could she go back the way she'd come? She stared down the gaping mouth of the tunnel. Could she even find the way again? This was how people got lost in the Maze of the Dead and ended up leaving their bones for the next generation to find. So, the only other option was to yell for help and hope for the best.

Before she could muster the courage to call out, the catacombs shook with a violent rumble. Moments later a cloud of dust bloomed out of the darkness behind her. The air filled with a ghastly green haze. It had to be him. Blasting through the walls with that sickly green fire of his. She'd left him empty-handed, and now he was coming for her.

Yvette felt her way around the walls, searching for another way out, a hole or crevice she could slip through, but there was nothing, only the bars. There was no time to call out and hope someone had a key. She'd have to make the jump through the bars. Either that or face that powder-sniffing fiend and his boot-licking minions. She stood with her back against the wall and summoned her magic, calling it forward, asking the All Knowing for the power to withstand the pain.

She shimmered and fizzed, her body transforming once again into glittery dust as she willed her body toward the iron and her only chance at freedom. If only the bars were a little wider apart. If only the metal didn't burn so hot.

Behind her a magical orb of green light emerged from deep inside the tunnel. Yvette pushed against the resistance, forcing herself to complete the transformation. She squeezed her eyes shut, concentrating on seeing her body on the other side of the gate. Searing heat pressed against her as her ethereal body slid between the fiery metal. She gasped at the pain, uncertain she could endure another second. She dared to open her eyes. Only halfway through! If she stopped now, she'd sizzle to death. The green orb grew nearer even as a man's voice from farther back in the tunnel shouted. Yvette summoned an absolute will to survive and squeezed through to the other side, the pain nearly stealing the breath out of her with its intensity.

A woman ran down the stairs, her high heels clicking on the wooden steps. She gaped at the still effervescing young woman collapsed on the stone floor, turned in the direction of the shouting and the green light coming from the catacombs, then quick as lightning scooped up a handful of cellar dirt. "Maze of darkness, plague and bones. There's nothing to see but iron and stones," she said and blew the dirt into the air.

Just as the green light threatened to explode into the end of the tunnel, bringing the wrath of the madman and his henchmen, the air filled with the scent of lemon verbena. The bars wavered as if seen through a heat wave, and the echo of running feet faded. But before the sound died out completely, Yvette heard what the man had been shouting as he ran to catch up.

Rings had found the book and was ready to bargain. For her.

CHAPTER THIRTY-ONE

Faint lamplight shone through an opening in the curtains as the cabriolet pulled up in front of Alexandre's curiosity shop.

"What a marvelous location." Marion stepped out of the carriage, her eyes lit up from the adventure of slumming it in the narrow back lanes of the city. "Now, where is this witch friend of yours?"

"This way." Elena took Jean-Paul's hand when offered. She knocked three times on the shop door, and the old man let them in. "My fiancé and his mother," she explained when his bushy brows shot up over the rims of his pince-nez.

"How do you do." Marion extended her hand.

Elena could tell by the way Alexandre stalled after their introductions that he had found the trace of an aura around Marion. Perhaps there was a shadow of witch blood running through the woman from some distant great-grandmother after all.

"*Enchanté*, madame. Do come in." Alexandre extended his arm toward the shop. "Welcome," he said to Jean-Paul, shaking his hand. "I'm afraid we're in the middle of a situation, but do make yourself at home."

"The book's well and truly gone?" Elena hoped the old man might have merely misplaced it.

"It's gone. And that's not all. The young scoundrel stole a revolver as well."

"Enchanted?"

"Almost certainly."

Elena closed her eyes in disbelief. "He'll get himself killed one way or another before the night is through."

"I'm sorry, did you say the gun was enchanted?" Marion wore the most delightful smile at learning such a thing was even possible. "What then does it do?"

"Let us hope we don't find out," Alexandre replied and escorted the curious mortal to sit in the overstuffed chair beside the front counter.

"Give me a moment." Elena removed her hat and set it aside. She was going to need all her concentration if she were to find the young man based on their brief acquaintance. "I'm going to try and get a location on Henri," she said. "I only hope we can find him before he trades that book away."

"How are you going to do that, dear?" Marion nearly sprang out of her chair when inspiration struck. "Oh, are you a medium as well?"

"She's quite well endowed with the gift of shadow vision, madame," Alexandre explained, "but her aura suggests it does not extend to necromancy. Lucky thing, that."

Jean-Paul took a step back and whispered, "*Maman*, let her concentrate."

Marion made a motion of locking her lips, then grinned and waggled an eyebrow in anticipation.

Elena closed her eyes and concentrated on the stone she'd given Henri. If it was still in his possession, she might be able to track it. Her mental vision narrowed until she felt herself go under, reaching, stretching to find a connection with the young man. When nothing surfaced, she tried visualizing his face, but without an emotional connection to draw her in, as there had been when she'd been desperate once before to find Jean-Paul, it was no use. The young man may have thrown the stone in the gutter for all she knew. She reeled herself back in and shook her head.

"I can't find him without something more personal of his, something with a strong connection to his psyche."

"Is the boy an artist by any chance?" Marion asked from her seat in the chair.

Now who was the psychic? "Yes, he is. How did you know?"

Marion bent forward. "I know I'm not supposed to speak—tick-a-lock—but I couldn't help noticing the satchel at my feet. A quick peek inside revealed a few sketches. One of them is signed Henri Perez. Is that our man?"

"His portfolio! He left it. Oh, Marion, thank you."

Elena took the leather satchel, knowing how much the young man's drawings meant to him. She hugged the sketches to her chest and tried again. This time her mind zoomed through the shadow world, emerging in a strange underground room with open bottles of gin on the table. A bronze statue of a woman with bat wings appeared in a corner, and a human skeleton propped up in an open coffin leaned against the wall. Several men had abandoned their drinks to circle around a young man holding a small silver revolver.

Henri. She'd found him. If only she understood where he was.

When Elena was conscious again, she had no more faith that they'd find him than before as she relayed the scene she'd discovered herself in.

"Describe everything you saw," Jean-Paul insisted.

"It must have been an illusion. There were caskets as tables. Bat wings on a woman. A skeleton and player piano. It makes no sense."

"Only to those who don't move within the city's social circles." Marion's eyes lit up with mischief. "There are marvelous adventures to be had in these sparkling champagne times we're living in, if one knows where to look."

"*Maman*, you know this place?"

"Of course. Who doesn't know about Hell's Mouth? It's perfectly situated at the base of the butte." She swung the young man's satchel on her arm. "We'll take my carriage, shall we?"

CHAPTER THIRTY-TWO

Yvette hadn't thoroughly passed out from the pain of squeezing through the metal bars, but there were squidgy moments she couldn't quite recall. Like how she'd ended up sitting on a damask fainting couch inside a rather exclusive perfume shop. Surrounding her were urns brimming with botanical oils, dried rose petals scattered on counters, and glass shelves showcasing dozens of delicate bottles, not unlike the one tucked inside her bodice for safekeeping. The heavenly scent worked like a transfusion to revive her, replacing the dank catacomb air in her lungs with the flowery scents of jasmine and lavender.

"They gave up and turned around almost immediately once they thought they'd hit a dead end," said a woman in a powder-blue suit. The pearl buttons on her jacket alone were worth more money than Yvette had ever earned in her lifetime.

"Thank you," she said and tried to stand. "I should probably go." But as soon as she said it, she wobbled back down onto the sofa.

"That was a very brave thing you did back there. Most *Fée* wouldn't have attempted to slip through iron bars."

Fée?

"The iron left several burns on your left arm, but this salve should help take the sting away." The woman dabbed a lavender cream on Yvette's skin. The balm dissolved immediately into a shimmering coating where several blisters oozed, red and angry.

"You're a perfume witch."

The woman nodded. "Priscilla Gérin. This is my shop. I was working on a secret new scent when you burst through my cellar. It's none of my business, of course, but I assume they were trying to trap you for profit?" She dabbed at a burn on Yvette's neck. "Why some men think they can treat the *Fée* like they're magic tokens to be cashed in is beyond me."

A flicker of fear darted across Yvette's thoughts, the sort that told her she was on the verge of a truth she wasn't yet ready to know. "Why do you keep calling me one of the *Fée*?"

Priscilla put the cork back in the jar of salve and did a quick up-and-down glance at Yvette. "Did you hit your head too? Poor thing. Can you tell me what day of the week it is? Who the prime minister is?" When Yvette's lip began to curl into a snarl, the witch pulled back. "You're serious? I just assumed . . . I mean . . . you transmuted earlier." She stared at Yvette as if she ought to understand. "You illuminated. Well, mostly. My grand-mère was a half-*Fée* witch too."

Half-Fée *witch?*

"When my sister and I were little, she'd illuminate in front of us as a treat when we stayed at her house in the summers. Alas, I have none of her talent for affecting glamour. Only those with enough *Fée* blood can do that."

A half-*Fée* witch? Is that what she was? "But there are no fairies here anymore. Isn't that what everyone always says?"

"Oh, I don't think they'd ever truly leave for good. There are pathways for those who want to come and go."

The news stunned Yvette so that she stared dumbfounded, her hand over her mouth. Did that explain the strange code in the book that no one understood? Was her mother a *fairy*? A quick memory of a woman bathed in rapturous light flashed in her mind, followed by a glittery chill that she was seeing a reflection of her true self for the first time. *Your kind*, her captor had said. Is that what he'd meant? And the goblins too?

"Your grand-mère, did she come from this other place?" Yvette asked. "Do you know if they speak their own language there?"

"It would have been her mother who came from the realm of the *Fée*. But, yes, my grand-mère knew the fairy names for all the flowers and trees."

"I have to go," Yvette said. Despite the wave of dizziness that came over her, she stayed on her feet. "I'm sorry I can't repay you for everything you've done for me."

"Nonsense. Besides, your friend there already paid me."

Friend?

The black cat came out of his hiding place beneath the fainting sofa. He purred and rubbed his cheek against Yvette's leg.

"Oh, Monsieur Whiskers, you waited for me." Yvette scooped the cat up in her arms, despite his prickly reservations, and hugged him to her chest, burying her face in his furry collar. Unsurprisingly he smelled of rose, hibiscus, and a dose of musk after crawling around the floor of the perfume shop.

"Thank you, mademoiselle." She waved to Priscilla as she carried the cat out the door. "Thank you, a thousand times, for everything."

Out of sight of the glowy eye of the streetlights, she set the cat down on the pavement and explained the predicament. The book, *her book*, was out there somewhere in the night. Now, more than ever, she suspected it was the key to something spectacular. Something people were willing to lie, steal, and abduct a young woman for. The key to what, she still didn't know. But if the men in the maze were to be believed, Rings had somehow gotten his hands on her book and was leveraging himself for a trade. Which meant something had gone terribly wrong with Elena and Alexandre to have lost possession of it.

"Right, Monsieur Whiskers," she said, thinking of the quickest way to get to the cabaret district without being seen. "It looks like this half-*Fée* witch needs to pay hell a visit."

The cat mewed and shook out his fur. Yvette found herself with enough coin in her pocket for a fare on the Metro, so she took off for the nearest underground station, the feline doggedly trotting behind at her heel.

CHAPTER
THIRTY-THREE

"Put the gun away, Henri. We're all friends here." Rings held his palms up in a half-hearted plea for a truce. "We put the word out we've got the book, like you said after you busted in here. The buyer will show up soon enough, with the girl, and then we can all go our merry way."

"You tried to have me killed. I don't think I'll be taking orders from you anymore."

"Yeah, funny about that." Rings nudged his chin toward the young man in the back tearing at his thumbnail with his teeth. "Theo swears he was attacked by some voodoo woman and her pet dragon. Dirty trick, sticking a man full of drugs in a fight like that."

Theo shrank inside his coat near the bat-woman statue. Rather than dispute the claim and convince any of them about the power of witches, Henri owned it, keeping the gun pointed at Rings's chest. "And still not as dirty as leaving one of your own to bleed out in an alley."

Rings shrugged off the accusation as a waiter dressed in an undertaker's coattails and top hat, his face painted deathly white, entered the room with a tray loaded with drinks and sloshing a bucket full of used mop water. Any regular customers wanting to sit in the Underworld had been redirected to the two upstairs rooms of the cabaret while Rings and his gang awaited the outcome of the trade. And though Henri was at a standoff against everyone in the room, there was no reason they couldn't have a shot of gin to calm the nerves and keep the mood even. After all, he only had three bullets. A happy hostage was less likely to jump out of desperation or false heroics.

"Any word?" Rings asked the waiter as the man set the bucket down at Henri's side as requested.

"*Non*, monsieur. I'll be sure to escort your guests in when they arrive."

"There, see, everything's moving along just like I said it would." Rings shoved a glass toward Henri. "May as well enjoy yourself while we wait."

The drink was tempting, but he was alone in a room crawling with slippery snakes. One false move and he'd be swallowed whole. He had no doubt the others were armed and would shoot him on the spot if he dropped his guard for even a second. Best to keep a steady hand on the gun aimed at the boss's heart. What he would do *after* the buyer came for the exchange, he had no idea. That was the problem with acting on impulse.

"It's a lot on the table to risk for a scrawny gutter rat like Yvette." Rings scratched at the stubble under his chin, then glanced back at Theo. "Then again, he took a peek and says you had a dozen drawings of her in your bag. Can't say I hadn't thought of jumping on that tender flesh myself some days. She's used, but there's still plenty of wear left on that girl, that's right."

He winked at Henri like they were men talking over the tread left on a set of tires. The tactic almost worked. Henri wanted to bloody the man's nose until the cartilage crunched under his fist, but he knew that was the game.

"I always did take you for a double-crosser," Rings said, his voicing rising dramatically. "Stealing from the one person who protected you, who kept you safe when the streets could have chewed you into a thousand pieces. I gave you your pitiful life, and now you want to rob me of my reward. You work for me. You owe me!"

Henri tightened his grip on the gun. He hadn't thought of taking the money too. His only concern had been getting Yvette free, but the idea was sounding better and better the more the old thief spoke. Might be enough money in the deal to make a proper run for it. Maybe take a steamer across the ocean and start over. Fresh canvas and all that.

No use in tipping your hand, though. "Finish your drink, Rings."

The men sat in tension-wire silence, everyone's eyes on the gun as they sipped their gin, until the lights quickly flickered. That was the signal. The buyer was on his way down. The mood immediately shifted into high-stakes uncertainty. Henri patted his jacket again and removed the book with his free hand. He readjusted his grip on the gun, his hand grown damp from sweat, ready to fire if he must.

Three bullets. Christ almighty.

"Stand up and turn around," he said to Rings. The crew of thieves lurched in their seats as Henri pressed the nose of the gun to the back of the man's head. "A little extra insurance so no one gets the wrong idea."

A moment later a trio of men entered the subterranean room. One with a flat cap and devil mask, one in a bowler and skull mask, and one wearing the hooded robe of the grim reaper, as if playing their part in the cabaret's hellish theme. So, the monsieur did not wish to be identified. A waste of time. Henri couldn't care less who he was or why he wanted the book. All he wanted was Yvette. But where was she?

Even from behind, he could tell Rings sported a devilish grin on his face, knowing the odds had heavily tipped in his favor. "Greetings, monsieur. I'm sorry I cannot shake your hand, but, as you can see, we have a small situation we're dealing with."

The reaper remained silent. His escorts pulled their weapons.

"Easy," Henri said. "I know you don't care if I blow this man's brains all over the floor. Don't really care myself. But I do think you want this little treasure all in one piece." Henri dangled the book over the bucket of mop water. "Any move toward me and it goes in the slop. Shoot me, it goes in the slop. Then good luck reading the message from fairyland."

The reaper betrayed a second of panic at the mention of "fairyland," nearly lunging forward to save the book. Instead, he held up his hand, motioning his men to back off and put their guns away. So, it really did have a secret message in there about fairies. That was something to bargain with.

"You're right," the reaper said. "We can settle this like gentlemen."

"Easy enough. Show me Yvie and the money you were going to give to Rings, and we'll call it a day well spent." Henri grinned, cunning and sharp.

"Backstabbing bastard." Rings shook his head like a desperate man looking for a way out and swore he should have killed Henri himself.

Henri waited for one of the men to go get Yvie, but no one moved. Which meant they didn't have her. Either they hurt her too badly to bring her, or worse, killed her. Or she got away. Knowing Yvie, he was banking on the latter.

"The girl isn't actually *here*." The reaper was trying to cover over the truth the same way the monger on rue de Giardi tried passing off his day-old fish as fresh caught. "Come with us. A gentleman's agreement. You give me the book, and I'll take you to Yvette."

"And the reward money for finding the book? Have you left that behind as well?"

When the reaper didn't answer, Henri let the book slip an inch through his fingers, catching it by the corner at the last second.

"Yes, yes, I have the money!"

Henri tapped the end of the pistol against Rings's head. "How much he tell you he's going to bring?"

"A thousand." Henri tapped the pistol again, only harder. "Okay! Ten thousand."

The men in the room gasped. Rings had obviously been lying to them about the amount of money they were waiting on. Everyone agreed the boss got the bigger cut, but cheating your own men out of their share? That's a good way to get your throat slit in an alley when you're coming around the devil's asshole.

"Is that right, boss? You brought ten thousand with you?" The reaper affirmed it with a slow nod under his hood. "Tell you what," Henri replied. "You put that money out where I can see it, and I'll consider your proposal."

No one moved. Henri thought he'd overplayed his hand. But then the reaper reached inside his robe and drew out a thick leather wallet the size of a mackerel and set it on the coffin table. Henri had never seen such a fat take. Of course, that got him wondering. If a man like the reaper, after dealing with petty thieves inside a shabby cabaret, was willing to give up ten thousand cash for a book no one can read, one had to wonder what the payoff was.

In the end, Henri's practical street-thief nature took the route it knew best.

"Done," he said and tossed the book over the reaper's head. Like a bump-and-run on the street, he used the misdirect to swipe the wallet and dash for the exit.

Right away he faced a split-second decision: go up the back stairs and be pinned in the alley at *le trou du cul du diable* or break for the street up front and be gone for good.

With youth and adrenaline pumping his legs, Henri ran for the front stairs of Hell's Mouth.

CHAPTER
THIRTY-FOUR

Marion Martel was not taking refusal well.

"What do you mean it's off-limits? I wouldn't advise getting in the habit of turning away one of your best customers."

"I'm sorry, madame, but the Underworld is closed at this time for a private party." The waiter, dressed in the costume of a red devil with a pointed tail and horns, made it clear he would no longer argue the point.

"Very well, we'll take Hell."

"This way, madame."

Elena and Jean-Paul exchanged matching raised eyebrows as Alexandre took Marion's arm and escorted her down the hall.

The corridor glowed orange and black, as if the fires of Hades licked at the customers' heels. A few feet down it led to a room similarly outfitted with fat candles that shone behind orange theater gels in the shape of flames. Sconces had been stuffed with a light sulfur-infused incense that added the distinct scent of damnation, while a piano played a sardonic tune, mocking the listener with the occasional off-key note. And yet Elena observed how everyone seemed to be having a great time. Dancing and drinking and devil-may-care laughter filled the room with the atmosphere of a doomsday party. Even Marion swayed to the music as she ordered a bottle of champagne from the red devil.

"*Maman*, we're not here to entertain ourselves."

"I know, dear. But I always order a bottle of the bubbly. It's expected."

Jean-Paul shook his head in disbelief at his mother. "How often do you come here?"

"Oh, once or twice a week." She picked up a menu designed to look like a Ouija board and coyly fanned herself with it. "It has a certain energy I find exhilarating."

Six months ago, Jean-Paul likely would have stormed out of such a place, scorning any homage to the paranormal. Life with Elena had opened his eyes to other worlds, ones he was not so quick to dismiss anymore. He turned to her with a resigned look and asked, "Is she right? Is there supernatural energy here?"

For the most part the cabaret was a mortal gathering place for vice, but in the corners, under the eaves, and in the wispy cobwebs suspended from the ceiling, a thread of magic wove itself into the atmosphere, imbuing the space with a tinge of genuine sorcery. "There are witches here. But I don't think we need to worry about them. Their energy is relaxed, cheerful."

"And drunk," Alexandre said, pointing at a man and woman in the corner laughing at an imp brandishing a lit sparkler as though it were a sword. "You can tell by the warp in their auras. But there is another witch somewhere nearby. The energy is much sterner."

"We need to find a way downstairs," Elena said. "Now."

"What fun! The caper continues," Marion said, clasping her hands.

Before Jean-Paul could stuff his mother's enthusiasm back in the bottle, a commotion erupted in the corridor between Heaven and Hell.

"Stop that man!"

Elena jumped from her seat. "I think I just saw Henri."

More than a scuffle, the disturbance outside Hell was quickly turning into an all-out brawl. In the middle of it stood Henri, surrounded by four thuggish-looking devils in cheap suits. Were they after the book? Henri pushed off one man and made it a step closer to the door before a second one dragged him back and punched him in the stomach.

"Jean-Paul, we have to do something," Elena said as a crowd closed in on the scene.

"Short of aiming a fire hose, I'm not sure what I can do against a mob."

And then they had him. Henri was pinned against the front door. His nose was bleeding and his right eye had begun to swell. Before Elena's mind could land on the right words for a spell, a burly sort of man parted the crowd. He got to the middle of the floor and reached down to pick up a pistol. Each of his fingers was adorned with a ring. The rag-and-bone man.

"Looks like you dropped something, boy." The man made sure to point the gun at Henri's face as he spoke. "But you always did have clumsy fingers when it came to the game."

"He was always better than all of us, and you know it."

Atop the stairs, Yvette stood outside the room to Heaven. She glared at Rings without a hint of fear or forgiveness in her eyes. The onlookers bent their necks to see who had spoken, then held their hands over their mouths in wonder as she began to glow ever so softly.

"No, Yvie! Go. Get out!"

Yvette ignored Henri's plea as she walked down the stairs, her skin pulsing.

"Your boyfriend here sold you out." The heads of the crowd turned in unison back to Rings. "Led us right to you. Then he stole your book and tried to backstab me and the crew."

"Let him go."

"He's got to pay the price, Yvette. Those are the rules." Rings pressed the gun to Henri's forehead. He grinned at Yvette, then pulled the trigger. No hesitation, no warning, just a squeeze. A woman screamed, and a beat later another laughed when the barrel on the gun began playing "Clair de Lune" as it turned slowly around like the drum on a music box.

"You threatened me with a toy?" Rings lashed out, hitting Henri on the temple with the butt of the gun. The young man crumpled to the floor as Rings threw the useless weapon at him.

Yvette exploded with light, illuminating as if she were powered by a thousand electric bulbs.

The crowd cheered, ready to be entertained. "A *féerie!* Oh, bravo."

Yvette jumped off the bottom stairs, confronting Rings and his crew as they bent down to rifle through Henri's pockets. Her body shone even brighter until the men were forced to back away and shield their eyes with their arms. When they were nearly blinded from her luminescence, she focused her energy into a fine point, like a knife extended from her hand, and aimed it at Rings's heart. Elena, fearing Yvette was about to run the spike through the man's chest, rushed to intervene, but then the young woman stopped her advance.

Rings stared at Yvette wide-eyed, as if searching for an electrical cord that might explain the light shining off her. "How are you doing that?"

"On your knees." She shouted with the fury of an angry goddess, taking Elena by surprise at the ferocity in her voice.

The men, mouths utterly agape at what they were witnessing, fell to the floor at her command. Yvette trembled as she held on to the swell of energy. The crowd, though still convinced they were watching a performance, took an instinctive step back. Elena wished to retreat as well, but this was no fairy play. The intensity of the young woman's energy continued to build. She feared Yvette had channeled something she didn't yet have the experience to control.

"Yvette, can you feel the wave of energy flowing beneath your grip?"

The girl nodded, uncertain at first, but then more firmly. "Yes, I think so, but it's getting harder to hold."

A man tried to run. Yvette's hand followed him, zapping him off his feet as if struck by a live wire. Rings and his remaining crew shrank to the floor and covered their heads.

"I need you to breathe gently." Elena took a step closer to Yvette. "Ask the power inside you to subside. Summon the All Knowing for help, if you need to. Focus on lowering the flow of energy so we can help Henri."

Yvette nodded and took three shallow breaths. The funnel she'd created crackled and arced, sending random sparks shooting out of its center.

"Deep breaths, Yvette. Inhale, exhale."

Out of the corner of her eye, Elena saw Jean-Paul and Alexandre splash the contents of an ice bucket on a stray spark that had landed on a tablecloth, burning a hole.

Yvette scrunched her face in concentration and inhaled, filling her lungs. The light quivered as it began to lose its centrifugal force. She took another breath and another until the light storm softened into a radiant glow.

Once the threat had receded, the men got to their feet and ran as if making their exit from the stage. The crowd clapped and cheered before returning to their champagne and fantasies in Heaven and Hell, the show apparently over.

As the mob dispersed, Yvette rushed to where Henri sat on the floor, cradling his head.

"You got away," he said when she knelt beside him. "I knew you would." Then he noticed the strange burn marks on her arms. "Are you all right? Did they hurt you?"

"I'll be all right. Always am," Yvette said, absently rubbing the marks on her arms. "But it looks like you got popped a good one."

Elena joined them, returning Henri's satchel of drawings to him, and dabbed the blood from the young man's forehead with a borrowed napkin. "I'd rather not make a habit of patching you up twice in one day," she said, surveying the damage on Henri's face.

"Is he okay? That's a lot of blood."

"He'll have a lump on his head for a day or two, by the look of things, but I think he'll recover."

Elena asked a waiter for a glass of water and some mint leaves from the bar to soothe Henri's wound, then turned her focus to Yvette's arms. So, it was the comté after all, recalling what Isadora had said about Yvette's mother and her need to wear gloves in public.

Elena looked at Henri. "Did you give him the book?"

"Wait, *my* book?" Yvette's skin radiated noticeably, rising with her anger. "Was Rings telling the truth?"

"No, I . . ."

"Then what's that money for?"

Henri saw the wallet sticking out of his pocket. He tucked it away, then patted his jacket on both sides, growing more worried, as if something was missing. "I didn't, I swear. I gave him another book. I took two from the shop, but the real one, the one with the feather in it. It's gone. It was here in my pocket, I swear. It must have fallen out during the scuffle."

"You tried to double-cross him?" Yvette paced with worry. "Oh, Henri, he's desperate for that book. He thinks it holds the key to some fortune he had stolen from him. When he figures out you gave him a dummy, he'll be back. He loves throwing fire around."

"He's a fire witch?" Elena searched over the heads of the people for the exit. "We've got to go. All of us."

Henri ignored her, crawling across the floor to search for the dropped book. As people continued to mill about at the bottom of the stairs, patting him on the back and congratulating him on his performance, he stretched his arm out to feel behind the statue of a half-goat, half-man figure. His fingers came up with the tossed revolver but no book. He was just about to search behind an oversize funeral urn when the stairs from the Underworld exploded with light. A blaze of green fire churned in the air, as odorous and malevolent as anything the decor had tried to replicate of hell.

The walls caught fire, and no one mistook the flames as part of any *féerie* play.

CHAPTER
THIRTY-FIVE

The eerie glow of green flames pulsated as they shot out, striking a second wall and setting it afire. Even a mortal's dim perception of magic appreciated there was only death to be found from sticking around to see what would happen next. Shrieks of panic ensued, followed by a rush for the exit.

"He's here," Yvette yelled. "We've got to get out or he'll kill us all."

Smoke thick with the smell of sulfur and brimstone snaked through the hallway.

And yet.

Elena watched the flames lick the walls, climbing, searching, and yet not actually devouring the structure. The flames appeared to singe the wallpaper here and there, yes, but it was spellfire. A sorcerer's trick. The smoke was real, an added touch to sell the illusion and empty the place of witnesses, but the fire had no appetite.

Elena stuck her hand in the flame. "It's only a spell. The comté isn't going to do anything that might destroy the book."

"Where's Henri?" Yvette darted in and out of the corridor, covering her mouth against the stench. "He was just here."

Elena squinted through the smoke, finding it harder to see or breathe. They had to leave soon or the place really would become a death trap.

"Elena, we can't stay any longer," shouted Jean-Paul as he watched his mother and Alexandre rush toward the exit.

"We have to find Henri." Elena poked her head inside Hell while Jean-Paul checked behind the giant funeral urn one more time. Her eyes watered and her lungs burned as she called out for the young man. "Damn the book, Henri. It isn't worth anyone's life."

Just when she didn't think she could swallow another breath of smoke, Henri ran out of Hell holding up the book. "Found it!" he shouted triumphantly. Yvette and Jean-Paul joined them and ran for the door and the sweet promise of fresh air. At the exit, a ball of flame burst in a shower of green sparks and black smoke. When the haze settled, the comté appeared before them in a black robe, like a cheap magician in a disappearing act. Two devils stood at his side, pointing pistols while he balanced a ball of green flame in his hand.

"And then all the rats ran for the door," the comté said. He tossed the ball of fire in the air. Behind them, new flames leaped ten feet high, only these were no illusion. Real heat from the fire pressed against their backs, lifting the hair at their collars and cutting off their only other way out.

"What do you want?" Yvette screamed.

"The book, obviously." The comté narrowed his eyes at Henri. "Now, or I will bring the roof down on all of you."

Henri shook his head, stubbornly refusing. The floor trembled as a green flame leaped up behind him, scorching the back of his jacket as he ducked to evade the heat. He slid the book out of his pocket, looking from it to Yvette, not sure what to do. He held it out toward the flame.

"Henri, no! It's the only thing I have left of my mother."

The comté stretched his hand out, green light arcing, ready to leap from his fingers. "Give me the damn book or I will burn her!"

"Let him have it," Elena said when Henri threatened to hold the book closer to the fire.

Yvette fumed. "Are you crazy? I'd rather see it burn."

"You don't need it anymore," Elena said, imparting enough calm so Henri and Yvette would trust her. It was the only way. "You know who you are, Yvette. You know what you were meant to be. That's what you wished for, and now you know. You're Cleo's daughter. One of the *Fée.* No matter what, you were given that much."

"But . . ."

"We need to give him the book, Yvette."

Yvette's face perspired from the rising heat. Elena could see her struggling, but then the young woman nodded. She grabbed the book from Henri and shoved it at the comté. "Here, and I hope you choke on it," she said.

"At last." The comté, teeming with the bloated euphoria of triumph, waved his hand. "*Extinxit ignem.*" The archaic spellwords dowsed the fire and cleared the air of the lung-stinging smoke. And though that immediate threat was extinguished, his two devils kept their guns pointed while the comté greedily licked his finger and peeled back the first page to check for authenticity. He wet his finger again, the same as he had the first time Elena was introduced to him, and turned another page.

"There should be seven pages with gold lettering," Elena said, encouraging him to check them all. "We had only begun to decipher them. But perhaps you already know how to do that?"

"Of course I do," he snapped before turning another page. "I've spent eighteen years waiting and preparing for this moment."

"So you could rob a young woman of her one and only tenuous connection with her family?"

"If her mother wasn't such a coward, she could have visited anytime."

Yvette exchanged a look of confusion with Elena. Was it possible? Did he know where her mother was? Was she still there, still alive?

"May I ask how you learned about the book?" Elena watched as the comté licked his finger and turned another page. "It was kept hidden in a wardrobe, forgotten for years." The longer she could keep him engaged, the better their chance of walking out the front door.

The delighted sneer returned as the comté peeled away another page.

"It may not surprise you to learn that artists often have a difficult time containing their egos. Especially when they think they're being clever. The man who painted the letters in this book made the mistake of boasting to a fellow painter, probably while drunk. It took a little 'persuading,' but he finally gave up the man's secret."

Henri's head jerked up. "Tulane's friend, Guillome. He was found dead soon after Tulane disappeared. The authorities said it was a suicide." Henri's face betrayed his newfound doubt.

So, he'd known all along the mother would find a way to communicate. He'd been waiting and watching for years for Yvette to claim the book the minute she was old enough. "You knew she'd receive that book on her sixteenth birthday," Elena said, watching his breathing as he studied the pages. "You sent a man to her room that night to find it."

The comté pushed back the hood on his robe and loosened his tie, his face damp with sweat. "Know your enemy, mademoiselle. The first rule of victory." He turned the last page. "The *Fée* have their quirks. The sixteenth birthday is significant. The age of independence, adulthood. She cost me three more years of searching and waiting when she murdered the man I'd sent."

"Good," Yvette said.

He looked up briefly. "You can blame her mongrel blood for her impertinence."

Elena noted the Magus Society ring on his pinkie finger, which she was certain he had not been wearing at the séance. "Until she was caught and put in jail. Then you had her. Only she escaped. Later you thought you could force me to give up her location by threatening my livelihood. Let me guess—the Minister of Records is a friend and fellow sympathizer."

The comté drummed his fingers against the back of the book, knowing exactly how the ring advertised his proclivities and associations. "Most would not prove so loyal to a murderess," he said.

"Perhaps not, which is why you needed to scare me into believing I was destined to meet my mother's same desolate fate." She shrewdly stared at his face, seeing now what he'd done. "The séance was a masterful display of ventriloquism, by the way."

"A simple voice illusion, which you so gullibly believed."

"Yes, but thanks to your ploy I was forced to explore my mother's craft more deeply," she said. "So many notions about poison I never would have considered, if it weren't for you."

He was beginning to catch on. His tongue darted over his teeth and his brow beaded with sweat. The comté coughed and pressed the sleeve of his robe against his neck. "You've done something to me."

"I'm not sure the All Knowing favors this endeavor of yours. You look a little peaked, Marchand."

"You've drugged me. With the book," he said and dropped it as if the pages might bite his hands off.

Sirens wailed from several streets away. Soon there would be a fire engine and certainly the police. But with the whiff of spellfire still floating on the air, there was a fair chance the Covenants Regulation Bureau would send a man to investigate the illegal use of magic against mortals too.

The comté slumped to his knees. Elena bent to pick up the book, careful not to touch the corners of the pages.

"You're not dying," she said. "It's merely a neurotoxin, of the batrachotoxin variety to be specific, an alkaloid embedded in the skin of certain frogs. Fortunately for you a milder version can be found on the feathers of a rare bird species from the tropics." She spread the pages of the book open and let the feather from the *apothicaire toxique* flutter out. "I happened to notice on our first meeting that tendency of yours," she said and licked her forefinger. "As a precaution I infused the book with a spell, in case we came to such an impasse. And here we are. The paralysis ought to be temporary, though I suppose I could have doubled the potency of the spell with a word or two. Lucky for you I'm a vine witch, monsieur, and not a *venefica* by trade. Despite your best efforts to change that."

"Shoot her," he replied before falling on his side, motionless.

"Boss?" The two devils lifted their masks, looking from Elena to the sound of sirens on the other side of the door. They lowered their guns a hair in indecision, and she snapped a ball of fire to life in her palm as a warning not to raise them again. After second thoughts, they stuffed their weapons in their jacket pockets and bolted for the basement, presumably to find a back way out.

The comté's glassy eyes stared up at Elena as the front door opened and a brigade of firefighters and police officers stormed the building.

"Elena, what should I do?" the girl pleaded.

Yvette. There was no time to run. No time to hide her. If the authorities recognized her, she'd be taken into custody. Eventually executed for murder. Unless.

Elena gripped Yvette by the arms. "You've got the blood of the *Fée* in you. You must use that power now. Let your charisma shine from within. Use your charm. Your guile. Manipulate with your allure, if you must. Glamour is part of the power your mother gave you. Use it, and we may yet see our way out."

CHAPTER THIRTY-SIX

Yvette braced herself as the fire brigade charged the front door to search for the source of the foul-smelling smoke still lingering in the cabaret. *Les flics* followed, waving their batons and ordering everyone out. She faced the men as they ran in, letting the fizzy, glowing sensation under her skin seep from her like moonlight the way Elena had said—eyes forward, a hint of a smile, and a slight drop of the hip and bend in the leg. Several of the police officers tipped their *kepi* hats at her and grinned as if mesmerized. She winked, and the men's faces lit up with hope and eager desire. "*Enchanté*," they said. She tried a more seductive smile, and the mortals practically melted into puddles of adoration. One of the firefighters removed his brass helmet with the feathered cockade and asked her and the others if they would kindly sit outside with the remaining witnesses. Sorry for the bother. And wasn't it just the loveliest of evenings, despite the fire?

Charm. Guile. Glamour. Yvette's body pulsed with the magic of the fair ones. She knew, if she desired it, she could lead a mortal down any path she chose—to greatness, to folly, even to death if she willed it. What kind of power was that? The sensation chilled her, and she had to go sit under the streetlights beside the others to settle her thoughts.

"If we're lucky, they'll let us go after giving our statement," Elena's man said as he leaned against a lamppost.

And then what? Could she leave the city? Escape and never return? Was her stolen wish fulfilled because her magic had been revealed? But what about her mother's book? The message inside? There was so much more to discover; she could feel it. The wish wasn't done churning its magic.

The cat, who had waited for Yvette at the back of the club after she'd climbed through the upstairs window to get inside Heaven, trotted out from behind a mailbox. He sidled up to her, rubbing his fur against her leg and purring like mad. His green eyes stared, insistent.

Alexandre, seated cross-legged on a bench, studied the animal from behind his spectacles. "That is a most unusual feline," he said.

"He's a stray, but he follows me everywhere."

Alexandre adjusted his position to get a closer look. "Out of curiosity, have you fed it?"

"When I can. Mostly I think he fends for himself. Why?"

"Any unusual good luck lately?"

Yvette smirked and shook her head slowly, waiting for the old man to catch up.

"Right, of course. It's been a challenging week for you, no doubt." He continued to stare as Yvette petted the cat. "A stray, you say? And yet he seems to be wearing a collar. An unusually decorative one as well."

With everything going on, Yvette hadn't given it much thought. He must have belonged to someone at some time, but the way he followed her around, she assumed he'd been abandoned like so many other strays that roamed the alleys and bridges of the city.

Moonlight caught on the silver collar. Just for a second, whether because of their talk or some other force, it glittered as if infused with magic. The old man noticed too.

"May I?" he asked and unclipped the collar's fastener. The cat purred softly in Yvette's arms as the shopkeeper inspected each link under the glow of the streetlight. "Good heavens," he said at last, the color draining from his face. "Elena, you need to have a look at this."

Alexandre waited for her to walk over, then let the collar dangle from his fingers to display each twinkling link under the streetlamp. Elena's mouth fell open at the sight.

"What? What is it?" Yvette strained to understand what they were seeing.

"Your friend has been hiding a secret." Alexandre pointed out the swirly decorative marks on one side of the link and a corresponding letter of the alphabet on the other. He pulled a lead pencil from his pocket and licked the tip as he set to work.

"You could have spoken up earlier," Elena said to the cat, who merely swished his tail.

"But what does it mean?" Marion asked, leaning in.

"It's the key," Elena said, opening the book between her and Alexandre. "It means we can translate the message Yvette's mother left her."

Yvette held the cat's face in her hands. "But how did *he* get it?"

"I'd say someone very much wanted for you to discover the message contained in that book and then sent this handsome whiskered fellow to make sure it happened."

Yvette added the idea to the pile of things already knocking her for a loop.

Meanwhile, Alexandre took the glass cake knife out of his pocket and glanced through it as he began marking out words to test the cipher. "It begins with 'Dearest One,'" he said.

It was happening. A message from her mother. Yvette began to glow with anticipation. Elena had to tell her to tone it down lest she attract the wrong sort of attention.

Down the street, firefighters carried the comté out of the cabaret on a stretcher. They'd soon confirm there'd been no fire, only smoke. Afterward they'd simply have to let everyone go. And then she could spend the rest of the night holding the book and rereading the message from her mother. Her mother! She wasn't a stray left alone in the world after all. She had a mother who cared enough to send her a letter.

Elena and Alexandre had jumped ahead to the pages with the gold lettering on them, thinking they'd been highlighted for a reason. With the aid of the cat's collar, they were able to work quickly and determine they were instructions of some sort.

Yvette was half listening to them argue over the direction of a curl of one symbol versus another when a man approached the comté's stretcher just as he was being loaded into the back of an ambulance. There was something familiar about the slouch of the man's hat, the shortened height, the full-moon face. When it came to her, shards of ice backed up in her veins.

Yvette turned away quickly. Behind her hand she pointed in the man's direction and whispered to Elena, "He's here."

Elena followed the direction of her finger and blanched at the sight. Inspector Aubrey Nettles of the Covenants Regulation Bureau. They were directly in his line of sight. If he recognized Yvette, she'd never be free again.

"What is it?" Jean-Paul asked, seeing Elena tense.

"Nettles. I knew he'd show up sooner or later."

"What do I do?" Yvette begged as a voice inside her whispered she could run. She always had.

CHAPTER THIRTY-SEVEN

Inspector Nettles took out his notepad and began jotting something down. The comté ought to be too rigid with muscle spasms to speak, but perhaps she'd fumbled the dosage. At any rate, she had to get the girl out of there before the inspector took notice.

Jean-Paul took Elena by the elbow to pull her aside. "I know we talked about this."

"I can't do it, Jean-Paul." She put her hand over his, pleading. "I'll sell potions from the back of a wagon. I'll leave the vineyard to you, but I can't do it."

He looked up at the night sky and shrugged. "Neither can I," he said and turned them around so that he shielded Yvette from the inspector's view with his body. "You've turned me into a sympathizer of witches and fairies, you know."

"It really is for the best, darling." Elena placed her hand against his chest, and even that brief contact with his beating heart set a course correction for her mood. She brightened and smoothed the front of her gown, ready for action.

"What can't you do?" Yvette asked, having overheard.

"Turn you in." Elena peeked over Alexandre's shoulder to check his progress. "The Minister of Lineage and Licenses stripped me of my vine witch status because of my family bloodline, though he's willing to renew it in exchange for me telling the authorities where to find you. Blackmail, pure and simple, done at the comté's behest to flush you out. But I couldn't do it. Not when you're on the verge of becoming everything you were meant to be."

"Oh," Yvette said, her face falling, seemingly at hearing her fate had rested in someone else's palm all this time.

Alexandre finished translating the instructions and cleared his throat. "Henri, where are Tulane's paintings kept on display?"

"At the Musée Couloir."

"Right. I think we need to be on our way," Elena said. "Before Nettles sees us or we lose our nerve."

Yvette scooped up the cat and grinned.

They escaped in Marion's cabriolet. Henri and Alexandre were forced to ride alongside the driver, but it proved a happy inconvenience, as Henri knew the quickest route through the city. Delivered at the foot of the *jardin* outside the museum, they hurried down the hedged-in sidewalk, darting swooning night moths busy dipping their proboscises deep into one flowery gullet and another. When they arrived at the door flanked by two enormous pillars, out of breath and restless with the vigor of rushing through the night air, no one anticipated the disappointment a single dead bolt could bring. They had forgotten about the time, too inebriated from the adventure to make it a concern.

"Closed?" Yvette sized up the metal hardware on the door.

"All this way for nothing." Henri stared up at the grand pair of doors, the ones he'd claimed to have walked through a hundred times. He slapped his hand against the thick oak.

"Careful, you'll alert the guards," Elena said.

"Iron or steel?" Yvette asked, wiping her hands together. "On the locks—iron or steel?"

"Steel, I think," Henri said. Jean-Paul agreed.

Yvette nudged Henri aside and placed her hand against the metal. "It doesn't burn," she said. With new determination she pressed her palm flat against the lock. "You keep your secrets, and I'll keep mine. Open for me, and we'll get along fine." The lock slid open. She looked over her shoulder at everyone and grinned. "Never fails."

"Good heavens," Alexandre said. "Are we really breaking and entering the Musée Couloir?"

"He has a point," Jean-Paul said. "There are priceless treasures in there. If we're caught, we could all go to prison. Perhaps we should return tomorrow during museum hours."

"Spoilsport." Marion pushed forward and tested the door. It creaked open slightly, daring them to enter.

In the garden, a flashlight beam swept the grounds.

"We can't turn back now," Marion said. "How will the girl ever know the truth about her parents? Her birthright?"

The six of them exchanged questioning looks. It was a criminal endeavor to be sure, one that would likely come with a steep price if caught. The decision wasn't to be taken lightly. They seemed to be on the verge of a common answer when the overwhelming scent of burnt citrus infiltrated the air. A cloud of incense settled between the giant pillars. From it a woman cloaked in flowing scarlet-and-gold garments emerged, eyes gleaming in the dark.

"Hello, Sidra," Elena said.

Marion sucked in a breath of astonishment.

CHAPTER THIRTY-EIGHT

"What are you doing here?" Yvette asked, waving away the lingering smoke in front of her face.

"We have come to the final entrails of your stolen wish, girl." Sidra swept past her, trailing the scent of lemon skins left to toast in the coals of a fire. She stared up at the heavy oak doors of the museum, pushed them wide open, then signaled everyone to follow in a way that made the gesture feel like an order.

The group followed within a cloud of smoke that encircled them like a veil. A guard passed in front of them, and they froze in fear. He gave the air a sniff, as if he'd caught an unusual scent, but then walked down the opposite hallway, unaware of their presence.

"Are we in a dream world?" Marion asked.

Sidra shushed the mortal and led them down a hall lined with columns the size of tree trunks and a great overhead arch from which a row of dimmed chandeliers hung. The walls featured life-size murals of famous battles done in heavy oil paints and mounted in gilded frames. Turning down another corridor, they walked among hazy water lilies, golden haystacks, and a vase full of droopy sunflowers. Henri and

Marion both sighed and stared in wonder, modern disciples before the canvas altars. Finally, Sidra walked them up a carpeted flight of stairs wide enough to drive two Metro trains side by side. On their right, they entered a square room with a single electric chandelier, a velvet bench, and a rope line strung in front of three paintings shimmering from the precious metals infused in the pigments.

"It's Tulane's room," Henri said and slipped his hand inside Yvette's. He pulled her away from the others to show her the first of the three paintings. "Here she is, Mademoiselle Delacourt," he said. The woman in the painting was kneeling in a field of flowers, her face tipped up and smiling as a man in a fanciful robe kissed her cheek with the passion of someone in the throes of love. Beside it was another painting featuring the same woman, but where the other showed passion, this one depicted the serene love of a mother and child lying on a bed of green grass. Flowers sprouted like halos atop their golden heads.

"Do you think that's my mother?" Yvette asked. "And . . . and me?"

Henri squeezed her hand and took her to stand before the third painting. This time the woman's eyes were closed as golden tears streamed down her flawless face. As with the others, a hint of crushed gemstones glittered within the painting.

"It's a spell," Elena said. "To mesmerize the eye." The vine witch held her hand out as if testing the air. "I'd wager it's the same shimmering energy as at Le Maison Chavirée." Elena looked at her then with a strange expression of concern. "We didn't have a chance to tell you yet. Tulane. He's your father, Yvette. He and your mother ran to get away from the comté."

"My father painted these?"

Seeing the paintings in person made the hollow space inside Yvette's chest sink with longing. She wanted to run her fingers over the gloss of the paint, feel the texture of the canvas, sense the magic on her skin, and know that her parents had once held the same picture in their hands, but Henri held on tight.

"There's an incantation in the instructions," Alexandre said. Behind him the jinni sealed the entrance to the room with a smokescreen, making them invisible to any mortal passersby. "I believe you are meant to speak it before the paintings."

"Me?" Yvette took the paper Alexandre had transcribed the message on. "Now?"

"There's no time to waste. Simply read the words out loud as written." Elena spoke softly, with an aura of reverence. "Visualize your power as you speak. Open your heart. The All Knowing will see your intentions and help you attain the thing you seek."

The thing she sought?

Yvette stepped up to the painting of the couple in the midst of their kiss. She studied the faces, imagining the people behind them seeing her as a grown woman for the first time. For a moment she lost her nerve, her knees cut out from under her by shame at the things she'd done to survive as a child left behind. Resentment began to show its teeth, but she shuttered the emotion away. She hadn't come this far to turn heel at the first sign of discomfort. She faced the painting, opened her heart, and read the words on the piece of paper.

"Feather, flower, quarter moon, offered with a mournful tune. Dragonflies and threads of gold, messengers of the gods of old. Affix your wish and let it soar, crack wide the light beyond the door."

She waited expectantly, her heart racing and her palms sweating. She listened for a presence in the room, for a voice to speak.

But there was nothing. No whoosh, no tingling, no instant parents. Just one more disappointment.

"Apparently I can't even do a spell that was written for me," Yvette said, grinding her jaw to keep from crying.

"If I may." Alexandre asked to see the paper again. "It's possible in our rush to interpret the words, we missed the meaning."

Elena joined him and then slapped her forehead, cursing her limited vision. "Yes, of course. It isn't merely an incantation. It's also a list of elements for the spell."

"Precisely." Alexandre tapped his finger on the first line. "I believe in addition to speaking the words, you are to gather the items and present them. Fairies do love an offering."

Yvette took the paper back, studying it. "But I haven't got any of this stuff."

Marion spoke up first. "I believe it called for a feather," she said and plucked the ostrich plume from her hat. "You may have mine."

"And I have something that should do for the flower." Elena reached in her purse and produced a handful of dried rose petals she'd collected on her first day in the city.

"A promising start," Alexandre said.

Jean-Paul spoke up next. "Hold on. I may be able to provide a suitable moon." The others cast a doubtful eye, until he unclasped the moon-and-star cuff links that had been his father's.

Could they truly have all they needed to cast the spell? Yvette felt a flutter of optimism sail into her heart. But what of the other items? Music, a dragonfly, and a golden thread? Surely, they were out of grasp. Or so she thought, until Henri stood, grinning like he'd just stolen a fresh loaf of bread.

"I'm still feeling the rattle to my brain from being hit with this little trinket, but I know it plays a lovely tune when fired." He removed the revolver from his waistband, pointed the muzzle toward the floor, then pulled the trigger. "Clair de Lune" played softly as he handed her the musical gun.

She held all the items needed for the incantation in her arms, all but the last two.

"Your hair," Marion said. "It's as gold as any thread. Perhaps you could use that?"

"Yes, that may do," Elena agreed. "Given its stubborn resistance to being anything other than the color it is." She gently removed three long strands from Yvette's head, plucking them out by the roots.

They laid the items below the center painting. Remarkably, each person had contributed something from the list. Well, nearly everyone.

Alexandre seemed to realize he hadn't anything to offer. And then he smiled and tapped his walking stick twice against the floor. "Your dragonflies, mademoiselle," he said, and beside him Elena's dress fluttered to life. The reed grass swayed, the moon glowed softly, and the dragonflies beat their wings and lifted off the gown, shimmering and iridescent as they circled the room. "The dress had already been enchanted, though the little devils usually only fly around the shop at midnight. A small charm to confuse them about the time," he said.

Yvette held her finger out to draw a dragonfly to her. The largest of them landed, its wings cantilevering in perfect stillness. "That's everything, isn't it?"

"But what about her?" Marion asked, nudging her chin toward Sidra.

The jinni folded her arms. "The girl has already stolen everything she needed from me."

"The wish." Elena turned to Yvette. "Write down what you wished for," she said and tore off a corner from the paper they'd used to transcribe the spell. Henri provided a stick of charcoal, and, with it, Yvette wrote down the thing she'd folded inside her heart all those weeks ago. Then she rolled it up, tied it off with a filament of her hair, and attached it to the body of the dragonfly, who proved a patient messenger as he buzzed to sit on her shoulder.

"All right," Elena said. "Try it again."

Yvette took a breath, looked at all the items arranged on the floor before her, and read once more the incantation left for her in her mother's book. Again, she wasn't sure if it had worked, but then the dragonfly took off from her shoulder. He zoomed toward the painting, landing at the feet of the couple. There he crawled across the canvas, moving his wings in mechanical precision.

Slowly, as if thawing from a frozen sleep, the scene in the painting began to move. Yvette took a step back, scared of what she might have unleashed with her words. She looked to Elena for reassurance.

"It's only the wish and fairy magic binding together," Elena answered, though she, too, kept a wary distance.

The woman in the painting blinked as her eyes adjusted to the lack of light. Yvette glowed ever so softly, helping to illuminate the faces of those in the room. The man in the painting watched the dragonfly buzz over his head, then turned to smile at her.

"Daughter."

After all the years Yvette had secretly wished for this moment, she thought the word, once uttered, would fit her like a crown. Raise her up. Give her a sense of legitimacy, purpose. Instead it pinched like new shoes stiff from disuse.

The couple seemed to intuit her confused emotion. They straightened and stepped closer to the edge of the painting.

"We've been waiting for you for so long," the woman said.

Her mother.

"I've been waiting too," she said and took a curious step closer.

Her parents.

They stood before each other, searching for recognition. And it was there in the color of the eyes, the shape of the nose, and the roots of the hair. The bloodline tying them together showed in their faces, and yet they were just as far apart as they'd ever been, divided by a canvas of magic.

"Where are you?" she asked, reaching out to touch the frame.

"In my father's realm," said her mother. Behind her a stag leaped across the grass.

"Can I come in?"

"Careful with your words, Yvette," Elena said.

"Why?"

Her mother smiled softly. "She's right to warn you. Words spoken in the fairy realm carry the value of currency. Words have weight and meaning beyond the mortal world's understanding of language."

"Like promises?"

Her mother's brow tightened ever so slightly. The word had struck the way she'd intended it. Yvette might be ignorant about magic, but not about people. That's all she'd done her whole life—study others, trying to figure out who she belonged to. And she knew how to defend herself against them all.

"I never promised I would return."

"No, instead you abandoned me here. Alone." Having her parents stand there as if they were real, speaking as if they cared, and yet still a world away only churned up the pain she'd lugged around since she was a child.

"We didn't abandon you," her father said.

"Never," her mother said, stepping nearer to the painting's edge. "Please, we've been waiting so long to explain."

Yvette's mother studied the frame of the painting as if surveying its strength. Her father encouraged her, saying the magic was strong and the portal would hold. She stepped out of the painting, floating to the ground in a halo of fairy light. The image of her in the painting had not fully captured the luminescence of her skin, the grace of her movements, or the warmth of her eyes when she beheld Yvette in her gaze from five feet away.

Cleo Marchand, famous dancer, socialite, and runaway fairy mother, stood on the museum floor in full flesh and blood and magic. Her gown was made of blue taffeta and silk the color of a summer sky, with silver thread woven throughout so that it caught the light from every angle, no matter how bright or dim. She acknowledged those in the room with a greeting of hello.

"I must have seen her dance at the Palais Opéra a dozen times," Marion gasped, unable to contain her awe.

Tulane followed, stepping out of the frame and leaving behind the fanciful multicolored robe depicted in the painting. He emerged instead wearing a tailored black jacket and a pair of pressed trousers, white shirt buttoned up to the collar, and a tie that matched the blue sky of Cleo's gown. At the sight of him, the cat mewed and jumped into his arms, purring as he rubbed his head against the man's neatly trimmed beard.

Henri hugged his satchel to his chest, amazed into silence at the sight of his idol.

"I see you've met my cat, Minuit," Tulane said to Yvette. "I sent him back to watch for you. I knew he wouldn't let me down."

"You sent him to find me?" When her father nodded, she reached up and scratched the cat behind the ear. "Is he some kind of fairy cat?"

"He's a matagot."

That got Alexandre's attention. He approached and looked again at the cat through his pince-nez. "I suspected as much," he said, taking a closer look at the space above the cat's head. "They've a reputation for graciousness once they're offered hospitality."

Yvette recalled all the times she'd found a stray coin right when she needed it, and her heart opened just enough to let a crack of hope in. She didn't know how to feel toward the couple standing before her in their fine clothes and their shining charisma. They'd left her behind, so why come back now? Her curiosity proved stronger than her anger, and so, while Elena directed the others to take a seat on the velvet bench, she agreed to listen when her mother offered again to explain.

"I was a foolish girl playing a dangerous game when I first came to this world," she began. "We shine here too brightly for most mortals. They stare wide-eyed without knowing what it is that draws them to us. The glamour befuddles the average human quite easily."

Her mother touched a finger to the line on Yvette's jaw where the *étouffer* had stifled her magic. Yvette's skin warmed immediately, as if her cheek had been sun-kissed.

"They removed the scar," she said, pointing at Elena and Alexandre.

"It was done to protect her," Cleo said with a nod to the witches. "To hide her. I couldn't have her shining in this world without anyone to teach her how to control her power."

"Why didn't you take me with you?" Yvette asked.

Her mother's hand trailed from Yvette's cheek to the burn mark on her arm. "I see you've already met with his particular brutality."

Yvette rubbed her arm, chilled at the recollection of the iron band around her body. Her mother mimicked the gesture on her own arm as if in sympathy.

"Some men are born with the seed for cruelty in their hearts," she said. "It only grows with the passing of time, the roots reaching out to ensnare every part of their soul. But one can't always tell the extent a man's heart has been compromised until after they've been hopelessly trapped within his grip."

Cleo explained how she'd been allowed to travel freely between worlds since she was a girl, the privilege of a daughter of the fairy court. A weakness, she knew, but she'd grown enamored of the mortal world and the way she shimmered in it. The way men stared. The way women smiled in curiosity. How children laughed with joy when she patted them on the head. And how her body moved here, dancing and thrilling audiences with her fairy lightness. So she'd decided to stay, mimicking the mortal ways as best she could, accepting the attentions and support of an *abonné* while a young dancer at the ballet. She felt herself lucky that she'd attracted a witch who might at least understand her strange, luminous manner.

"It was only after he insisted that we marry that I glimpsed the sinister forest growing inside his heart."

As she spoke, Cleo walked around the room, breathing in the museum air, letting her fingertips linger on the frames of the paintings and the velvet ropes, as if reacquainting herself with the scents and tactile sensations of the mundane world.

"He despised mortals," she said, casting a brief apologetic glance toward Jean-Paul and his mother. "Especially any that had attained more than his family had. He resented the rules that prevented the magically endowed from profiting off their abilities. When his family's money ran out, he devised a spell that allowed him to steal from wealthy mortal families without leaving a trace for the authorities to track. Duplicity has always come naturally to him."

She stopped in front of Henri, taking in his appearance—the cut on his head, the bloodstain on his shirt, the familiar, protective glance he made toward Yvette. "He used a gang of street thieves to steal jewelry, cash, coin collections. And paintings," she said, shifting her gaze briefly back to Jean-Paul's mother. "He empowered them with a sort of urban camouflage so they could easily slip in and out of the upscale residences of his acquaintances unseen. Taught them how to open locks with a few cleverly crafted words. He needed the money to keep up appearances with his fellow *bon chic*, you see. But more than that, he enjoyed taking from mortals."

"He claimed *you* stole from him," Yvette said.

"The gold, yes." Cleo turned to face Yvette with the youthful grace of the dancer she'd once been, her back straight and poised. "He'd encountered a mortal woman whose wealth exceeded his by a thousandfold, her money kept, in part, in solid gold."

"Oh, I'll bet she means Madame Chevalier," Marion said. "Over a million in gold was taken. An absolute scandal."

"Yes, madame," said the fairy, and Marion blushed at the attention. "He was quite proud of that one. It was going to set him on a whole new path for squandering wealth he hadn't earned."

Tulane joined Cleo at her side. "By then we'd already met and fallen in love."

"But I had remembered that the woman's treasure was the result of my father's generosity. A fairy blessing bestowed on someone who had shown kindness by championing a city rose garden many years prior." Cleo smiled at Elena. "I believe you still have some of the petals drying in your purse. May they bring you luck."

"I'm sure they will," Elena said.

The fairy faced her daughter again. "I'd already bore you into the world when the gold was stolen from the woman, my darling. Marchand knew you were not his, but he refused to release me. He did not approve of divorce, though I was nothing more than a sparkling trinket on his arm to him. But one that he, and no one else, would possess. So, yes, when I learned of the stolen fortune, I saw an opportunity."

"You took the gold and chose your freedom over me."

"No!" The fairy's quick anger at the accusation rattled the frames on the walls. Her halo flashed bright and harsh, sending orbs of light to crash into the walls. "The gold was used to buy our way back into my father's realm, more than enough for the three of us to live out the rest of our days there in peace. Only . . ."

Cleo took a moment to let her anger recede, letting her inner light return to a shimmer. "Your grandfather is a fair man, but he is also a king. He cannot skirt the law, not even for his own blood."

King?

"He accepted the gold as our offering," Tulane said, setting the cat down. "He was pleased to have a fairy blessing returned rather than see it go to a thief, and so he allowed me to join Cleo and live within the realm, even though I carry only witch blood."

"But he would not allow you to join us, my darling," said her mother, eyes glistening. Yvette looked anew at the painting of the tears trailing down her mother's face. "Because you were born here in the mortal world, he would not let us make that choice for you, not until you were old enough to decide for yourself what magic you were willing to give up or to gain. And yet your father and I had already agreed to the pact. We were trapped by fairy law. *We* had to enter the realm and remain there, but you could not."

"The law is an ass," Elena said.

Tulane hid his laughter behind his hand. "I may have said something similar to Oberon," he said. "Still have the scar to prove it." He pointed to a spot behind his right ear.

Oberon?

Cleo approached Yvette and took her hand despite her daughter's initial resistance. "We were given seven days to place you. I could not risk Marchand finding my only daughter and holding her hostage, so I turned to an old acquaintance, one whose path had veered far from the comté's ambitious social circle. Yes, she was ill prepared to take on a child, let alone one who was a vessel of untapped magic, but Isadora was the best choice I could make with the time I had. And she promised to keep the book safe for you until your sixteenth birthday. According to fairy law, that was the day you would be old enough to decide for yourself."

"But he did find out," Yvette said, swallowing back tears of her own. "He sent someone. To find me. To find the book. He knew about the code inside. He knew it would lead to you. And the gold."

"Yes, he was always clever that way."

"I killed the man he sent. It's why I ran. Why I never knew about either of you. Or the book. Or about my scar. Until now. And now you've wasted your time. You waited all these years to learn your daughter is a murderer."

"Oh, no, Yvette, you mustn't think that." Tulane stroked her hair as one might calm an upset child.

"But it's true. They can arrest me at any moment. I'll go back to prison."

"Listen carefully," her father said. "Oberon granted me permission to cast a looking-glass spell on your sixteenth birthday. We wanted to be there when you learned about your legacy and made your choice. We were both watching from the mirror in your room, eager to reveal the message concealed in the book, when the man attacked you." Tulane took gentle hold of Yvette's shoulders. "You did not kill that man. It was *my* spell. I saw him hurt you, and my anger took over. Emotions are more mercurial in the fairy realm. I couldn't stop myself. *I* sent those scissors flying into that man's neck, not you." Tulane stepped back, pulling his hand down over his mouth as if he could wipe away the shame of admitting what he'd done. "I'm so sorry."

Yvette slumped down on the velvet bench, as if every truth that had been holding her upright until that moment had been removed. She'd lived with the idea that she was a murderer for three years. She'd believed it. Let it define her life and the shape of her thoughts. Who was she if not the girl who had murdered a man on her sixteenth birthday? The girl who had always been shit at magic? Who had run feral as a cat in the narrow lanes of the butte from the time she could button her own shoes?

But as she sat on the bench with Henri gripping her hand for support, her light eerily glowing as the power of the *Fée* continued to pulsate within her, she recognized the glimmer of truth. She was Oberon's granddaughter. Even as ignorant as she was about magic, she knew who the king of the goddamn fairies was.

And if the choice was hers to make, she'd take being an abandoned fairy over a failed witch any day.

"That's an interesting version of events," said a man's voice from the hallway in response to Tulane's confession. "After all, who doesn't love a good fairy tale?"

CHAPTER THIRTY-NINE

A short moon-faced man with wispy blond hair stood in the smoke-filled doorway, a wand poised threateningly in his hand.

"Did you think I hadn't seen you all scatter from Hell's Mouth?"

Tulane moved protectively in front of Yvette. "Who is this man?"

"Inspector Aubrey Nettles of the Covenants Regulation Bureau." Nettles flashed an official ID at the artist, one adorned with moons and stars above his name. "Interesting what you said about being the one to cast the spell that killed that man. I always did wonder how a young woman without any magical aptitude could have mastered a defensive spell in the very moment she needed it most. Alas, she already confessed to the murder."

"But I didn't know it wasn't me!" Yvette protested.

"Don't say another word to him," Jean-Paul warned. "Any of you."

The exchange made Nettles look sharply around the room. Among the fairy lights still floating from Cleo's anger, he spotted the jinni, also wanted as a fugitive. Sidra revealed her inlaid teeth, grinning at him like a predator about to take a bite. Before he could form the words for a custody spell, she poofed off in a cloud.

As the inspector's eyes searched the room for a telltale sign of which direction the mist traveled, warmth flooded the space between Yvette's breasts where she'd kept Sidra's bottle stashed for safekeeping. She hoped her alarmed expression would be taken for the fear of being arrested rather than surprise at having a jinni dive below her *décolletage*.

"You," he said to Yvette, "will not be so lucky. You're under arrest, and I'm taking you into custody." For emphasis, he pointed the wand at Elena and Cleo, as if warning them not to meddle with their magic.

"You will do no such thing," boomed a man's voice that resonated with the power of a rushing river cascading over heavy boulders.

The man stepped through the empty frame on the wall. But not a man, exactly. He was taller than most mortal men and wore a crown of antlers protruding from his temples. His robe, which swept behind him in a long train, appeared to be made of moss, with threads of russet and gold, azure and scarlet, woven throughout to mimic the colors of a forest floor. And yet it was no imitation. The robe was alive with tiny winged creatures that peeked out from behind leaves and flowers, rocks and lichen, as curious about the mortals and witches staring at the robe as they were about them.

"Father," Cleo said.

"King Oberon," Tulane said, unable to hide his surprise.

Both he and Cleo bowed their heads in deference to the King of the Fairies as he halted in the center of the room. Jean-Paul and his mother sat dumbstruck, hands over mouths, while Elena and Alexandre made the sign of the sacred pose before lowering their gaze. Yvette and Henri cowered, too, though she kept her eyes on Oberon, watching for which way the king's mood swung.

"*Merde*," Nettles said under his breath and swallowed.

"This charade has gone on long enough." Oberon moved so that he towered over the inspector. "It was amusing at first, but I've grown weary of this jape involving my granddaughter."

"Your . . ." Nettles stumbled for the next word before discovering his tongue did still work. ". . . granddaughter?"

One of the winged creatures from the robe flew up to Oberon's shoulder to whisper in his ear. The king nodded as he listened to the chittering. "I'm informed she is the three hundred and fifty-seventh of my descent."

"Er, congratulations," Nettles said, apparently unsure of where to point his wand any longer.

"Smacks of injustice, does it not, to arrest someone for a crime they did not commit?" The rest of the creatures in Oberon's robe tittered before darting back to the safety of their hiding places. "Indeed, I demand she be relieved of all incrimination in this dubious affair."

"But she's still a fugitive, and our court system requires—" Nettles began, but even he heard the absurdity of his statement as he faced the fairy king and so cut himself off.

"It's me you need to arrest," Tulane said, holding his wrists out before Nettles. "Let my daughter go, and I will confess to the crime before your court."

The inspector hesitated, as if watching for evidence of a trap. When he looked at Oberon and Cleo, there was no argument, no sign of outrage. "This is what you want?" he asked.

"No," Yvette cut in. "Of course not. Tell him." She looked at her mother, at Oberon, but their faces remained impassive as the inspector took out his rune cuffs and placed them on the artist's wrists, cutting off his access to magic. "You're going to let him get arrested? You have to do something."

"We've spoken of this day many times," Cleo said with a wistful look toward her lover. "He was always prepared to turn himself in to free you of this burden."

"But you can't. Not now. I've only just found you both."

"That, my daughter, is sometimes the price of love."

Love? All she felt was pain and confusion. Once on the verge of having all she'd wished for, she was now faced with the sacrifice of her father. If that was the price, it was more than she could bear.

She sensed Oberon's gaze upon her. His eyes were narrowed and his lips pursed, as if gauging the validity of her outburst. Oberon closed his eyes and inhaled, only to open them again in mild surprise. "This one's moods are astonishingly capricious."

"Oh là là, are you really going to stand there and let him turn himself in? They'll take his head if he's convicted!"

Oberon turned to Cleo in an aside. "She gets that spark from her grandmother," he said. He then looked at Tulane. "Were you aware of this deadly aspect of the law when you volunteered to turn yourself in for the sake of the girl's freedom?"

"It is the fate of all those convicted of murder in this country," Tulane said. "That or exile to a penal colony."

Monsieur Whiskers mewed and leaped into Tulane's arms despite the restraints. The artist held the cat close in the crook of his elbow and whispered in his ear to watch after Yvette.

"I do not like to measure one man's value against another's," Oberon said after a moment of contemplation. "There's a certain vulgarity in assigning worth to any individual life when each represents a piece in the mosaic of the whole." He approached Nettles. "And yet I find I can no longer accept the risk to this man's life, he whom I know as a good fellow, in payment for the murder of a man who sought first to do great harm to another that I love."

"But the law requires . . . ," Nettles began.

"The law is an ass," Oberon said to much snickering from his robe's hitchhikers. "Or so I am oft reminded." The King of the Fairies then walked up to Tulane, threw off his manacles without so much as a spoken incantation, and instructed the artist to take his place once more beside his daughter. "If exile be an acceptable punishment in the eyes of your law," he said to Nettles, "then you have my honor that this man will never again have the freedom to leave my realm, whereupon he shall be confined to a piece of land beside a river where the moonlight is just a little too harsh against the trees in autumn. He'll never be able to paint it with any satisfaction as long as he lives."

Nettles opened his mouth to explain. "But we have a process. A court system. The matter must be officially adjudicated."

Oberon's lip curled in a snarl eerily similar to Yvette's whenever she stared down an idiot in her path.

"I . . . I'll write up the report," Nettles said in defeat, picking up his broken manacles off the floor.

Oberon nodded as if the issue were settled. "I expect my grand-daughter to be fully exonerated in the matter. However, if your paper-pushing superiors in the Bureau have any objection to my decision concerning her father, they are free to send an extradition request to my representatives." The creatures in the robe again exploded in gales of laughter. "I'm sure they'll give it its due attention."

"Of course, Majesty."

Oberon, apparently grown bored with the trifles of mortals and witches, announced he was ready to return home for a good long walk beside a meadow. He gently tapped Cleo's chin when she thanked him, then told her it was time for Yvette to make her choice. "See that it is done," he said.

The King of the Fairies gathered his robe around his body, bid his farewell, and shimmered into nothingness through some invisible gap between worlds. A trail of tiny trilling voices followed in the wake of his leaving until they, too, dissipated into silence.

Still stunned by his reprieve, Tulane cradled the cat in his arms and kissed Cleo's temple. Then they both looked at Yvette with cautious optimism.

"We hope to get to know you better, and for you to know us," Tulane said, gazing at his daughter as though he saw only the brightest, shiniest parts of her. "It's uncanny, but you do have your mother's eyes."

"But perhaps your father's stubbornness," Cleo teased.

Harmony. That's what surged inside Yvette when she looked at them. The notion was as foreign to her as a family dinner, yet she thought it was one of those things a person could get used to, like cold baths in the summer and long, starry nights in winter.

"Would I live with you?"

"Everyone lives where they like there." Her mother took a step nearer. "But it would be easier to teach you if we were to share the same roof of stars. You need to know how your power works. How to control your glamour. How to guide it. How to give back in exchange for what you have been given so you may stay in balance."

"Would I have to stay there forever? What if I didn't like it?" She stole a look at Henri. "Could I come back?"

Cleo held a finger to her lips. "It would be wise to spend as much time there as you need to discover the answers to your questions, but you should know the hours and days work differently in the *Fée* lands. Sometimes moving fast, sometimes slow. 'Forever' is not a term we use."

Yvette glanced at Elena, hoping for advice. "What do I do?"

"It's what your heart wished for when you weren't looking," Elena said, taking Yvette's hand. "That's the truest kind of magic. Be with your family, and discover your lineage."

Even as she said it, Yvette knew the truth. To know her mother and father and learn their magic was what she'd waited for all her life. She just hadn't counted on the moment requiring so much courage to say yes.

She let go of Elena's hand and, as if mustering the nerve to jump off a cliff, nodded at her mother. "I choose to go with you."

As soon as she spoke the words, Monsieur Whiskers jumped from Tulane's arms into hers. She cuddled the cat against her chin, relieved to have something alive and warm to bury her face against. She looked around at the faces of the people, witch and mortal alike, who had helped her, each in their own way, to arrive at this moment of having everything she'd ever dreamed of. They smiled at her, eager to see her take the next step, and so Yvette said her goodbyes, shaking hands and thanking everyone for their wishes of good luck. But when she came to Henri, her heart nearly somersaulted with regret. Aside from Tante Isadora, she'd known Henri the longest of anyone.

"Oh, Henri, I have to go."

"Couldn't you stay just a little while longer?" He reached in his jacket and pulled out the leather wallet. "Or I could go with you. I can pay." His hopeful gaze darted to Cleo and Tulane. "I have the money," he said, offering the bills he'd taken from the comté. "Take it."

"Your paper money has no value in my father's realm," Cleo said, her words imbued with sympathy for the damage being done to the young man's heart. "And it is not a place where mortals easily adapt."

Disappointment came naturally to *les enfants* who haunted the back lanes of the butte. Always had. But to see it float in Henri's eyes now nearly had Yvette changing her mind.

His offering hung between them a second longer before he put his money away.

"I'm so sorry," she said.

"No, you did it, Yvie. Like you always said you would. You found your magic." He wiped the corner of his eye with his cuff before reaching into his satchel. "I think I captured you best in this one," he said, handing her a charcoal sketch. "Maybe you could take it with you instead so you'll think of me now and then?"

Yvette recognized the palm-size drawing—the girl sitting on the steps of the butte, overlooking the city. They were practically still kids then, yet he'd shown her without a trace of a scar. The omission was why she hadn't been sure the picture was of her the first time she saw it. But now she wondered if he'd ever seen the flaw in the first place.

She took the sketch and waited for him to meet her eye again. "Henri, you can't stay in the city. They'll come after you. Run. Go somewhere Rings and his goons can never find you."

"But—"

"Promise me."

The truth seemed to settle inside Henri. He let out a breath and shrugged the satchel up on his shoulder. "I always did want to take a ride on one of those big steamer ships across the ocean," he said, as if knowing he was being forced to accept a consolation prize compared to the one standing before him.

On impulse she leaned forward and kissed him. With both hands he held her face and kissed her back. Then they both promised they'd find each other again. Nothing was forever, not even goodbye. She folded the kiss and the promise into her heart, tucked the drawing between her and the cat, then told her parents she was ready to go.

Inspector Nettles stood before her brushing his thumb over his fingertips, as if ridding himself of the feel of being left empty-handed. She remembered then about the stowaway jinni hiding in the bottle between her breasts and waved at the inspector as he turned to leave.

"*Au revoir*, mademoiselle," he said and doffed his hat at her in defeat before turning on his heel and disappearing through the fog at the door.

At the thought of truly being free, Yvette's body filled with buoyant light. Her skin glowed ever so softly as a humming energy surrounded her. Already she could feel a tug inside her heart, beckoning her home to a place she'd never been. Her mother leaned in and asked her to picture that particular glimmer of light when the sun glints off a ripple of water. The image caught in her mind, her bones and veins fizzed with glittery energy, and the next thing she knew she was skimming across a wave of ultraviolet into the realm of the *Fée* to live under a roof of stars.

CHAPTER FORTY

Minister Durant blinked back, his mouth forming a small O shape as he read the form drawn up by Jean-Paul and signed by Elena.

"But this is absurd." He leaned forward and thumbed through the codebook. "There is no precedent for this."

"Oh, but there is," Jean-Paul countered. "LeBlanc in 1789 and Gaultier, 1791."

When he hadn't been able to find an obvious appeal to her dilemma through the law, Jean-Paul had followed a hunch and searched the official lifecycle records. It was seeing Yvette and her mother reunited that had given him the idea to take a look at Elena's genealogy. Though with Elena, sifting through her complicated lineage was like tugging on a thread and having a lifetime of loose notions come undone.

After checking the official records, he'd discovered Elena's father had originally worked the vineyard atop the butte before the vines died off from the phylloxera. In the same place where people now dumped their broken crockery, animal carcasses, and rotten vegetable peels. Then Raul met Esmé, bought a wagon, and devoted his time to her art when the vine no longer called.

Elena had never known any details about her parents other than the scattered memories that rose up through her consciousness when she caught the scent of ground-up foxglove or heard the distinct music of tincture bottles clinking together. That, and the revelation they'd been poisoners. Murderers hanged for their crime. Yet only one had been a true *venefica*, which made swallowing Jean-Paul's solution bittersweet. Like accepting unripened fruit on the tongue, only to have the mouth pucker in regret.

Durant bristled at being contradicted. "But there hasn't been a renouncement of a bloodline since the Revolution. Certainly, some leaned on the loophole to get out of military service—witches were sometimes conscripted for their healing abilities or their proficiency with fire—but LeBlanc and Gaultier were branded cowards and banished from society for denying their blood." He shook his head in that bureaucratic way meant to signal the matter was closed. "I understand how you must feel, Mademoiselle Boureanu, but it's out of the question. Your blood is your tether to your magic. Your legitimacy. Without that—"

"Without my mother's blood I am a vine witch, and nothing else."

Durant narrowed his eyes and drummed his fingers on the desk. "Yet your father was a known potions witch as well, so I'm afraid—"

Jean-Paul placed a yellowed deed of registration that was dated fifty-one years earlier on the desk in front of the minister. "In fact, Raul Boureanu was registered at birth as a vine witch and remained one until the day he died."

Durant studied the legal document, his lips tightening with each witchmark of authenticity noted in the margin. He shoved the registration back at Jean-Paul. "It would appear your application for exception has merit. *If* you truly wish to renounce your mother's bloodline forever."

"I do," Elena said. And while she understood severing the tie to her mother would dampen her instincts concerning poisons, it was the only way to regain the life she'd created for herself in the vineyard. She would always guard the shards of memory she had of her mother and father. The people who cradled her in the back of the wagon as a small child, who gave her warm milk and honey and crushed lavender sprigs to put under her pillow when she couldn't sleep. And she would remember, too, the single miracle grapevine left leaning against the wall in the place where her father had once respected the art of winemaking.

But she was a vine witch, and no one was going to deny her who she was meant to be.

⁂

The next morning, having already packed, Jean-Paul answered an expected knock at the door of his mother's apartment. Pedro entered, carrying a canvas wrapped in an old bed linen under his arm.

Marion instructed the artist to set the canvas atop the sideboard in the main salon, where the light was favorable. "I'm so eager to see what you've come up with," she said, clasping her hands beneath her chin. "Elena, aren't you absolutely aquiver with excitement?"

Elena certainly was curious to see if the vision-altering spell she'd used on the poor artist would show up in the portrait. That he was talented was without question, but how his perception had been affected by the magic remained to be seen.

"Your portrait, mademoiselle." Pedro bowed, then removed the cover, beaming with pride.

Revealed beneath the cloth, painted in hues of blue and black, tan and white, and a hint of pink and red, was a rendition of a most unusual face. All three leaned their head to the side. The usual features were all present and recognizable, but their placement was at odds with what most accepted as normal human anatomy, with one eye low, one eye high, the nose in profile on the right where the ear should be, while the lips were perched on the left. It was as if the artist had painted Elena from three different angles, only to smoosh all the perspectives into one abstract replica of a face. And yet the image was Elena without a doubt.

"What do you think?"

Jean-Paul scratched the stubble on his jaw. "I'm . . . not sure I know how to put it into words."

His mother took a step closer, tilting her head from one side to the next. "Well, I love it," she said. "It's brave. Bold. Just like my new daughter-in-law. The way you threw convention out the window to follow your vision, Pedro, is why art exists. Don't you agree, Elena?"

She supposed there had always been a danger of the spell colliding with the unique magic of the artistic mind. The collision seemed to have created a hybrid optical illusion. Or perhaps it was the result of the artist having to coalesce her physical self, the photographic representation, and her supernatural being into one portrait. Not an easy task, that. Yes, in that respect she did rather like the painting. The perfect mix of magic and mortal genius, reminding her of the complex tension between the born self and the created self and the trick of finding one's balance.

Satisfied, she hooked her arm through Jean-Paul's and stared again at the portrait. As they contemplated the artist's future—and how best to get the canvas home—a fairy-light touch brushed against her cheek, warm as sunshine. She looked, but there was nothing there but the glint of silver light reflecting off the decorative pin in Marion's hair.

ACKNOWLEDGMENTS

Publishing a second novel is in many ways a different experience from the first. The process is less formal and the learning curve a little easier to navigate. And yet one thing does not change: gratitude for those who make the entire endeavor not only possible but worthy. I am, of course, indebted to my agent, Marlene Stringer, for creating the opportunity that allowed me to write the second book in The Vine Witch series. I am also grateful to my editor, Adrienne Procaccini, for allowing me to tell my fairy-tale fantasy stories in all their quirky glory.

In addition, I wish to thank those whose editorial input was invaluable in shaping the final version of *The Glamourist*. To Clarence, thank you for your critical feedback and for knowing when to make me dig just a little deeper. Much thanks to Jon for your dedication to getting even the tiniest details right and knowing why it matters. To Laura, Karin, and Kellie, thank you for your brilliant attention to the written word and making it look like I know what I'm doing.

A special thank-you also goes out to Micaela Alcaino for her beautiful cover art, and to the team at 47North for their wonderful production and design. I am grateful for all for the amazing work you do. And, as always, a huge shout-out to my family. Thank you for your support and continued encouragement.

ABOUT THE AUTHOR

Photo © 2018 Bob Carmichael

Luanne G. Smith lives in Colorado at the base of the beautiful Rocky Mountains, where she enjoys hiking, gardening, and a glass of wine at the end of the day. She is the author of *The Vine Witch*. For more information, visit www.luannegsmith.com.